W9-DFR-801

Middle Ground

Middle Ground

KATIE KACVINSKY

Houghton Mifflin Harcourt
Boston   New York

Copyright © 2012 by Katie Kacvinsky

All rights reserved. Originally published in hardcover in the United
States by Houghton Mifflin Books for Children, an imprint of
Houghton Mifflin Harcourt Publishing Company, 2012.

For information about permission to reproduce selections from this book,
write to Permissions, Houghton Mifflin Harcourt Publishing Company,
215 Park Avenue South, New York, New York 10003.

www.hmhbooks.com

The text of this book is set in Adobe Garamond.

The Library of Congress has cataloged the hardcover edition as follows:
Kacvinsky, Katie.
Middle ground / written by Katie Kacvinsky.
p. cm.
Sequel to: Awaken.
Summary: In 2060, seventeen-year-old Maddie is sent to a Los Angeles
detention center and subjected to brainwashing to get her to accept a
world in which nearly all personal interaction is done online.
[1. Brainwashing—Fiction. 2. Government, Resistance to—Fiction.
3. Science fiction.] I. Title.
PZ7.K116457Mi 2012
[Fic]—dc23
2011048035

ISBN: 978-0-547-86336-8 hardcover
ISBN: 978-0-544-10480-8 paperback

Manufactured in the United States of America
DOC 10 9 8 7 6 5 4 3 2 1
4500439617

Dedicated to Graham
for reminding me to slow down, walk, and explore.

PART 1

New Life

Los Angeles, September 24, 2060

I have over one hundred online profiles. They link me to thousands of people who link me to thousands more and together we form an anonymous world. My life is ruled by stars and thumbs and tomatoes and points and carts. I can rate my friends. I can know anything. But sometimes I don't want all the answers. I want to cleanse my mind of knowing because I never have to wonder or imagine or think or reflect. I never have to remember or organize or plan. It's all done for me. But doesn't that just make me a marionette?

I'm ready to cut the strings.

I've made it my goal to start deleting my profiles, one each day. It's my new detox plan. My mom always says you need to weed your life every couple of years, of things and even of people, or it all piles up and accumulates, and it's impossible to stretch out when so many things are competing for space to grow.

I'm keeping some of the sites, the ones that inspire me and encourage me and put people in my path who are irreplaceable. The ones who value my time instead of squandering it. But I need more than this life. It's all communicating on the surface, living on the sur-

3

face—*it's like low-calorie relationships. Well, that isn't filling enough for me. I've never had the willpower to diet. I'd much rather feast.*

U-DESIGN-IT PROFILE: DELETED

I can design anything I want with this site. I can sit inside the mouth of a volcano. I can ride down a lava flow. I can be a director and a cook. I can wrap my arms around a star. I can walk on top of the arch of a rainbow. I can lift a building with my hands and place it here or there. I can play God in this place. But at the end of the day, have I really done anything? Or am I just full of hot air? Do I deflate when I log off?

MAKE-YOURSELF-OVER PROFILE: DELETED

This site is a personal shopper. Commercials tell me what to own. Celebrities tell me what to look like. But isn't it what we do, not what we own, that makes a difference? Isn't it how we treat people, not how we appear, that makes us attractive? If we could see only internal beauty, what would people look like? Who would the supermodels be?

DS-MEET-ME PROFILE: DELETED

I can meet you. But I can't hear you smile. And that's my favorite sound, how his skin and breath and lips change when he smiles. It can't show me that each hair on his head insists on growing in a different direction, so it's always a mess, even after he combs it. It can show me his hair is dark brown, but it can't show me that it lightens just above his temples. It can't show me that he prefers to sleep on his stomach with both hands tucked under the pillow, up to his elbows. It can't tell me that when he walks into the room I will feel calm and nervous and elated and relieved all at the same time.

People are like places: you don't truly know them until you take the time to visit and experience them in person. I prefer to be a traveler.

Life is three-dimensional, but there are other dimensions we can't see, can only feel, and those are the ones I want to explore.

❁

I'm learning that the real world is full of land mines. I've set a few of them off. It's full of mistakes, and of actions and words you can't take back. But I'm also learning that mistakes may open more doors than they close.

CHAPTER one

Clare and I changed at Pat and Noah's apartment in Hollywood. She was in town visiting for the weekend and we both agreed to celebrate by getting dressed up and going clubbing in L.A. We got ready in Noah's practice studio, crowded with guitars and amplifiers and speakers stacked up to the ceiling. I squeezed into a red dress that Clare loaned me. It was tight and low cut, something my dad would probably ground me for wearing, which was reason enough to embrace it. I slipped my arm under the silky strap, watching the tattoo of a bird on my wrist happily soar through.

Clare's black strapless dress sparkled with tiny sequins. We sauntered down the hallway like we were strutting down a catwalk. When we turned into the living room we found Pat and Noah just as we'd left them over an hour before—sitting on the couch wearing jeans and T-shirts and working off their manly testosterone by battling it out over a soccer video game. I now understood why guys played video games—they needed something to do to kill time while they waited for girls to get ready.

Pat and Noah shared a typical bachelor pad: every inch of wall space was covered in digital screens, and every piece of furniture was black leather with built-in drink holders, back massagers, footrests, and video-control pads. The bottom cushion of one seat was propped up to reveal a minifridge (since taking four steps to the kitchen was such an inconvenience).

Clare cleared her throat, and Pat's eyes flickered toward us. He paused the game and stared for a few seconds, confused, like we were strangers who'd let ourselves in without knocking.

"Wow," Noah said. "You two look amazing."

"What's the occasion?" Pat asked.

Clare raised her arms like it was obvious. "Aren't we going dancing?"

"Yeah," Noah said. "But we're just going to Nino's."

Clare's shoulders sank and she shook her head.

"What's Nino's?" I asked.

Noah blinked with surprise. "You've never heard of it? It's a virtual dance club. It's going off tonight."

My face fell. "It's virtual? Isn't the point of going out to be around people? There's got to be real dance clubs in this city."

"There will be people there," Noah said. "It just makes getting rejected by women a little easier for Pat."

"You're hilarious." Pat snickered.

"Maybe *your* ego needs some rejection once in a while, Noah," Clare informed her brother, whose band, the Managers, had been getting national attention since they recorded their latest album in L.A. Clare made it a priority to deflate his star status whenever she got the opportunity. "How many girls call you on a typical day?" she asked.

Noah brushed some shaggy dark hair out of his eyes. "You mean call or text or voice-text or videochat or message or contact?"

Clare groaned and ran her fingers through her short brown hair. "This, I haven't missed." Pat's phone beeped and I noticed his eyebrows arch when he checked the screen. He started to type a message.

"Who's that?" I asked him.

"Probably Noah's latest groupie," Clare offered.

"Don't talk about your mom that way," Pat responded. Before Clare and Noah could throw out a reply, I grabbed Clare's hand and pulled her toward the door.

"Let's get out of here," I voted. "Nino's sounds . . . interesting."

"There's a hundred-dollar cover," Pat said as he continued to type on his phone.

"A hundred dollars?" Clare and I said together.

"It's the hottest club in L.A., a hundred's cheap," Noah said. "I'll treat. It's my idea anyway."

"For that price, it better come with model escorts," I said.

Pat turned off the wall screen and grabbed a jacket. "You won't be disappointed," he promised.

❖

The four of us piled into a ZipLimo and headed downtown to Third and La Cienega. Noah insisted the trick to getting celebrity treatment in L.A. was arriving in style. ZipLimos were in limited supply in the city, but Pat knew a promoter who reserved one for us.

We swiped our fingerprints before the shuttle took off. My dad had set up a temporary fake profile connected to my fingerprint so police wouldn't be able to track my movements, but my father still had constant access to my whereabouts. I was still on his leash.

Clare ran her hand along the leather upholstery, and blue interior lights cast an electric glow inside the tight space. I leaned back in the seat and absorbed the smooth acceleration of the car. I was learning I needed motion in my life. I craved it, as if the movement outside of me charged movement inside. It reminded me I was more than a stationary object. I had legs for a reason. I wasn't meant to be molded to a chair.

Pat sat next to me, and his jacket sleeve brushed against my arm. I scooted over to give him room, or maybe because I felt safer putting space between us. In the four weeks I'd been in L.A., I'd spent most of my time with Pat. He was one of my only friends in town and even though I had my brother, Joe, he embraced the digital life—he worked, exercised, socialized, and dated on his computer. I'd seen him for only a few hours since I'd been in town, and I lived with him. But living had become so computerized, we rarely interacted in person. Even though we were divided only by three-inch-thick walls, we were living in separate worlds that clashed when they connected, like purple on red.

"You should move down here," I told Clare. I missed her energy. She was the friendship equivalent of a shot of caffeine.

"I have to get back in a few days. I have a date," she said with a bored expression, like a date was up there with vacuuming as her idea of fun. "I don't know why I bother."

"Which site are you using?" Noah asked.

"I prefer masochistic dating," Clare said. "You know, face-to-face. I met this guy at a coffee shop."

Noah whistled through his teeth. "Impressive."

Clare shrugged. "It beats those awkward online interview dates any day," she said.

We all shuddered at this. My parents didn't allow me to date, but I knew there were hundreds of match sites. They claimed they could pair you with your soul mate in thirty days or less, or your money back. They could go as far as genetic profiling, so you could see blueprints of your future kids. We wanted fast love. Drive-through dating. And we got it.

"I refuse to use dating sites," Clare announced. "Technology can now bring us love for six hundred dollars?"

"A lot of my friends like them," Pat said.

"It's because it's set up like a video game," Clare said. "You have to make it to level ten before you can virtually meet. And you have to rack up points in order to advance to the next dating stage."

Pat smiled. "Exactly. It's like playing online soccer, except I'm trying to score with a girl."

"Romantic," I said. "Don't worry, Clare. Someday you'll get swept off your feet."

"More likely by a train than a guy," she said with a shrug, as if this were her fate and she'd already accepted it. "We haven't heard from you in a while," Clare mentioned to Pat. I knew what she was referring to. Since he had moved to L.A. to help manage Noah's band, he'd dropped his friends back in Oregon.

Pat shrugged. "I'm taking a break from all that," he said.

"You're not going to fight digital school anymore?" I asked.

His hazel eyes met mine. "It's not the most dire concern in my life."

"Not when there's excellent music to produce," Noah added.

"So you're just giving up?" Clare asked.

Pat flashed her an annoyed frown. "No, I'm just not that dedicated. I have other goals besides racing to save America's youth from a world of digital prison," he said. Pat always had a sarcastic side, especially when he was in the presence of me and Clare, but he'd never spoken against fighting DS before.

"What if Justin needs your help?" I pressed.

Pat checked a message on his phone. "I'm not off the schedule completely. You can call me a seasonal employee. I help out when we're understaffed." He met my eyes. "Don't get me wrong, DS sucks, but now that I'm out of it, it doesn't seem as bad. School's just a part of life. You survive the monotonous boredom, you get out and move on. It's like your mandatory torture years."

"That's not why we're fighting it," Clare argued.

Noah's eyes were skeptical. "Hey, rebel twins, a lot of people actually like digital school. You don't know what you're up against."

He looked from me to Clare and laughed at our identical frowns.

"DS is easy," Noah said. "You don't have to waste time getting places. You don't have to put up with all the drama being face-to-face creates. You don't even have to get out of bed. I spent my entire high school career in my pajamas."

"Thrilling," I said. "There's a word for not getting out of bed all day. It's *depression*."

"You have more time to do the things you want," Noah argued. "It's not that bad."

"It's a trap," I said. "People don't know how to exist outside of it, that's the problem. People might not be experiencing drama, but they're also not experiencing anything else. It's taking over our entire culture."

"Hey, Debby Downers, can we talk about something fun?" Pat asked. "Besides, Maddie, it's not like you're committed to fighting DS," he reminded me. Just as he spoke, the limo turned the corner onto Third Street, and a neon billboard sign for Club Nino blinked down at us. A long line stretched along the side of the building, and the crowd turned to gape at the limo when we slowed down in front of the entrance. Some people were already poised to take videos, hands up and phones ready. Noah opened the door and we were greeted by a short bouncer in a suit and tie who held a scanner in his hand like a gun ready to fire at anyone who dared question his guest list.

"Bouncers," Pat mumbled under his breath. "They think they own the city."

The bouncer asked us if we had reservations, and judging from his deadpan expression, we could have shown up hovering in a spacecraft and he wouldn't have been impressed.

I started to shake my head but Pat announced we needed four seats.

"We're at capacity," the bouncer said. "You'll have to get in the back of the line."

Pat shrugged. "All right, if you want to turn down a member of the Managers. It might hurt your image, but that's your call."

A few girls in the front of the line had already recognized Noah and started yelling his name. When he turned to wave he was greeted with shrieks and a swarm of lights from camera phones. A dozen glittery dresses bounced up and down.

"Come on," Pat said, and pulled at Noah's sleeve. "Isn't your music label throwing a party tonight?"

The bouncer's tight frown relaxed. "Wait, let me see what I can do," he said, his tone changing from snobbery to flattery in less than a second. "I might have a few VIP seats open." He typed on his screen, mumbled orders into his earpod, and, after scanning our fingerprints, ushered us through a side door and then up a flight of metal stairs. Noah turned and waved once more to his fans and was answered with shrieks so loud it made Clare cringe next to me.

"I think the trick to getting celebrity treatment is to actually be a celebrity," I told her as we walked inside.

A security guard led us down a narrow hallway. The ceiling lights were a frosty yellow and I looked down at a see-through plastic floor, lit up underneath with colorful rotating lights. Techno music seeped through the walls, and bass pulsated the ground. I grinned and thought maybe the hundred-dollar cover charge was worth it.

When we pushed open a heavy door into the main dance room, my smile quickly vanished.

CHAPTER two

Club Nino looked like a dark movie theater. Seats took up the entire space, and the room was packed full of people staring up at an empty black screen that filled the front wall. Their eyes were hidden behind silver glasses and all of them wore thin metal MindReaders. People were rocking and laughing and nodding their heads to the music but I couldn't figure out what was so entertaining. I turned and grabbed Clare's hand.

"What is this?" I yelled to be heard over the music, and a staff member tapped my shoulder and pointed to a screen on the back wall listing all of the club rules, the first being NO TALKING. I frowned back at her. What kind of a club didn't allow you to talk? With a hundred-dollar cover? I felt a pang of guilt that Noah had just dropped four hundred bucks to take us out when I would have been happier watching them play video games at home. At least we could have had a conversation.

An usher escorted us to four open seats in the back of the room. The seats had enough space between them so people could get in and out and waitresses could drop off drinks without obstructing anyone's view. We sat down in the cushiony armchairs and I watched Pat to follow his lead. He opened a flap on his armrest and took out a pair of glasses, so I did the same. I put them on and jumped in my seat. Like magic, the screen at the front of the room filled with people.

A laser light show showered over the dance floor, where a pack of glittering digital bodies moved to the music. Groups of people flirted and mingled around the club. I blinked at the movie-screen party happening in front of me. Clare nudged my arm and motioned for me to put on my MindReader, hanging on a hook on the side of the chair. I slid on the silver headband and adjusted the sides until the small foam edges fit snug against my temples. I opened up the other armrest and pulled out a thin flat computer screen that automatically snapped on with my touch. A young woman appeared on the personal screen, tall and gangly and beautiful. She wore a long, silky red dress and sat on a slender white couch. She smiled and as words traveled out of her mouth, they were spelled out on the screen like a cartoon caption.

Welcome to Club Nino the caption read, and she waved at me. I waved back, as if she could see me. She talked me through the instructions after offering to skip ahead if I already knew how to log on. After I set up an account, she leaned back on the couch cushions, clasped her hands in her lap, and told me it was simple. My thoughts would appear on this personalized screen and I could press Send to enter them into Club Nino (the huge wall screen in front of me) or delete the words if I didn't want people to read them.

Try it! She encouraged me with an inviting smile.

This is stupid, I thought. I smiled as my thought illuminated on the screen in front of me. I pushed Send and looked up to see my message floating on the bottom edge of the giant screen, but I didn't have a body, so the words hung suspended in the air.

I stared at my message and wondered why I was invisible. I could see Clare out on the screen, and Pat and Noah, who were already surrounded by a pack of women. My instructor must have sensed my distress. She appeared on my computer and calmly explained I needed to add my image to the wall screen. She told me to imagine what I looked like and my body would appear.

I scanned the crowd at Club Nino. Some people had decided to go naked, although their privates were blurred out. The guys were all muscular and athletic (or maybe they just fantasized they were). Most people did opt for clothes, and judging from the looks of them, I was attending a virtual fashion show. There wasn't an overweight, unattractive person on the screen. Every girl had glitter highlights, gleaming skin, and makeup. Some girls had styled their hair in twists and braids; others left it long and shiny. One girl had straight platinum-blond hair that fell all the way to her ankles, nearly sweeping the floor. I wondered if that impeded her dance moves. Even some of the guys had glitter highlights. One word: *lame.*

Everyone dressed in the latest trends: plastic, shiny pants for the guys and metallic denim jeans and neon-colored spandex tops for the girls. It was the best-looking room of people I'd ever seen, but no one stood out. They blended together like a catalog. Even Clare had dusted some glitter makeup on her face that I know wasn't there earlier and she suddenly changed her dress color from black to neon pink and made herself about four inches taller.

What's wrong with being ourselves? I thought, but I deleted the comment. I knew the problem: it was boring to be ourselves because we came flawed and ordinary. We all wanted superpowers and stage presence. Each of us wanted to turn heads and leave an impression. Technology allowed that—it made us architects. I decided the only way to entertain myself was to add some shock value to the atmosphere.

I closed my eyes and imagined how I looked in the morning, with no makeup on, in my sweatpants and a holey T-shirt. As I visualized it, my body appeared on my personal screen. I looked tired and my eyes were a little puffy and I had ratty bed hair. Perfect. I laughed at my image, and, for a final touch, I added some leopard slippers. I hit Send and my body was teleported to the giant screen, larger than life, like I was suddenly a movie star.

Nice look, Maddie, but don't you think you're being a little vain? Noah said to me. He walked over and stood by my side, where his comment floated between us in the same cartoon caption the model spoke with.

Suddenly, a stranger approached me.

I didn't know sweatpants were in style, he said with a grin.

He was a little shorter than me, with brown hair and glasses. He was wearing a gray button-down shirt and dark slacks. At least they weren't plastic.

Sweatpants are the new denim, I thought.

He smiled. *You want to dance?*

I frowned up at the screen while my body stalled.

What? I asked him.

Dance, he said, and pointed to the crowd in front of us to remind me we were at a dance club.

I blinked back at him, stupefied. I watched people move on the floor in front of me. Couples grinded. Some people were break dancing. There was a stage you could jump on and stand above the crowd, and it was full of women. They shook their chests and hips to an audience of guys goggling below.

The guy reached out and grabbed my hand to pull me closer. I immediately thought I didn't like that and yanked my digital hand away.

Sorry, he said. *I was just trying to show you.*

Let's take it slow, I thought. *I'm a digital-dance virgin.*

He grinned and told me it was easy. I watched with amusement as his body awkwardly moved next to me. I laughed out loud as his feet and arms bounced to the music while I stood next to him, still and rigid as stone. I pressed Delete over and over at all the sarcastic thoughts filling my personal screen so he couldn't read them: *Are you dancing or doing jumping jacks? Wow, I've never seen anyone hop up and down like that before. Where did you learn your moves, whiteboyscantdance.com?*

He inched (jumped) his way closer to me, but I backed up.

It's nice of you to give the socially challenged guys a chance, Pat said as he came up behind me.

Stay out of this, I thought back.

The music switched from techno to hip-hop and before I knew it I was being nudged into a mosh pit with my new bouncy dance partner. I almost lost my body in the pack of people leaping around me. I closed my eyes and focused on the beat and mentally convinced my feet to move to the music. My digital friend smiled and nodded to encourage me. I started jumping in the air with the crowd, and my dance partner was so overcome with excitement, he picked me up and threw me over his head. I watched with alarm as my body was caught and passed over the crowd.

This was not okay, even in a digital world.

I tried to get down, but the crowd was loving it. I noticed a dozen other people around the dance floor being body-passed. I narrowed my eyes as a guy ran his hand up my thigh when he passed me over his head, and I started to kick and squirm until the crowd finally got the hint and dropped me. I fell hard to the ground, right on my butt, and just watching it made me flinch in my seat.

I stood up and searched the screen for my dance partner. When I found him at the edge of the dance floor stalking his next victim, I stomped over and shoved him hard in the chest.

That wasn't cool, douche bag, I thought. He fell back a few steps, jolted by my shove or my insult or both. Even though I wasn't actually moving, I could feel the muscles in my arms tense.

The seductive host lit up my personal screen and gave me a stern stare.

I'm sorry, but violent or sexual contact is not permitted at Club Nino. This is your first warning. I frowned at her words. But it was okay for him to throw me up in the air like I was a rag doll?

I looked up at the screen and I was standing there, alone, with my arms crossed over my chest, looking pissed. My leopard slippers stood poised like they were threatening to bite the next person that approached me. I definitely wasn't giving off a friendly vibe. I took a deep breath and told myself to calm down, this was all just make-believe anyway. But that was the problem—I'd been make-believing for seventeen years. I was ready to start living.

Douche bag? Pat asked me. I could hear him laughing in the seat next to me.

I'm bringing that expression back, I thought. *It's a classic.*

Maybe you should sit in the Lounge for a while and cool off, Pat suggested.

I asked him what the Lounge was and he explained it was a bar in the back of the auditorium where you could hang out if you decided you wanted to meet somebody face-to-face. I looked around at all the seats in the audience and didn't see a single one empty. Apparently face-to-face meeting wasn't a popular choice. Meeting in person was like waking out of a perfect dream—almost always a letdown.

I'm sorry, I told Pat. *I was really excited to go out tonight, but this isn't exactly my idea of socializing.* Pat and I stood close to each other on the screen.

Try not to take it so seriously, Maddie, he said. *Just have fun with it. Don't go all Justin on me.*

His name is a verb now?

Yeah, Pat said. *Other synonyms are* extreme, excessive, *and* overrated. I narrowed my eyes at this.

Thanks, Mr. Thesaurus. I deleted that one. I wasn't in the mood to start a virtual argument. Too much gets lost in translation.

I turned away and scanned the movie screen, searching for Clare. My stomach started to twist. Standing in that superficial crowd of people only magnified how much I felt like an outsider. I thought about Justin. This place would drive him crazy. If he were here right now, he'd probably instigate a riot.

More strangers tried to introduce themselves to me but I ignored them and walked over to Clare. She was dancing with a group and when I attempted to join in, she turned to me. My digital face was frowning and she guessed why.

Have you heard from him? she asked me.

No, not since I moved down here.

I know they're really busy, she said. *I talked to Scott and he said they've been working overtime.*

That isn't an excuse, I told her. *You can always make time for people. The point is, you have to want to.*

We're understaffed, Clare reminded me. *And it seems like more and more people are getting arrested every day. It's getting trickier to stop—*

Maybe this isn't the best place to discuss that, Clare? Pat interrupted us. I noticed several girls milling around him. I also noticed he didn't stray far from my side. *And Maddie,* he said, *you need to forget about him. The sooner you do, the less time you'll waste.* He turned away to talk with one of the girls standing behind him.

I closed my eyes. I hated that I was having this conversation on a screen for everyone to read. This night only reminded me why I wanted to fight digital school, why I detested where our culture was headed. I felt nauseated, like I'd felt last spring at the National Education Benefit when I watched a digital dance contest and realized people were addicted to the pixelated and perfected version of themselves. We were all losing touch.

I needed Justin right now. He could always explain things to me; he could comb out the confusing knots in my mind. I opened my eyes and looked out at the stationary sea of bodies sitting around me juxtaposed against the dancing characters on the screen. They hid safely behind their glasses and stared up at the party like they were hypnotized. I watched them delete corny or inappropriate thoughts before they were spoken. I hated that life was so censored. But most of all, I hated that tonight I was a part of it.

Music swam around me, so loud I couldn't concentrate. Blinking white strobe lights made the bodies on the screen look like shattered pieces. There was a cheer from the crowd as sparkle confetti fell from the digital sky, and people raised their arms and spun underneath it. In that huge space, I was the only girl standing alone. I read conversations spiraling around me.

You should meet us tomorrow for lunch.

Where at?

At this outdoor café in Amsterdam called Lucky's. It looks out over the canals.

Very cool.

Have you ever taken a virtual walk through the red-light district?

The what?

I watched people talk about sites and programs and chatrooms. Why couldn't I do that? Just blend in, be content to act like everybody else? I watched other conversations, people comparing brand names and clothes and bragging about grades and school. People didn't talk *to* each other, they talked *at* each other. It was a game of who could brag more. No one really listened to anyone else. Why is it that the people who talk the most sometimes have the least to say?

As I was considering this, another guy walked up to me and introduced himself as Jeff. He was cute but I couldn't get beyond his red hair highlighted with gold glitter.

Why are you dressed like that? he asked, and pointed to my sweats.

Baggy clothes make it less obvious that I'm pregnant, I told him. He blinked in surprise and hurried away without another word.

Good one, Pat said.

I can't do this, I thought. *Don't you people see this isn't real? You don't even exist, you're just living inside a fantasy. Wake up.* I sent my words and they lit up on the screen. Clare grabbed my hand, really grabbed it, and it startled me. She took her glasses off, and her eyes met mine. She leaned over in her seat and whispered in my ear. I could feel her breath touch me when she spoke and I could smell her hairspray and see a crease of concern on her forehead. She was so human, so real, it was reassuring.

"Do you want to leave?" she asked. I shook my head and focused on the club screen.

DS is killing us. We're not human anymore. We're more comfortable being robots. I sent the words and my thoughts continued to flow. My personal screen shut off and the host popped back on, smiling like we were old friends. She crossed her legs and her face turned serious.

We do not allow hostile communication at Club Nino. This is your second warning. One more violation and you'll be asked to log off.

I imagined what Justin would say in this situation, what he would do. I smiled as an idea took shape and grew until it cracked its shell. I deleted the thought before it had time to appear anywhere but in the privacy of my mind.

CHAPTER *three*

I logged out and turned off my computer. I could feel Pat and Clare both watching me but I avoided their eyes. I buzzed the Help button on my armrest and a few seconds later an usher came to my side. Her gold nametag said SUSAN on it. She crouched down and asked me what was wrong.

"My computer crashed," I said. "It won't let me log on."

She leaned across me and turned the computer back on. When the menu screen appeared, she scanned an identification card attached to her wrist by a stretchy rubber cord. She touched the employee page and typed in a password. I watched her fingers move deliberately over the keypad. It was too easy. She typed in *Nino1*. She tested a few of the functions and when they all worked she shrugged and logged out. She told me everything looked fine and to try again. When she walked away, Clare was staring at me.

"What are you doing, Maddie?" she asked.

I looked down at my screen. I didn't know what had come over me; it felt like someone in the room was daring me.

I restarted the computer and while I waited I took my wallet out of the purse I was sharing with Clare. Magnetic identification

24

cards were easy to override; I learned this piece of information eavesdropping on some of my dad's phone calls. When the main menu popped up, I touched the employee page. It asked for my identification, so I swiped the first magnetic card I found in my wallet—just an ordinary money card. I received an error message, which I expected. The computer said to try again or to enter my information manually. I took the second option. I typed Susan's name and conveniently her last name popped up next to it. I highlighted the name and clicked on it. This brought me to another screen with available options.

I scrolled down until I found the instruction I was looking for: Clear Club Nino. I assumed it would eliminate all the identities on the giant wall screen. I clicked on this function and the computer informed me only a supervisor had the authority to issue this command. I shrugged and hoped Susan was a supervisor. I hit the Clear Club Nino function. It asked for a password and I typed it in. I hit Enter.

With the press of a finger, the sea of bodies and colors pooling and flickering in strobe lights turned into a black canvas. The world stopped. There was a loud gasp from the crowd, heard over the pumping music.

At first, I was just as startled as the rest of the audience. I hadn't expected this to work. I never stopped to think about the possible outcomes of my crazy ideas, something that led to frequent problems in my life. There was a single icon blinking on the giant screen. Since I was still logged in, I let my mind run free. I couldn't pass this up.

How many of you think there's more to life than a virtual world? How many of you want other choices?

My words came out bold and bright over the screen. Since I didn't have an identity, the words hovered in the very center, like a warning. The techno music blared, the bass pumped, and I could feel the adrenaline kicking up in my chest. Heads turned, hands pulled off glasses in a synchronized motion, and people looked around the room. For the first time all night, people started to make eye contact. I felt myself smile.

"Who's doing that?" someone yelled in the crowd.

There's only one way to change the system: fight digital school.

Clare grabbed my hand. "Stop it, Maddie, you can't afford to get in trouble right now."

When I looked back at the screen my smile widened. There was another hanging bubble there.

I'm listening, it said.

Live outside your computers. Our minds are more than programs. Our bodies are more than extension cords. We might as well have been born with wires for fingers. That's how much technology controls us.

You're just trained, the other voice said.

"Stop it," someone yelled out.

Life is more than a show. It can't be entertaining all the time. It isn't real. And with those words, all the messages disappeared.

The techno music shut off and bright overhead lights snapped on. A chorus of groans and complaints filled the room. I sat back in my seat and slid my headband off with a sigh of relief. The room finally began to shift with human movement. Pat leaned toward me.

"That was stupid, Maddie," he said.

"I'm sorry," I said. "But at least people are actually talking now."

"So? You could get arrested."

Voices echoed off the walls. I wanted to know who the other person on the screen was and I looked around the room, as if he would be waving to get my attention.

Two bouncers followed a petite woman in a gray business suit down the main aisle of the auditorium. They stood at the center of the room and stared awkwardly at the crowd. The woman yelled out in a voice that sounded too strong for her small frame.

"We apologize. There's been a technical problem with our computers."

An annoyed grumble erupted from the crowd and she held up her hand.

"This has never happened at Club Nino. Until we can localize the problem, I'm afraid we're going to have to keep the wall screen turned off."

The audience shouted arguments about the cover charge.

"If you don't want to wait, we will be happy to reimburse you for your tickets tonight. Again, I apologize for the inconvenience," she said, and with that, she bolted up the aisle toward an exit sign with the two bouncers hurrying behind her.

Chairs squeaked and sighed as people stood up and started to move toward the exit in a herd. I felt a hand tug my dress.

"Let's get out of here before they localize the *problem*," Pat said. I nodded and stood up but before I moved a step a security guard blocked my way. He was at least a foot taller than me and built like a heavyweight boxer.

"You better come with me," he said in a deep voice that sounded as if it were buried in his massive chest. "We have a few questions for you."

I swallowed and attempted to look confident. I imagined I was wearing combat boots instead of high heels. "I don't think so," I said.

"We don't want to have to call the police," he said. "I'm sure we can handle this quietly if you cooperate." His eyes dared me to argue.

"I'm not talking to anyone until I call my lawyer," I bluffed. I had no idea what that meant but I'd heard the line in a movie once. It sounded intimidating. I looked over at Pat and he was shaking his head.

The security guard stood his ground.

"I didn't do anything wrong," I insisted.

"Then you have nothing to worry about," he said. He curled his meaty fingers around my arm, which he could probably snap without much effort. I sighed and let him pull me into the aisle. I looked over my shoulder at Pat, Clare, and Noah, who were watching anxiously, and I shrugged to show them I wasn't concerned. I hoped my acting was convincing.

He pushed me through the crowd, and people narrowed their eyes and pointed as we shoved past. Some people took pictures and videos with their phones while the guard yelled to get out of our way. I kept my eyes focused straight ahead. It started to sink in how much trouble I could get into for this. Playing a prank is one thing; getting arrested for it is another. The guard kept a tight grip on my arm, as if I'd try to run away in high heels. I wanted to assure him I wouldn't, since he was big enough to crush me to death with his pinkie finger.

I glanced back at the theater before we left. Groups of people were talking and laughing around me. They were face-to-face now, not face-to-screen. Instead of focusing on what I'd stopped, I noticed what I had started. A body at rest stays at rest until it's set in motion. I liked that I was the catalyst. My guilt rolled up into a tiny ball and pride kicked it away.

He led me into a dark hallway and at the end we stopped in front of a door with an OFFICE sign. He knocked twice and it clicked open. He pushed me inside and I stumbled in my heels but I held my head high. Thoughts spun through my mind. I wasn't guilty yet. They still had to prove it was me and, since I'd used the supervisor's information, I wondered how much leeway I had.

The club manager sat behind a behemoth metal desk that looked big enough to swallow her. She was small, maybe five two, but the security guard treated her with the respect a soldier shows his lieutenant.

"So, here are the two troublemakers," she said. I wrinkled my forehead at her comment. Two? Then I heard someone move behind me.

I turned and Justin stood up from a chair in the back of the room. My body froze when I saw him. The only part of me that appeared to be moving was my heart, which rocked in my chest. His brown eyes found mine for a split second but then focused on the manager again.

He took a few steps forward so he was standing closer to me. He was dressed casually for a club, dark jeans and a faded black T-shirt and black leather jacket. His hair was messy, like it was windblown. Hardly trying to impress anyone, Justin still managed to stand out, even in L.A.

One of the guards informed us the police would be here soon to read us our rights. A rush of nerves fluttered through my stomach. Justin tucked his hands calmly in his jean pockets. His face didn't show a hint of concern. I'd forgotten how much I missed his unwavering confidence. In his presence, I felt stronger, like his energy was contagious. He kept his dark eyes on the front of the room and I faced forward and wondered what annoyed me more: that I was about to get arrested or that I was standing so close to Justin but had to keep my hands off him.

CHAPTER four

"Do either of you have anything you'd like to say before the police arrive?" the manager asked us. I knew she was waiting for an apology, for us to grovel on the floor and beg her to forgive us for shutting down her digital dance emporium.

I couldn't help myself. My thoughts were being excavated.

"I think your hundred-dollar cover charge is ridiculous and your club is lame," I told her, which she answered with a sneer. Justin shifted next to me and he cleared his throat.

"I'm really sorry," he said in a low voice that sounded sincere. I stared at him, amazed to see a look of apology on his face. I turned back to the manager and saw the tight line of her lips had softened. She nodded and her accusing eyes fell on me.

"We know which screen those words were coming from," she said huffily. "And we know who was sitting at those computers."

"It was a mistake," Justin cut in. He offered her an innocent grin. "I was just trying to shake things up."

She shook her head. "Not at my club. Club Nino is a place to make friends and feel safe."

I had to tighten the muscles around my mouth to keep a

straight face. Yeah, what a great place to make real, genuine friends. More like a place to be digitally molested.

"It isn't a floor to start a political debate," she added and stared at me. "Speaking of our cover charge, do you have any idea what you've cost us tonight?"

"We can cover the losses," Justin offered.

"What?" I mumbled under my breath, and glanced over at him.

The manager tapped her long fingernails on her desk as she contemplated this. We heard clattering outside and the door swung open. The muscular security guard who'd escorted me earlier stalked through.

"Trey, can't you use the wall screen instead of barging into my office?" she asked.

"They're still down," he pointed out, and she gritted her teeth. She told him to turn the screens back on but he said it was too late. The auditorium was empty.

"The Lounge is way over capacity," Trey said. "And people are hanging out in the streets, blocking the shuttle tracks." Through the open crack of the tinted office window, we could hear people laughing and shouting outside.

The manager stood up with a heavy sigh and followed Trey.

"You two can wait right here and think about what you did," she said as she passed. "We've lost over fifty thousand dollars tonight, thanks to your little shenanigans. Don't think you can get away with that kind of behavior at Club Nino."

I coughed to suppress a laugh that was climbing up my throat.

She turned to Trey. "I want you to stand right outside this door."

He nodded. "Yes, ma'am." He reinforced her threat by glaring at us before he slammed the door closed behind him. I blinked at the office door and suddenly everything was quiet. I felt the air around me charged with a familiar energy. I turned and met Justin's eyes.

"Did she really just say *shenanigans?*" he asked.

"Must be the new crime lingo for a misdemeanor," I said.

There was a grin on his face. I had fantasized about seeing him for weeks but it usually played out a bit more romantically than the current situation—standing in a dimly lit office awaiting a fine or possible arrest from a power-tripping club manager.

His eyes never strayed from my face and I waited for him to say something, but he seemed content to stare at me. Questions rolled through my mind: *Where have you been? Why haven't you called? Have you thought about me once? I've thought about you one or one thousand times.*

"What are you doing here?" I asked. He studied me for a few more seconds, probably trying to guess what I was really thinking.

"I'm headed to San Diego, so I thought I'd surprise you. Pat told me where you guys were going." He raised his hands in the air. "Nino's? Seriously, out of all the great places in L.A., you guys choose Club Frat House?"

"Hey, this wasn't my idea," I said. "And considering I just shut the place down, you could say I'm not a huge fan of it either."

He shook his head and his eyes found mine again. "What bothers me is you're not even remotely worried you're about to get arrested."

"I was worried, but now you're here," I said simply.

He frowned. "You think I'm always going to magically appear and get you out of trouble?"

I thought about this. "It's more like you magically appear and I get into trouble," I corrected him. "You're like my antivenin to the lethal bite of authority."

"Great," he said. Justin's gaze trickled down to my dress and he raised his eyebrows. "That isn't what you were wearing on the screen," he pointed out.

I felt myself blush with embarrassment. He must have been thinking I looked ridiculous, so overdressed. I crossed my arms over my exposed upper chest.

"I didn't know we were going to a virtual club," I said. "How long were you in there anyway?"

His mouth turned up at the corner. "Long enough to see that I'm *extreme, excessive,* and *overrated.* That last word hurts a little."

Before I could respond, we were interrupted by footsteps outside. The door buzzed open and we both faced forward solemnly, like two children who've been given a time-out. The manager streaked past us and sat down behind her desk, her face frazzled.

"Well," she said. "This is certainly a scene. Now the news is here." She lifted a lanyard holding several keycards from around her neck and set it on the desk. She worried her fingers through her brown shoulder-length hair and studied her flipscreen.

"The good news is we turned up information about you two," she said. "Paul Luddite and Rebecca Riggs?" she said with a coy smile and waited for both of us to nod in agreement. "In case you forgot, we scan all our clients' fingerprints when they come into this club. That's the advantage of technology. We have access to all of your information. If you two were so smart, you would have thought of that."

The door opened again and Trey peered in.

"You can at least knock, Trey," she barked at him. Justin and I exchanged amused glances.

"They want to interview you," he said. She raised her eyebrows and tried to appear annoyed, but her eyes were bright.

"Television?" She stared down at her blouse and ran her fingers over some wrinkles on the sleeve of her jacket. "I just need to run to the restroom." She grabbed a small cosmetic bag out of her desk drawer. As she passed us, she said over her shoulder that she would be back to deal with us later. The door slammed loudly behind her.

The noise from outside the window escalated and we could hear the crowd cheering. I looked over at Justin and he was still watching me.

"Paul Luddite?" I asked him. "Interesting name choice. Any relation?" He smiled, his dimples appearing.

"You've heard of them?"

"I've read about the Luddites. They were rioters in Britain in the 1800s. They protested against the industrial revolution because machines were taking over human jobs."

"That's right," Justin said.

"They were called machine breakers," I said.

"It has a nice ring to it," he said. "Speaking of protesting, we can walk away from this pretty easily, maybe with just a fine, if you'd at least attempt to look sorry."

I tapped my foot on the floor and considered this. I could smell his leather jacket. I could hear it wrinkle every time he moved. I looked down at his hands, just visible under the cuffs. The sooner they let us go, the sooner I could touch him. That was definitely motivation. "They won't call the police?" I asked.

He shook his head. "These kinds of clubs let underage kids in all the time—so they can't call the police; they could get their license suspended. They're just trying to scare us." He took a step closer to me. "So, do me a favor," he said. "No more arguing. Just suck it up and say you're sorry."

"But they have nothing on me," I said, testing him. "It could have been a computer virus, even hacked in from an outside source, and since I'm sure the hard drives are all connected—"

"Maddie," he said, and just the sound of my name from his lips made me smile. "We're arguing with a bar manager. Suck it up and admit defeat this time. You've got to choose your battles once in a while."

I looked down at the ground and pouted. He did have a point. "Fine," I said. "I just have issues about backing down."

He pressed his finger under my chin and lifted my face toward his. He smiled and it made his dimples stand out. All the reasons to argue drained away.

"Did I mention your rebellious streak is a huge turn-on?" he asked, and I managed to shake my head. He brushed my hair back, behind my shoulders, and his eyes seemed to ask me something. Then, slowly, he lowered his head and touched his lips to mine. I grabbed his waist and pulled him closer but we were interrupted again. Heavy footsteps stomped outside the office door and Justin lowered his head farther until his lips were warm on my neck. He ran his hands down my back. We could hear Trey and the manager arguing on the other side of the wall.

My heart was going to explode if there was one more distraction. I untangled myself from his arms and crossed the room and grabbed the manager's stack of keycards off the desk. I examined the control panel next to the door and I saw it was the same security system my parents used at home. I scanned the manager's card and started to reprogram the commands.

First, I dead-bolted the doors. While I was at it, I reprogrammed the controls for the water sprinklers, the fire alarm, and the emergency lights.

"You have an interesting way of apologizing," Justin noted.

I shrugged. "If I'm already in trouble, I might as well have some fun," I said. "Besides, technically it's Rebecca Riggs's fault." I threw the keys on the floor. "Finally, we have some privacy."

Neither of us hesitated this time. He grabbed my face firmly in his hands and pressed his lips hard against mine. He wasn't soft or careful or slow. This kiss was heated, like he was making up for lost time. I fell against him and he backed up until we hit the couch on the side wall of the office.

Voices shouted outside and someone must have tried to open the door because it set off the fire alarms. A repetitive wail filled the room and the lights blinked on and off, but we ignored it and fell onto the couch. He pulled me on top of him and held my face in his hands, but he didn't kiss me. He just drank me in.

"Oh, damn it!" we heard the manager scream.

Trey and the manager shouted over the wailing siren, and Justin sighed and looked at the door. Even in all the commotion, I didn't want to move. I didn't want to break this moment. He ran his fingers over my lips.

We could hear pounding and yelling and someone turned the door handle, which set off the overhead sprinklers. They snapped on and a steady shower rained over us. Justin grabbed my hand and pulled me off the couch.

"Was this really necessary?" he yelled over the sirens, but he was laughing. I shielded my eyes from water spraying in all directions and followed him to the office window, large enough for us to crawl through.

We were both soaking wet by the time he lifted the window and pulled out the screen. He climbed out onto the sidewalk and offered me his hand to join him.

CHAPTER five

I bent over awkwardly in my heels and tried to brush off drops of water that had gathered on the silky fabric of my dress. Justin shook the water out of his hair and grabbed my hand tightly in his. The sidewalk outside was packed with people. I didn't recognize a single face from the wall screen. It was like seeing people you'd met at a Halloween party without their costumes for the first time. They looked normal—flushed skin, crooked noses, huge lips, small lips, pale, tan, skinny, curvy. What they saw as imperfections was what made them original.

Security guards from Club Nino were trying to keep the growing mob off the train tracks. A group of guys rigged speakers to a microphone and pumped music around the crowd. The party had officially moved outside, and it seemed from the landscape of smiles that people didn't mind. A group of girls tried to pull Trey and another guard into their dance circle. It was like seeing wild animals set free to do what nature intended. People opened apartment doors and windows to see what all the commotion was about. The mass was only growing.

A reporter interviewed the manager in front of the club entrance, and her voice echoed around us, like lyrics to the techno music. Her face was projected on a screen draped over the side of a building, where the live newscast was being shown, and her voice filled the air through speakers mounted on top of the news ZipShuttle.

"Now, this looks like a real dance party," the reporter noted, and she was answered with a cheer. A camera panned the audience. "Do you think this will push more face-to-face dance clubs to open?"

The manager gushed from all the attention.

"I certainly hope so," she said, and the audience applauded her. "I'm just thrilled my club is a place where people can express their feelings openly." Justin and I looked at each other and rolled our eyes. We skirted around bodies clustered together and I noticed eyes stop on Justin like they were caught in a web. Girls ogled him but he didn't notice the stares. His eyes were focused ahead.

"I thought you'd want to stay and enjoy all this," I said, and pointed around us. He squeezed my hand tighter and his eyes scanned the area like he was my bodyguard.

"I never trust the news," he said. "And I don't want you around any cameras."

"I look that bad?" I joked.

He glanced at my long hair, still dripping at the ends, and his eyes took in my revealing dress. "I think your dad would imprison you on your dress choice alone," he said. "And breaking the law doesn't help your record." I couldn't argue with him. It was easy to forget about my dad's watchful eye when I was a thousand miles away. But I knew he was always following me.

We turned the corner and at the end of the block we found Noah, Pat, and Clare waiting for us next to an empty ZipShuttle.

Noah extended his arm to slap Justin's hand and Clare offered him one of her signature hugs.

Pat regarded our clothes and hair. "Why are you two all wet?" he asked.

"Some idiot pulled the fire alarm," I said.

Pat looked at me. "Club etiquette, for future reference," he said. "If you're not having fun, you can just get up and leave. You don't have to shut the whole place down."

"Got it," I said.

"I didn't mind," Clare said to me. "You were brilliant." Pat and Noah were less grateful and I caught Pat's eyes shift to my hand, still wrapped tightly inside Justin's.

"Brilliant," Noah mimicked. "I was hitting it off with the hottest girl there until you got *bored*."

"That's some serious cock-blocking," Pat pointed out to me.

"I'm sorry," I said, and looked at Noah. "I'm sure there will be plenty of skirt-dropping women in your future."

He shook his head with disappointment. "You didn't see Christine."

I raised my eyebrows and was about to point out that he hadn't actually *seen* her either when three girls came around the corner and interrupted us. We all turned as they approached and one of the girls waved. She was short and stocky and her platinum-blond hair was frizzy with tight curls.

"Hey, you still want to come to the party?" she asked, and Noah's forehead creased.

"Do I know you?" he asked. She walked closer, and in the dim streetlight she wasn't unattractive but she definitely wasn't model material. She and her friends had a style my mom and I called *overcooked*, which is where everything is overdone: the hair, the makeup, the clothes. It ruins whatever is naturally there.

"I'm Christine," she reminded him. "I'm a little shorter in real life," she added with a grin, and judging from Noah's alarmed expression, I could see that wasn't the only thing about her appearance that was different.

One of the other girls checked out Pat and Justin. "You're all invited," she said.

I watched Noah and could practically hear his thoughts: *I think we'll pass.* Before he could comment, Clare spoke up. "He's dying to go. It's all he's been talking about."

Noah shot a look of hate at his sister. "Um—"

"We were actually saving this shuttle for you," Clare added.

"Excellent! We can all go together," Christine insisted, and she and her friends climbed inside. Pat started to argue, but Clare pushed him toward the door.

"You still made the party," I said to Pat. "I guess this is a truce, right?" I added with a peace sign.

"You're dead to me," Pat said, but there was a grin on his face that made me laugh.

Clare followed behind him. "This I have to see."

I grabbed her arm before she stepped on the shuttle track. "You don't have to go," I said.

She lowered her eyebrows at me. "I think you two could use some alone time," she whispered and looked over my shoulder at Justin. "Have fun tonight," she said. She winked at me and climbed in the shuttle after Pat. The doors beeped closed behind them. The shuttle sped down the street and left Justin and me alone on the sidewalk. Distant techno music drifted through the air. A familiar electricity hummed around us. I turned to see Justin watching me.

He tugged my hand. "Let's walk," he said. The streets were empty except for an occasional train. A mural of billboard lights surrounded us. There were so many constant advertisements and flashes of color it made the streetlights obsolete. I missed Eden, where the world was quiet and reachable and my mind was clear.

"How are you?" Justin asked me.

Three simple words that most people answer with *Fine* or *Good* or *Great* or *Fantastic,* and then the conversation moves on to movies or food or shows or anything else easy to talk about. But I could never answer Justin's questions with simple one-word replies, and they didn't lead to easy conversations; he always saw through me and pulled me out of anywhere I tried to hide.

I wanted to tell him life was perfect, that a city of twenty million people was the most fulfilling place to be. I wanted to tell him living in L.A. was a constant stimulus, a high, a current of lights that pumped energy into the air like an electric charge. I didn't want to tell him I missed him and that I saw his face everywhere, on strangers and wall screens and even on the tiles in my shower.

He watched me and waited for a response like he could see my thoughts twisting together and breaking and pulling apart.

"You told me once that missing people is a waste of time," I said. "So, I don't miss you at all and I don't miss Eden and everything in my life is fabulous and if happiness were tangible I would be so heavy with it, it would be crushing me."

I looked at him and smiled.

"You have the most bizarre way of being honest. Okay, my turn," he said. "I miss you." The words sounded strained coming out of his mouth, like it was difficult for him to admit it or, more likely, difficult for him to feel it. "And I know I told you it's a waste of time, but in the past few weeks, I've learned it's unavoidable."

"You know, it's not a bad thing," I said. "It's not a weakness, like if you had a poor immune system."

"I'm just not used to it," he said. "I've never missed anyone before and it's brutal. It's a huge time suck. If I told you how many times a day I've thought about you, it would seriously scare you."

I smiled but more than anything I was relieved.

"Everything comes back to you; it's like this vacuum. It's so *irritating*," he said through a grin.

"Thanks?" I said.

"That's why I needed to talk to you. I don't know how to do this. I don't know how to be a *boyfriend*." He said the last word slowly, giving it three syllables.

He stared at me with a deadpan expression and my stomach flipped at the word *boyfriend*. It was strange hearing it come out of his mouth because I'd almost skipped this stage. I already knew I wanted to be with him forever. I decided not to verbalize this small detail. I didn't want to send him into cardiac arrest. I needed to be careful with Justin. He acted as solid as stone but when it comes to emotions, we're all made out of glass.

"Well, if you care about someone, it usually involves *communicating* with them. You know, calling, texting, messaging . . ."

Justin pondered this. "That's what proves I care? That I check in with you?" I nodded and he asked me how often. "Once a week? Twice?"

"Haven't you ever watched a television show?" I asked him. "Or seen a movie? Communication's a pretty big deal. To everyone. It's how we're reassured people are thinking of us. That they care. That they haven't, for example, moved on and forgotten we exist because all they think about is fighting digital school."

He stopped walking and leaned his back against the wall of a brick building and stared at the ground.

"I know your job comes first right now," I said. "But relationships take effort. If you want them to work," I added.

He nodded thoughtfully while he absorbed this, like I was

some deity revealing hidden secrets of the female soul. I felt like I was just stating the obvious.

"Huh," Justin said. "So that's how a healthy relationship works, according to television?"

I smiled. "Okay, this isn't a debate. It's very simple. If you cared about me, you'd check in with me. You'd want to know how I'm doing. That's how it works."

Justin was fascinated. His eyes were wide, as if this were truly new to him. And then I thought about it. Justin didn't have any close friends. He'd never dated. He didn't understand how to be close to people. He only knew how to distance himself. That's how he handled his relationships; his parents had brought him up to think separation was normal.

He repeated my last sentence slowly. "That's how it works."

I stared up at the starless sky. He inspired me to build friendships every day, but when it came down to a real, intimate relationship, I felt like I had to hold his hand and teach him how to walk with baby steps.

"How do you think dating works?" I asked because I was equally intrigued by his take on it. He shoved his hands in his coat pockets. We started walking again.

"It doesn't work," he said, and his voice dropped a little. "Does it?" His eyes stared straight ahead and I felt doubt begin to prickle down my spine.

"Then what are you doing here?" I asked, and my voice came out unsteady. The wind whipped past us and it was warm, but I still felt a chill run down my arms.

"I've been thinking about what you said before you moved to L.A. You told me you loved me."

My heart started to race, but I wasn't embarrassed he brought it up. I was proud I had the courage to admit it. "I do love you."

He looked more confused than happy to hear this. "That took some guts to say."

I shook my head. "It was a relief to say. It was a lot harder trying to hold it in."

"No one's ever said it to me before."

I stopped walking and he kept on but looked back at me over his shoulder. His face held no emotion, like it didn't matter to him either way, like love was just a place, just a location on a map that you either visit or pass by. If you don't experience it then you won't ever know what you're missing.

"What about your parents? Don't they say it?"

His forehead creased as he thought about this. "Maybe when I was little. We just don't say it. I think it's more assumed."

"Assumed?"

"It's how we operate."

"Operate?" I repeated. "You're a family, not a business plan."

He grinned at me and we started walking again. I was quiet while my mind tried to assimilate this foreign idea. "I have a question for you," he said. "How do you know when you love somebody?"

I felt something inside of me shrink when the words left his mouth. It sounded like a rejection.

"You don't have to ask yourself. You just know it. It's like religion; it's like believing in a god. You can't explain it. No one can tell you you're wrong. It just is."

"Do you think it's temporary?" he asked.

I shook my head. "Not if it's real. Do people stop believing in God because they miss church for a few weeks? You'll always believe." I cocked my head to the side. "Haven't you ever told someone you love them?"

"No," he said. "Never."

I gaped at him. "What?" I asked.

He laughed at my response. "What?"

"That's unbelievable."

"Why? I've never felt it before. Some emotions you just don't feel. And I'm not going to say it if I don't feel it."

"You think you're immune to feeling love?" I asked him.

"I don't know. Maybe I don't have that emotion. Some people never get jealous. Some people never get angry. I used to think love was ownership, like it weighs people down. It makes people dependent. I guess that's what keeps me from feeling it."

I felt a heavy thought hovering between us. It finally registered what he was trying to say. I'd let my sappy mouth go on a love crusade only to have it drive me off a cliff. Because he didn't feel that way about me.

A row of ZipShuttles hissed by, crammed full of people leaving the club. I wanted to be inside one of them, to be anywhere but trapped in my skin. I wanted to escape this moment. I wanted to log off, press Delete, fast-forward out of this.

"There's something I wanted to talk to you about," he said. "That's why I stopped by. I don't want to drag out this distance thing any longer than necessary."

I nodded but I couldn't look at him. My face burned hot with anger and humiliation and went cold at the same time. It was all starting to make sense. That's why he hadn't called the past few weeks. He'd realized this could never work. He never told me he loved me because he didn't. Maybe he was right; he wasn't capable of feeling it. But he'd wanted to put some distance between us first. And he had the decency to break things off in person even though I wished he'd just done it over a message.

I took longer strides. There had to be a train stop coming up. I focused on signs ahead of me, not on my thoughts, not on something tightening inside of me. I focused on the fastest way to escape.

"I'm looking for an apartment down here," he said, and the words didn't make sense. "What do you think about that?" he asked.

I looked up at a digital billboard advertising a diet plan. It showed a couple sitting on a beige couch sharing vitamins instead of eating a meal together. They watched a wall screen instead of each other. Their kids played on the white carpeting with electric learning pads. It made me feel lonely. I stared back at Justin, so confused I could barely think straight. Hadn't he just told me this wasn't going to work?

"Why would you look for an apartment?" I asked with annoyance. "You've never had your own place before."

My tone made him hesitate. He ran his hands through his hair. "You're right," he said. "I never felt the need to, until now. I always thought having a home would be like dropping an anchor. And my life doesn't settle down very often, so what's the point?"

"Exactly," I agreed. "What's the point?"

He looked bemused. "I want to be here," he said.

"You want to live in *Los Angeles?*" I sighed. What a lovely idea. First he tells me he wants to break things off, then he says he's moving to the city I live in. And he's hoping it won't be awkward if we run into each other. That's just great. *A* for *awesome.*

"I think you're nuts," I said.

His eyes widened. "Why's that?"

I stopped walking and pointed out the endless trail of advertisements around us, built so high up they practically covered the sky. "This place is everything you despise. It's completely plugged in. There's noise everywhere. They don't have trees here. They don't even have fake ones. They'd get in the way of all the digital billboards."

"Yeah, but—"

"You'd hate it here," I said, and glared at him. This slow-motion breakup was grating on my heart. I just wanted him to say it and get it over with. He stared back at me with surprise, like I'd tried to slap him. Then a thought entered my head, like a quiet knocking, like a reserve parachute opening and snatching me up seconds before my body would have collided with the ground.

I held up my hand. "Wait a minute," I said. "Rewind. Start over. You're in town to look for an apartment?"

"I was just considering it, forget it," he said quickly, like he'd already dismissed the idea.

"Why were you considering it?" I asked.

He looked at me then, really looked at me, with the same intense stare he gave me at the club. It was a stare that, I realized, wasn't trying to mess with my mind; he was just trying to make sense of his own.

"Because you're here," he said. He paused for a second and then spoke his next words slowly, like he was getting used to the idea. "I've been thinking a lot about you, and me, the past few weeks." He stopped because he was tripping over his words. I started to smile. It seemed like I was the only person who could make his smooth confidence waver.

"You want to live here to be close to me?" I said for him.

"Yes," he said without hesitating. He watched me carefully. "This isn't a fling, Maddie. What's happening here—I don't do crushes. I want to make this work. Because you're worth it." He took a few steps closer to me. "I figured since you told me you loved me a few weeks ago, you'd be okay with the idea."

I inhaled a breath of relief. "I'm sorry. I thought you were breaking up with me," I confided. Justin walked up to me and we were both smiling. He ran his fingers under my chin and lifted my face.

"*You're* the one who's nuts," he informed me.

He leaned down and kissed me, and I realized Justin's decision would change everything. This move wouldn't be temporary. He was moving more than his life. He was moving his heart. Putting it closer than down the road from me. He was putting it right in my hands. Right where I'd wanted it since the first day I met him.

CHAPTER Six

An open ZipShuttle came to a stop next to us and Justin pulled me inside. We scanned our fingerprints and fell onto the car seat. I broke away from his mouth long enough to mumble the address to Pat and Noah's apartment, where I was crashing tonight, and then I was pulling at Justin's jacket because it wouldn't let me close enough to his skin. He pushed me back against the plastic seats and started to climb on top of me when a high-pitched ring interrupted us. Justin peeled his lips away from mine. We looked at the wall screen in the front of the car and a yellow light informed us we had a message waiting.

"Are you on call tonight?" I asked.

He shook his head. "No, but we should take it."

He reluctantly slid off me and I sat up and adjusted my dress, which was nearly stretched off one shoulder. Justin touched the screen to accept the message. I froze when an image of my dad stared back at me. He sat behind his desk in his office, a place I knew too well. I swallowed and met his eyes. Even through the wall screen, he could use them like weapons.

49

"Hello, Madeline," he said, his voice steely and formal. The screen lit up the dark space around us in a white glow, exposing everything. I hadn't spoken to my father in months. During that time, I convinced myself I was brave enough to stand up to him. Now I wasn't so sure.

"Dad," I said, trying to compose myself after the shock of seeing him.

He looked at his hands, clasped calmly in front of him. "Interesting prank you pulled tonight," he said with a small smile.

I looked at the clock on the corner of the wall screen. It was almost 1:00 a.m. "Do you ever sleep?" I asked him.

He sighed. "I might sleep a little better if my daughter's behavior weren't lethal to my career."

"Dad—"

He held up a hand to silence me. "What you did tonight was very foolish, especially considering your situation."

"No one can prove it was me," I said. "I didn't use my real identity on the computer. I'm not stupid."

He laughed at this. "No, you certainly are not stupid. That isn't the problem. It would just please me if you'd focus your intellect on more law-abiding goals." His eyes passed over me and concentrated on Justin for a few seconds. Disdain crossed my father's face, like Justin was a kidnapper holding me hostage. Justin stared back at him with indifference. He could repel emotions as easily as my father could.

"I'm not trying to fight *you*," I told him.

"Encouraging kids to drop out of digital school isn't fighting me?"

"DS is corrupt," I said. "It's gone too far. It trains people to be so plugged in, they're addicted. By the time kids are done with school, they can't unplug. Ever. You started a disease."

"You don't understand what I'm trying to do."

"You're blindfolding people," I said.

My dad took a deep breath. "People need to be controlled, Madeline. There need to be rules to maintain any kind of order in this world. I'm trying to make this country a peaceful place. I want you and Joe and everyone else's children to be safe. That's all I'm trying to do. I wish you could accept that."

"And while you're so busy rescuing people you forget to listen to them. You forget they want choices, that they're human."

"And you forget that you're crushing your mother's happiness. Do you forget that she's worried sick about you? That you're tearing your family apart?"

"That's not fair," I said. "This isn't all my fault."

My dad's eyes fell on Justin again. "It's interesting how trouble always finds you when you're with certain people." Justin's hand squeezed mine tighter. He had never spoken a word to my father and he seemed determined to keep it that way. "I'm getting tired of bailing you out after you make mistakes, especially when you associate with people who drag you down to their level."

I tightened my lips. "If you're so disgusted with my life, then just stay out of it," I said, but I regretted the words as soon as they left my mouth. I didn't want distance from my father. I wanted acceptance.

My dad stared back at me. "I can't do that. You're my daughter."

His words stung because I didn't feel like his daughter. I felt like he saw me as something he needed to fix, something that had come loose but with the right winding and tightening would lock safely into place again.

"That doesn't mean you own me."

"No, it means I love you," he stated, but with no emotion. It made my jaw clench. He was using love to make me feel guilty. Love was just a chess piece to him.

"This isn't a rebellious streak I'm going through, Dad. You can't fix me with threats and counseling and grounding me. This is who I am. Maybe we need to work together, not against each other all the time."

He stared at me. "Sometimes I think you don't even regret what you did when you were fifteen," he told me.

"I don't know if I should regret it," I told him. "Maybe I did the *right* thing. Maybe that's what I'm trying to prove."

My dad rubbed his forehead between his fingers. "I thought sending you to L.A. would give you a fresh start. I thought it would keep you away from the people who are trying to take advantage of you. I hoped you wouldn't take your liberty for granted this time."

He said goodbye and switched off his connection. The wall screen turned a blank gray. I looked at Justin and his face was sympathetic. He leaned his forehead close to mine and pulled my hair back behind my shoulders.

"It's nice to know the family accepts me," he said.

"They're not too accepting of me these days either," I reminded him.

"Your dad has a point," he said.

I frowned and asked him what he meant.

"Maybe he'd agree to listen if you weren't associating with me." He grinned but it stopped before it got to his eyes. "You realize I'm number one on his shit list."

"You're number two; I'm number one," I said, and he smirked.

"Sorry I tried to steal your number-one status," he told me and the next thing I knew my body was shoved against Justin's chest as the ZipShuttle brakes scraped against the tracks and the car screeched to a stop. Justin grabbed a handrail at the edge of the seat to keep us from slamming into the wall. In the beam of headlights we saw someone in a black hooded sweatshirt standing in front of the car. Every ZipShuttle had a heat sensor to detect animals or pedestrians on the tracks in order to stop the car, but I'd never seen it happen before.

The hooded figure jumped off the tracks and ran to the side of the shuttle and banged on the door.

Justin slid the door open and a boy fell through and yelled for us to go. The door beeped closed and Justin ordered another address while the boy collapsed into the seat across from us. I instinctively tightened up and pulled my legs away from him.

His hood slid back far enough to reveal a kid, younger than me and Justin. He was breathing so hard his eyes were pinched, and sweat dripped off his chin. He reached up and used his arm to wipe sweat off his forehead and that's when I noticed a handcuff dangling around his left wrist, although his right hand was free.

Justin leaned closer to him while the shuttle picked up speed and asked him what happened, but the boy was still panting for air and couldn't speak. Justin took his phone out of his pocket and used it to scan the kid's fingerprint. Once the boy realized what Justin was doing he jerked his hand away and tried to elbow Justin in the head. Justin grabbed his arms and pinned them down against the seat.

"Nice swing," he complimented him.

"Go to hell," the boy managed to say through his gasps.

I raised my eyebrows and quietly watched him, impressed he had the nerve to be so defiant. But staring at him, I understood how he felt, because I'd been in his shoes—running, handcuffed, trusting no one but the space inside my own skin. When you're helpless it forces you to be callous. It's a natural shield. His hard eyes looked back at me and I could see a mixture of desperation and anger. I noticed the gold emblem of the LAPD on his handcuffs.

Within seconds, Scott's face appeared on the ZipShuttle

screen. While Justin was better at hands-on work, Scott handled the technical side of fighting digital school. Computer systems have dozens of languages and Scott was fluent in all of them. He was surrounded by a row of computer monitors and he yawned lazily at our image. His feet, clad in white socks, were propped up on the desk.

"Background check?" he asked, and Justin nodded. He threw a few potato chips in his mouth and mumbled, "I thought you were off tonight?" Scott's eyes trailed down a long list on one of his monitors. "His name's Jeremy Stevens."

Jeremy looked up.

"He was arrested in Ventura two hours ago for committing, uh-oh, code two twenty-seven."

"What is that?" I asked. Assault? Attempted murder? Rape?

"He was trying to break into the DS grading system," Scott said.

Jeremy stared at Scott with surprise. The hood slid all the way off his head and sweat dripped from his short blond hair down the side of his face. He creased his eyebrows and surveyed my dress and heels, Justin's casual clothes, and Scott's face on the wall screen.

"Who are you guys?" he asked as his breathing settled.

Scott chuckled at something else on his screen. "Looks like he was trying to alter some test scores. Most of the classes he was failing were in computer science," Scott said. "Go figure. You usually have to understand the system in order to break into it." He laughed again.

"Screw you. Sorry I'm not some cyber nerd," Jeremy retorted.

"We prefer to be called cyber gods," Scott clarified.

I looked at Jeremy. "They were going to put you in a detention center for that?" I asked.

"It was his third offense," Scott added.

Jeremy rested his head on the back of the car seat. "I hate digital school." He groaned. We all smiled at him. At least he was in good company.

"Looks like you were smart enough to get away on your own," Justin noted.

"More like paranoid enough," he said, but before he could explain, we heard car tires screech around the corner, and police lights flashed behind us. I bolted straight up in my seat but Justin didn't flinch, as if he'd been expecting it. I frowned down at my shoes. I wasn't dressed for sprinting from the cops tonight. Justin must have read my mind.

"We won't have to run," he assured me. He looked up at Scott. "I need a car."

"I'm on it," Scott said.

"And will you call an ambulance?"

I looked from Scott to Justin and wondered why we'd need one.

"Let me know how it turns out," Scott said.

He threw another handful of chips in his mouth and the screen snapped off. Justin dimmed the interior lights of the shuttle, but the police car was so close behind us the blue and red lights illuminated the space like we were back on the dance floor in Club Nino. Jeremy looked down at his lap, and failure hung over his face. He told us to stop the car.

"I'll turn myself in," he said.

Justin looked insulted. "We have a no-surrender-to-the-cops policy," he told him. He squatted next to the exit door of the ZipShuttle. There was a red emergency latch along the side with white letters that read PULL ONLY WHEN ZIPSHUTTLE IS IM-MOBILE.

"Hold on," he said to us, and pointed at handrails next to our seats. I curled my fingers around the metal handle and looked back at the cop car. The headlights were inches away, and a blinding glare filled the car. Blue and red beams orbited inside of the shuttle, and sirens screamed so loud my ears vibrated at the high decibels.

Justin checked to make sure Jeremy and I were ready. He pulled the lever down and I braced myself. The force of the car stopping so suddenly threw me out of my seat and knocked me to the floor, but I managed to hang on to the handrail. A crash shook the car as the shuttle derailed. We ground off the track, sending up sparks around us as the iron burned hot against the pavement. Metal bent with a wrench, and a dark object flew and smashed against the side of the train's window.

The screeching and shaking stopped but I was afraid to lift up my head from where I had it pressed into my arms, dreading that the shadow that had collided with the train was a body. I heard movement across from me and a warm hand squeezed my shoulder.

"You all right?" Justin asked me. I slowly peered up and nodded; Jeremy was already out of his seat, poised to run. I let go of my grip, amazed my fingers didn't leave indentions in the metal. Justin kicked the door open and told us to get out.

We jumped down to the street and I gasped at the totaled cop car behind us. I'd never seen an accident before. The ground was littered with glass and shreds of plastic, and the front end of the cop car was smashed and had disappeared underneath the rear of the ZipShuttle. The front window had been busted out and there were two white airbags filling up the space. The lights were still rotating, but the siren's sound was out. The ZipShuttle wasn't as badly smashed, but the back headlights were knocked out and the bumper was crumpled and folded underneath the car.

"We need to move," Justin told me. He grabbed my arm to lead me down the street. I pointed behind us at the cops.

"Shouldn't we check on them?" I asked.

"They'll be all right," he assured me. "That's what the ambulance is for." I could hear faint sirens in the distance. Before I could argue, a red sports car pulled around the corner and stopped inches from us. Justin opened the front passenger door, and the driver handed him something that looked like a switchblade. Justin grabbed Jeremy's wrist and aimed a red laser at the lock to free the handcuffs. He used the same laser to unlock the bracelet that was tracking Jeremy and threw it on the ground, then smashed it with his foot.

"You're lucky they didn't use a skin tracker on you. That's what they're starting to do these days," Justin said.

"A skin tracker?" Jeremy said.

"They embed it in your skin, like a tattoo. It lasts for a couple of days. We can't intercept people if they have them." He tossed the cuffs down next to the smashed bracelet. He was so unaffected by the accident it was disturbing.

"We were going forty miles an hour," Justin said, not looking at me but sensing my thoughts. "That's a ZipShuttle's top speed. Those airbags are designed to withstand blows at sixty. I've been in accidents worse than that, so trust me, they'll be okay."

I scrambled into the back seat and Jeremy climbed in next to me. The driver whistled when he saw the collision and the road full of debris. His dark eyes had the same detached look as Justin's, as if he'd seen this hundreds of times.

I looked back, and sure enough, I saw two policemen pushing free from the airbags. The hood of the cop car had flown off, and I assumed that was the shadow I'd seen smash against the window.

"Beautiful crash," he said. "I give it a ten."

Justin typed something on his phone. "Works every time," he said. "Cops haven't learned it's rude to ride someone's tail." He introduced the driver, Matt, to Jeremy and me.

Matt asked where we wanted to go.

"How about some food?" Justin offered.

"There's only one restaurant that's open right now," Matt said. "It's a pizza place called the Cliff, over by the river. Amazing thin-crust."

Justin said, "Deep-dish trumps thin-crust any—"

"Wait a second," Jeremy interrupted, and he leaned forward between the front seats. "Are you seriously discussing pizza crust right now? After what just happened?"

"This is a pretty typical night for Justin," I told Jeremy.

"I might still have cops after me," Jeremy said. "Shouldn't we be running for the border?"

"They won't find you," Justin said. "Your tracker runs on a wireless signal that I passed on to Scott, and he'll program it into a train, or a shuttle. It will buy us time to eat and then Matt will help you out from there."

Jeremy sat back in his seat, and his eyes passed over all of us. "Who the hell *are* you guys?" he demanded, and I started laughing. I had nearly been arrested *twice*. I should have been scared. I should have at least felt guilty for crashing a cop car. Instead, I was soaring. Rebelling had that effect on me; it was like a drug I was becoming addicted to. I liked the high.

"I'm Justin Solvi," Justin told him and grinned over his shoulder.

Jeremy nodded. "I've heard of you. The founder of the DS Dropouts. The Godfather of anti-DS. You have a lot of fans."

"I'm not the Godfather," Justin said. "But there's definitely a family history."

"I'm Maddie Freeman," I said, and Jeremy did a double take.

"Wait, Kevin Freeman's daughter?" he asked. "I thought you looked familiar. My little brother thinks you're hot. He has a digital poster of you up in his room."

"What?" I said. "They have posters of me?"

Justin nodded. "I've seen them," he told me. "You photograph really well."

"By the way, I heard you were supposed to take the night off," Matt said.

Justin nodded again and slipped his phone into his jacket pocket. "I was hoping to have a date."

"Sorry it didn't work out," Matt said.

Justin looked at me. "You don't mind, do you, honey?" he asked me with a smile.

"Not at all, sweetie," I said, and blew him a kiss.

CHAPTER seven

Matt parked on the roadside in front of the Cliff. The restaurant offered only outdoor seating; the entire deck was covered with a white tent, and underneath, the canopy was dotted with yellow twinkling lights, like a private sky of stars. Heat fans blew warm air around us and we followed the hostess to the back of the balcony. A handful of tables were occupied with nocturnal life—some people in dresses and clubbing clothes and other people casual in shorts and flip-flops. Matt and Jeremy sat on one side of our booth, and I slid in next to Justin. His arm naturally looped around my back, and his fingers played with the zipper on my dress. I did my best to study the menu but I had to force my mind to concentrate on food.

The Cliff was an appropriate name for the restaurant, since it was built on a rock overhang that had formed during the Big Quake, a massive earthquake that hit Los Angeles in 2037. People still talk about it. Half of the seaside hotels, houses, streets, and freeways slipped into the ocean. It was the largest natural disaster to hit the United States. All of the major highways were ripped up and spat out in the quake, as if the earth had opened its mouth and tried a bite of concrete but didn't like the taste. Underground subways in California have been banned ever since. Buildings have also changed dramatically since the quake. All the sky-rises (the one I live in included) are built on a layer of rollers, and the buildings themselves are made out of suber, a material that can bend and flex. Engineers declared these buildings indestructible in any natural disaster: floods, earthquakes, fires, and tsunamis. And they were proven right. There have been two substantial earthquakes since '37, and sky news coverage observed the buildings in all their synthetic glory, waving and gliding easily with the swaying earth, as graceful as dancers on a stage.

One of the most impressive consequences of the quake was a giant fissure that cracked through the city, beginning at the ocean and snaking its way to East L.A., forming a narrow canyon. Ocean water rushed in to fill the open crevice, which is now called the Hollywood River. Most people avoided the space but a few downtown businesses were gutsy enough to build in the exposed earth.

Golden lamps surrounded us, and the canyon walls blocked the wind. I could smell the dusty rocks and the salt water and I could hear the water lapping the sides of the bank hundreds of feet below.

We ordered, and then after the waitress brought our drinks, Justin asked Jeremy how he escaped from the cops. "What did you mean when you said you were paranoid enough to get away?" he asked him.

Jeremy took a sip from his drink. "I'll die before I go into a detention center," he stated, and his hard eyes said he meant it. "My best friend was sent to one last year. He lived next door and we hung out all the time with a couple of kids in my neighborhood. We all hated DS. He was in the detention center for only three months."

"What happened to him?" Justin asked.

"I don't know," Jeremy said. "He's home, and we've talked, but I haven't seen him. He says he's fine and he's happy but he won't meet me face-to-face. I stopped by his house once, and he wouldn't even leave his room to talk to me. We talked through a wall screen. And his parents say he's cured. But if being cured means dying like that, I don't want it," he said. "So I keep a tranquilizer gun in my room. I sleep with it. I carry it everywhere, just in case. I had it with me when the cops showed up."

Matt nodded. "We've done virtual interviews with former DC students. That's all they agree to — they refuse to meet in person, even though some of them used to lead face-to-face groups."

"And they all claim they're fine," Justin added. "But most of them are on antianxiety meds. It doesn't translate. No one who works at a DC is willing to talk either. It's the one system we haven't been able to hack into."

Jeremy looked around the table nervously, as if he thought we all expected something out of him.

"Listen, I really appreciate you all helping me out, but don't think I'm going to join your side or anything."

"It's not a side," Justin said. "It's a state of mind."

"Okay, whatever you want to call it, it's pointless. You know that, right?"

"Pointless?" I asked.

"Yeah. It's like having a local food drive to end world hunger. Your heart might be in the right place, but really, you're not even making a dent in the problem."

"I don't want to make a dent. I want to inspire a revolution," Justin clarified.

Jeremy smirked. "You can't fight digital school," he argued. "It's the law. You might as well overthrow the government while you're at it."

I narrowed my eyes at this but Justin only looked amused.

"You're right," I said. "We might as well quit. We'll just drop you off at the detention center on our way home."

Jeremy's smirk faded. "All I'm saying is remember who you're up against. It's not just the digital school; it's our society in general. And the government doesn't budge. It takes politicians twenty years to pass a new speed-limit law. You think you're going to change DS anytime soon? Good luck."

I watched Justin but he didn't look discouraged. When people argued about his mission, it only fueled him. He seemed to thrive on proving people wrong.

"So how come no one intercepted *me?*" Jeremy asked.

"We have to be selective these days," Justin said. "So many people are getting arrested we can't keep up. We intercept only people we think will join us. No offense," he added, "but someone who repeatedly gets busted for cheating isn't high on our list of people we want to recruit."

The waitress delivered a pizza, which she set on a metal stand in the center of our table. We passed plates around and scooped up slices, and the yellow cheese pulled apart like string.

"So what are you going to do if you actually win?" Jeremy asked.

"I'll have my freedom back," Justin said simply. "You think you're free? You're not. You live in a computer system. And you're conditioned to think it's the best thing for you. When it comes to technology, humans are as easy to train as rats in a cage."

"What happens if you lose?" Jeremy pressed.

"I don't see it as winning or losing. I'm just looking for a middle ground," he said. "I get that technology is convenient and has its benefits. We definitely can't live without it. We can't go back to living in caves. But most people are so plugged in, they're not even living in the real world. Our lives aren't grounded by anything. Being too dependent on something makes you a slave to it. And I sure as hell won't worship a digital screen. So I'm looking for a halfway point. A balance. It's not just about ending digital school. It's about having a choice."

❖

It was after three in the morning when Matt and Jeremy dropped us off at Pat and Noah's apartment. When we got inside, Justin checked the rooms, and everyone was still out.

"The party couldn't have been that bad," he noted. I found some blankets and sleeping bags in the hall closet and we spread them out on the floor in Noah's studio. The room smelled like electronic equipment.

Justin threw down some couch cushions for pillows.

"This is why I need my own apartment," he said as we looked at our makeshift bed. He tugged his coat off and put it over a speaker and dove down on top of the pillows. He flipped over and sprawled out on the floor and then placed his hands behind his head and looked up at me.

"I'm not tired," I said. "It's hard to get tired around you."

"Even after tonight?" he asked.

I shook my head. "There's always too many firsts. My first virtual club, my first attempt to shut it down, my first car accident, my first riverside restaurant. You're always there for my firsts," I said. "You're like the tour guide of my life."

He smiled. "It's a fun job."

I looked down at the hem of my short red dress. "I didn't bring pajamas," I said, and I could feel the blush warming my face.

"That dress wouldn't be very comfortable to sleep in," he

pointed out, and he kicked off his shoes, flinging them to the side.

"You're right," I agreed. It was tight but stretchy with spandex and I easily pulled it over my head, which left me in just my heels and underwear.

"Off," I said, and the lights snapped off. I slid off one shoe.

"On," Justin said, and the circular overhead light snapped on again to reveal me. He smiled.

"Off," I argued. This went on for a while, the light snapping on and off, until we both were laughing. Until he pulled me down on the soft blankets with him. We agreed to dim the lights.

❋

The next morning I sprinted into my apartment; I could smell coffee brewing so I knew Joe was up. I turned the corner into the kitchen, which wasn't much bigger than a storage closet, and Joe stood next to the counter, pouring a cup of coffee.

For a second I had a flash of my perfect life: Justin living in Los Angeles. Finishing DS and finally being free from my probation, my parents' control, and my past. Meeting my brother for coffee. Clubbing with Clare and hanging out at Noah's concerts. Trying to bring back face-to-face classes and jobs. For the first time ever, everything was falling into place, and my life was becoming a clear, solid picture that was focused and centered and colorful.

"Nice timing," Joe said, and started pouring a second mug.

"Sorry, I'm in a hurry." I had just enough time to shower and change before I met Justin downtown. He was leaving for San Diego tonight and I was determined to spend every possible second with him. We had a list of apartments to tour before he left.

"Give me five minutes," he said, and offered me the mug. "I want to talk to you." I glanced at the clock on the refrigerator wall screen and back at Joe.

"Okay, three minutes," I offered. I took the coffee and slid onto a stool next to the counter that separated the kitchen from the living room. It was so rare we spent any one-on-one time together, I didn't want to pass it up.

Joe studied the wrinkled T-shirt and shorts that Justin had loaned me and the plastic bag I was holding, which had my dress and shoes inside. "Where have you been?" he asked, and glanced at the tennis shoes that I'd borrowed from Clare's suitcase.

I considered skirting around the truth but reminded myself that Joe wasn't my dad. I took a chance.

"Justin's in town," I said, and felt a girlish grin brush my face.

His eyebrows rose. "That's who you were with last night? You told me you were going out with Clare."

I sighed and set the bag on the floor near my feet. Bringing up Justin's name around Joe usually sparked a heated debate. I couldn't blame Joe for resenting him — it was true that he encouraged my rebellious side. But that side was dormant only because Dad had smothered me with regulations for so long. I was just living in a shadow. It was interesting that two such vastly different men had had the greatest impact on my life.

"He met up with us," I said, like it wasn't a big deal.

Joe sat down on a stool next to me. "You know something, Maddie? I really don't think Justin's your type."

I fought a groan and took a sip of coffee. Do older brothers feel it's their birthright to screen who their younger sisters date? "You don't know my type," I assured him.

"I have some friends who are single, if you're looking for a boyfriend."

I couldn't help but laugh at the idea of anyone replacing Justin.

"Great," I said. "I'd love it if you'd pimp me out to your friends. Are you going to introduce me as your juvenile-delinquent little sister?" I knew I was being a brat but I was tired of my family condemning me for dating the most amazing person I'd ever met.

"I will if you act like one," he said, and his face was serious. "What about your friend Pat?"

"Pat?"

"He's into you. He's *unplugged*, as you like to refer to it. And he isn't running from the cops on a daily basis."

"That's no fun," I said, and Joe frowned. "He's Justin's cousin," I pointed out. "And he knows we're just friends."

Joe shook his head. "Guys don't want girls as friends," he told me. "If he's hanging out with you, it's because he thinks he has a chance."

"Whatever," I said, and took another sip. I told my brother it was none of his business who I dated. I never picked on the girls he liked. "Not that I care, but why don't you think Justin's my type?"

"Other than the fact he's leading a revolt against our father?" Joe asked. He scrunched up his face. "I don't know. He's kind of a hippie."

I set down my cup and stared at him. "People still use that term?" I asked, and Joe shrugged. "He is not a hippie. He's like James Bond in blue jeans," I said with a smile.

"Well, when your tree-hugging Bond boy leaves and goes running around trying to save the world, what are you going to do?"

"Probably help him," I said.

"So you've decided to join his side?"

"I'm leaning that way. Why fight gravity?"

Joe's eyes narrowed. "You don't learn anything from your mistakes, do you?"

"Mistakes are simply a matter of opinion," I said. "Joe, I've had full-time babysitters my entire life. I could really use a break. I know it's well intended and I appreciate you care, but there's a fine line between caring and controlling. And I'm very sensitive when someone's trying to breach that line."

Joe stared at me like he didn't recognize me. "Who are you and what did you do with my baby sister?"

I took another sip of coffee and gave him a proud smile. "I grew up, Joe. It's finally me."

He nodded slowly. "That's what I was afraid of." He rubbed his finger thoughtfully along the rim of his white mug.

"Paul called me last night," he said. "He saw footage that people took of you at the dance club. He was wondering why you weren't keeping a low profile since you're supposed to be in the LADC."

"Paul Thompson?" I asked, my throat already tight. "What did you tell him?"

"I told him the truth. That you were still hanging out with DS dropouts."

I stared at the ceiling. "Why would you tell him that, Joe?"

"He's a good friend. The Thompsons are like family to us."

"Paul Thompson wants to see me burned at the stake. His dad's my probation officer. What were you thinking? You should have just dropped me off at the LADC."

"What were *you* thinking?" he shot back. "Paul told me you helped out with an interception. And you crashed a cop car? This isn't funny anymore, Maddie. This is serious. You could have killed someone."

"That's what airbags are for. They're designed to withstand impacts at over sixty miles an hour."

"What are you, some secret agent all of a sudden? One of the cops is in the hospital with broken ribs and a punctured lung. How do you feel about being responsible for that?"

I looked down at my lap and felt terrible. "I'm sorry. We didn't plan the interception; it just happened. That kid stopped our shuttle and we were only trying to help."

"You help the wrong people," Joe insisted. "Don't you see that? Maybe you shouldn't be hanging around Justin anymore. The guy's bringing you down." He looked away from me and sighed. "I did some research and the LADC doesn't sound that bad. It's a rehabilitation clinic. It might really help you."

I stood up and tried to laugh but it got caught in my throat. It sounded like a whimper. "I'm getting out of here. Nice talk. Now I get to go into hiding again."

We were interrupted by a knock at the front door. I looked at Joe with suspicion, but he refused to meet my eyes. No one ever knocked on our door. For a second I foolishly thought it was Justin, but he knew better than to come up here; he knew where he wasn't welcome.

"What's going on, Joe?"

"You should get the door," he told me. "It's for you."

The muscles tightened around my lips. "Open," I told the sensor, and the door unlocked.

Two tall uniformed figures walked in. My first instinct was to run but my feet were locked in place. Damon and Paul blocked the only exit in the apartment. They stared at me and their faces held identical cocky grins.

"We meet again," Damon said.

"It's been a while," Paul added.

I glared at Joe. "You knew they were coming all along?"

"Sorry, Maddie," Joe said. "I just care about you. I don't want to see you throw your life away because you're too naive to know what you're doing."

I slumped down onto the stool and pressed my face into my hands. I wondered if there was a website where you could buy and trade brothers because my current one sucked. Disownyourfamily.com. I'd have to look into it.

"It was a cute prank," Paul said.

I looked up at him and rolled my eyes.

"Is this your new goal?" he asked. "To free the world one digital dance club at a time?" He laughed at his own joke.

"How thoughtful of you to come all the way down here to be my personal escort," I said.

He asked for my hands; I grudgingly raised my arms and he slapped metal handcuffs around my wrists. "My dad and I made a special trip down here to keep your arrest private. That way no one could intercept you this time. Nobody knows about this. We were open to working with you and your father until you almost killed a cop last night."

I stood up and Damon grabbed my biceps tightly with his hand. "You're about a month late for your registration at the LADC."

I mumbled that I preferred to be fashionably late wherever I went. I tried to play confident even though my hands were shaking. Damon's eyes pierced mine. His patience was gone.

"You don't speak unless I give you the privilege. You understand me, young lady?"

He squeezed my arm so tight I flinched and forced myself to nod. If there were two words together that made my skin crawl, they were *young lady*. Only adults used that expression and it was just to be condescending.

"Let's try this again," Damon said.

I glared at Joe before they hauled me out the front door. I wondered if it was a curse in our family to let one another down. I could feel tears brimming behind my eyes but I refused to let these men see me buckle.

I concentrated on one image. One face. I held that picture in my mind and it reminded me who was on my side. It gave me the courage to hold my head high as they dragged me down the empty hall to the elevator.

CHAPTER *eight*

I looked out the tinted car window and watched the scenery pass but I couldn't make out a single detail in the landscape. It was too hard to focus when my thoughts were spinning. The confined space in the car made it an effort to breathe. Panic always had this effect on me.

Just when I thought my life was falling into place, it was all pulled out from under me, like somebody yanking a tablecloth from beneath perfectly set dishes, toppling everything and leaving a disarray of chipped plates and broken glass.

The sound of voices raging in my head was the worst. Regret screamed at me for screwing up. *Why is it my destiny to be a perpetual screwup? Why can't I be a nice, easy, simple, obedient teenager who is content to wake up and go to school every day? Why can't I be satisfied with good grades and a clean bedroom and my own flipscreen and wall screen and social dates and movie nights and online friends? Why can't I be content with a structured, predictable life? Why do I have to take the risks? Why do I have to mess everything up that is neat and easy and laid out for me? There are so many clean paths trimmed and paved and I always have to run through the middle, where there is no path; there are vines and brambles and rocks and holes and I fall down and scrape the hell out of my life. For what? Kicks?*

I watched my world narrow in on all sides until it became so small I was trapped. I knew no one was coming for me this time. My arrest wouldn't be in the police listings for Scott to hack into.

I closed my eyes and imagined Justin waiting for me downtown. He had an even sharper intuition than I did. Maybe he would sense something was wrong. But by the time he figured it out, it would be too late. And I knew one thing: no one had ever escaped from a DC. No one had ever broken in. My future was officially carved in stone. That was the most unsettling idea of all.

Skyscrapers gave way to a warehouse district, and the car slowed down in front of an old abandoned shipping yard. A railroad track used to run through the area, but it was bent and uprooted in the Big Quake. Pieces of iron twisted and poked out of the ground like a giant fossilized reptile. Damon pulled the car up to the entrance of the detention center. He opened the back door and grabbed my arm to lift me out. I looked up and down the sidewalk, searching the area for anywhere I could run, just as Damon attached a second handcuff to connect his wrist to mine.

"Don't even think about it," he said.

I stared around at my new existence. A white sign read LADC in black letters and evoked all the warmth of a snarl. A tall electric fence encircled the deserted lot, and a low hum emitted from the charged lines. Behind the fence stood two buildings at opposite ends of an open, dusty lot. The one in the far corner was a small, single-story office building. Looming across from it was a modest sky-rise, about ten stories high. There were no windows, and I assumed, judging from the grainy, beige exterior, that it was made out of suber, like all of the modern skyscrapers built after the Big Quake.

Paul waited in the car while Damon pulled me toward a kiosk. We were greeted by a bored-looking security guard. He wore a black vest that said LADC across the chest pocket, and silver-coated sunglasses blocked his eyes. Damon shoved a registration card through an open window in the gate.

The guard uploaded the file and furrowed his thick black eyebrows as he skimmed the information. He told me to hold still and reached through the window to scan my eyes using a white laser that slowly measured each iris. It was for additional security; an eye scan was impossible to cheat. He examined his computer again and mumbled something into his headset. A few seconds later, he looked at Damon with a frown.

"We don't have her scheduled to check in," he said.

"She should be in your system," Damon said. The guard nodded but stated that a scheduled drop-off time was mandatory.

"It's a last-minute registration," Damon persisted.

"This isn't a hotel," the guard said. "We don't do walk-ins, you know that."

I perked up at this. If I could stall for an hour, that might be enough time. I knew Justin would be suspicious by now. He was probably at Joe's apartment, following my trail. He'd have Scott check the routes of every police car in Los Angeles. An hour was all I needed. Time could save me.

Damon glared at the security guard and guessed my thoughts. "I'm not going to sit around here and give somebody the chance to intercept this girl. You'll have to book her now and talk to Richard later."

The guard chuckled. "I'd love to, but the boss doesn't make exceptions."

"Get me your superior," Damon grumbled. "This girl isn't moving unless she's inside those gates."

The guard sighed and slammed the window shut.

Paul impatiently got out of the car and stalked over to see what was holding us up. He looked more determined than everybody to see me impounded. Maybe he was still bitter over my date rejection six months ago. I was tempted to tell him that holding a grudge was really unattractive.

We silently stood in the warm, dry air. I listened for noise inside the gates, for voices or movement or life of any kind. If DCs were rehabilitation clinics, surely they let students move around outside? Maybe visitors were allowed.

A few minutes later we heard footsteps approaching. A woman walked briskly through the courtyard. She was middle-aged, and her sandy blond hair was pulled back in a tight ponytail. She wore a simple white polo shirt that said LADC in the corner tucked into brown slacks. She had a collection of keycards on a lanyard around her neck and she carried a scanner in one hand.

"What's the problem here?" she asked, and eyed me through the gates. She didn't look a bit happy to be interrupted. She pressed her hands on her hips and narrowed her small blue eyes, which gathered wrinkles at the corners. I held her gaze and she raised her eyebrows as if she recognized me.

"She's in our system," the security guard said. "But we didn't have a check-in time scheduled for today."

She looked at Damon. "This is against company protocol."

Paul took a step forward. "You can take your protocol and shove it—"

Damon put a hand on Paul's chest and pushed him back. "Look, this is Madeline Freeman," he stated.

The woman nodded. "I thought I recognized you," she said to me.

I raised my shoulders in response. Great. I was a celebrity convict. Dreams do come true.

"She was scheduled to be dropped off a month ago," the guard

75

continued. "According to her file, she's been meeting with a psychiatrist in L.A. for evaluations. Her violation is still under investigation and charges are pending."

I raised an eyebrow at this information. My dad must have written the file. He had obviously been trying to keep me out of the detention center. But then why put me in now?

She huffed. "So, Mr. Freeman just assumes his daughter gets VIP treatment? Well, he isn't involved with the DC regulations. This is Richard Vaughn's area."

"Fine," Damon said. "If you have a problem with it you can contact Richard personally and he can call Kevin and you can waste all of our time. We'll wait right here."

She narrowed her eyes at this. Technically Richard was my father's boss. He was the one that funded digital school. But she knew as well as the rest of us that my dad always got his way. She backed up and told the security guard to open the gate. Damon unfastened my handcuffs and when the gate slid open, he waved me forward. I walked through and the entrance gates closed behind me with a metal clang. I could feel Paul and Damon watching me, but I refused to look back at them. Meeting their eyes would just seal their victory, and I refused to give them the satisfaction.

"Follow me," the woman said roughly, and turned toward the sandy courtyard. She took impatient strides and I tried to keep up with her while I searched the open area. There wasn't a single tree or blade of grass, just a dusty, concrete washout. When I pictured detention centers, I imagined a scene out of a prison movie: kids shuffling their feet, smoking, hanging their heads; people walking around in orange jumpsuits sharing a communal silence of regret. Instead, there wasn't a single sign of movement. There wasn't one footprint imprinted in the gravel.

"This isn't a sightseeing tour," she scolded, and I quickened my pace to catch up with her. We walked to the taller building, which she called the dormitory. I stopped and squinted up at the soulless sky-rise. She typed in a code and swiped a card, and the doors buzzed open. Her voice turned flat as an automated recording.

"Each floor is separated by gender. You stay on your assigned floor at all times."

I nodded and followed her into an elevator.

"The electric gates around the DC are live twenty-four-seven. I wouldn't recommend getting too close. The charge won't kill you. It damages the nerves in your spinal cord, but it leaves your brain intact. So you can think, you just can't move."

I stared at her. Friendly welcome speech. I wasn't sure what bothered me more: that the gates could paralyze me or that she was smiling as she told me. Scare tactics had been used on me for so long I was learning how to trap them and block them before they ever penetrated.

I just nodded my head solemnly. The elevator arrived at the fourth floor and we stepped out next to a utility closet. She opened the door and there were shelves full of clothes inside, neatly folded and stacked and arranged by size. She handed me dark green scrubs; my uniform, she explained. She also handed me a blue towel and some generic black underwear and sandals.

We continued down the hallway and she pointed out the bathrooms, two single units. She opened one of the doors and a light snapped on. It was an open space with a toilet in one corner and a sink built into the wall. A metal showerhead stood in the far end. There were no curtains; there wasn't even a mirror.

"Shower, change, and when you're done, hand me your civilian clothes," she told me.

She shut the door behind me. Before I let the silence loom and allowed more panic to set in, I hurriedly stripped off my T-shirt and shorts. I realized quickly that I had to live in this place from second to second. If I tried to think even a minute into the future, the fear would kick in and they would win. I had to stay in the moment. It was the only time I could count on.

I took off my underwear, folded everything, and set my clothes on the edge of the sink, next to a toothbrush holder. There was a metal hook over the door, and I hung up my scrubs and towel. I stood naked in the confined space and looked at the showerhead. My thoughts turned to documentaries I'd seen about concentration camps. I felt like I was standing in a gas chamber.

My teeth started to chatter. The linoleum floor was cold on my bare feet. But it was more than the cold space that felt menacing. It was the energy of this place; it felt like I'd stumbled into a void, as if the air were a vacuum that sucked out any hope inside of me.

I reminded myself to move. I turned on the shower and a heavy spray pelted my skin. There were three clear cylinders welded to the wall, labeled as soap, shampoo, and conditioner. I turned up the temperature until the water was scalding hot. I wanted to feel something warm, something that made my skin almost burn, but my feet refused to warm up. Air seeped out of the vent in the ceiling and blew a cool breeze, like icy breath, through the water. I was shivering by the time I was done, and the scrubs were so thin they felt like tissue paper over my skin; putting them on barely made a difference in the chill.

I came out of the bathroom and handed the supervisor my regular clothes. She wasn't wearing a nametag and I assumed she wasn't on a first-name basis with the students, but certainly someone had to be. Wouldn't someone have to interact with us? She stuffed my clothes in a yellow canvas bag with the number 415 printed on it in red letters and shoved the bag down a chute in the hallway labeled LAUNDRY. The space was so small, she had to push to get the clothes through.

I followed her down a narrow corridor, lit by one single ribbon of fluorescent lights that cut down the middle of the ceiling like an electric vein. Every door we walked past was shut. I tried to feel the energy of people but all I felt were walls. She told me all the rooms were soundproof so the students wouldn't be disturbed. *Or acknowledged,* I wanted to add.

I lumbered behind her; my sandals were a size too big so I had to drag them along the floor to keep my feet from sliding out. In my green scrubs I felt like a patient admitted to a mental hospital. Maybe that's what they wanted us to think. They wanted us to feel like we were sick, like we all needed to be healed. In our identical uniforms we were no longer individuals. The DCs disconnected us from our old lives in order to start us new again. They turned us off to restart us.

She pointed to a lens in the ceiling, a circular black bulb protruding in the middle of the hallway.

"We call it the Eye," she told me. "There's one on every floor, in every hallway, and in every stairwell. It provides better security than humans do because the Eye doesn't even need to blink. It watches your every move in this place."

She stopped in front of room 415.

"The rules here are simple," she said. "No talking to other students. No loitering. Keep your movements outside of your room to a minimum."

"What happens if I don't?" I wondered out loud.

She raised an eyebrow. "The Eye watches. People will be informed. Let's just say, you never make the same mistake twice in here."

She opened the door and I followed her inside.

"Your room doors are locked from ten p.m. to six a.m. If you need to get out at night for an emergency, you'll have to call security. And it better be a good reason. We run on routine in this place and we don't like interruptions."

The room looked like what I imagined a college dorm would: small, functional, with a metal cot in one corner and a desk in the other. Just enough sterilization to make you homesick. There was an open closet in the corner of the room with a clothes hamper in it. Every wall was covered in a digital screen, as was the ceiling and the floor. They weren't going to deny us technology—that much was obvious. It felt stuffy inside, since there were no windows, but the air was cool, circulating through a small vent in the ceiling.

She raised a scanner in her hand and told me to spread my arms and legs. I did as I was told and she passed the scanner along my body to make sure I wasn't hiding any kind of bug or tracker. When she was satisfied I was no longer contaminated with any ties to the outside world, she dropped the scanner and punched some numbers into the device.

I looked around the room and felt isolation wrap its cold arms around me. We had to be allowed some kind of human interaction. People will go insane if they're completely isolated. Humans are social; the administrators couldn't deny us some contact. Could they?

"Where do we eat?" I asked, hopeful there was a cafeteria or a commons.

"You eat in your room," she said, and pointed to a narrow metal window, inches above the desk. She told me there was a menu on my computer and whatever I ordered would be delivered through the slot. I stared at the rectangular space, a flat metal mouth, and nodded. Of course, the point of a DC is to keep you separated. Encourage distance. Reinstall you into the digital life.

She pointed to the keypad on my desk. "Your computer's programmed to answer any of your questions," she told me. "You'll be spending a lot of time together."

I stared at the keypad and felt a chill crawl over my skin. I could feel the confident shell around my chest start to crack.

She informed me my first counseling session was tonight.

"Counseling session?" I asked.

She nodded. "It's mandatory. You'll meet with a counselor routinely to help you adjust to the DC and discuss what brought you here in the first place so it doesn't happen again. We've never had anyone return to a DC once they're released," she added proudly. "We have a one hundred percent success rate. Not many correctional facilities can claim that."

The statistic reminded me of something my father often said, and it gave me one more reason not to trust her.

"Someone will be by tonight to escort you to your first session. After that, the elevator will be programmed to let you go there on your own when you have appointments. The counseling rooms are on the first floor of this building. The elevators are programmed to take you there."

She pointed to the pajamas on my bed: a dark green T-shirt, sweatshirt, and sweatpants.

"Throw your dirty clothes in there." She motioned behind me to the tall, square hamper in the closet. "We'll empty it out during your counseling sessions. You'll get a stack of clean uniforms and enough bedding to change your sheets every day. Any questions?"

I looked down at the bed. "I don't think I'll need new bedding every single day," I pointed out. It seemed a little luxurious for a detention center.

She was quiet for a few seconds before she answered. "Why don't you wait a day or two before you decide that?" she offered. "You might change your mind." I heard a noise down the hall and I turned my head in that direction. "Oh, one more thing," she added, and raised a finger, gesturing for me to follow her. We

walked down the hall and I heard someone around the corner.
The hall widened at the end, and we turned and entered a small
corner room that had a food machine set up against the back wall.
A boy was stocking the counter with clean mugs. He looked
young enough to be in digital school, but he was wearing a staff
uniform. He was tall and gangly, with dark hair cut close to his
head. Silver-wire-rimmed glasses slipped down his nose. He
pushed them up and grinned when he saw us.

"Hey, Connie." He addressed the woman standing next to me
with a single nod.

She frowned. "No using first names in front of the students,"
she reminded him and he nodded apologetically. She rattled off
that each floor had a food station stocked with water, tea, coffee,
and snacks. I looked back over at the boy while she was listing my
choices. Our eyes met and there was recognition on his face. His
blue eyes stared at me a little too boldly, and I figured he recognized me.

A single chair was tucked in the corner, black and metal and
hardly inviting.

"You take everything back to your room. This is the only place
to get warm food." She pointed to the soup and sandwich options. "All the meals sent to your room are cold. This is your one
luxury, so don't abuse it."

I almost thanked her but I had the feeling I'd get chastised for
it. Connie nudged me back into the hallway and we stopped outside room 415.

"Your tour's done," she said with a flat voice as she opened the
door for me and I stepped in. "Welcome to the LADC."

She shut the door and left me alone. I looked around at the
stark white walls and felt like I was stuck inside a dream, not quite
conscious, like I was hovering between two lives. It was strange

standing here without a single thing to connect me to my past life. It made me feel uneven. Unreal. A little transparent.

I collapsed down on my bed and stared at the white ceiling. I took in the new smells, a mix of clean sheets and electronics from all the digital screens. My clothes smelled like bleach. I listened for the new sounds. Every place has its own unique shifts and movements that you need to get accustomed to before you can relax. But I knew I'd never relax here. The only sound was choked silence. It slid over me like a shadow.

PART 2

Life, Simulated

CHAPTER nine

No one was going to save me this time.

I felt like a character in a video game, as if someone were watching my life and manipulating my movements with a remote control. I'd entered a world where I'd be running blindly through a barrage of obstacles and trying to dodge blows I couldn't see coming until they were already on top of me.

I sat on the bed and raked my fingers through my hair. Enough feeling sorry for myself. If there was one thing I'd learned from Justin, it was that change didn't come by throwing a pity party. You could sit around and wait for life to happen or you could get busy and make it happen yourself. So I got out of bed, turned on my wall screen to a blank document, and spoke out loud, recounting everything I could remember from the last few hours. It seemed important to think, to feel, to use my senses. I paced back and forth and imagined the walls away. I tried to picture the courtyard outside. I pretended I was an undercover journalist sent here to investigate the detention center. If I could capture every event that occurred inside of this place, maybe I could shed some light on what was going on and help other kids in my shoes.

I could view this experience as a lesson instead of as a punishment. It was a relief to put my thoughts in order and reflect on what had just happened. It helped everything make sense. I watched as my voice was converted into words on the screen and my sentences became paragraphs. I saw my story take shape, like a scroll unrolling in front of me.

I stopped talking and looked around at the walls. My words hung there, suspended, and I realized they weren't safe. Everything I recorded was property of the DC. They were probably reading my words right now. I tried to delete the paragraphs but they clung to the walls. I reached out, as if my hand could sweep them away.

I realized the DC could take anything from me. Even my thoughts. They didn't want us to reflect in here. They didn't want us to remember. They didn't want us to think.

❁

There was a knock at the door, and I opened it to find the boy I had met at the food station. His arms were full of sheets and scrubs, piled all the way up to his chin.

He walked in and crammed the clothes onto a single shelf in the closet. Then he glanced around the room.

"Wow," he said, looking at the wall screens still crammed with my words. "Working on a novel?"

"I think too much," I admitted.

"Well, this place will cure you of that," he said.

I looked around at the walls. "I keep forgetting I don't have to think. Computers do it for me. Thinking just gets you into trouble."

He studied me. "You're Madeline Freeman, aren't you?" he asked.

I nodded at his assumption. "Why do you look so surprised?"

"We never learn people's names in here," he said. "The staff refer to you all by numbers. I've never recognized anyone before." He tilted his head to the side. "Your dad couldn't pull a few strings to get you out?" he asked.

I shook my head. "No," I said simply, and glanced around. "With his connections I was hoping for at least a penthouse suite. But at least there's room service," I noted.

He stared at me like I was speaking a foreign language. Or maybe he wasn't used to people having a sense of humor in this place. He cleared his throat.

"Um, we're not really supposed to talk to the patients," he said, as if he had to remind himself. "That's why we never learn your names. It's a staff rule not to get personal with anyone."

You mean, not to treat us like we're human? I wanted to ask. He motioned for me to follow him and started walking down the hall toward the elevator. I glanced up at the black bulb as we passed under it and imagined eyes inside, yellow and unblinking, staring down at me.

He scanned his keycard and the elevator door opened. I got in and leaned against the metal side. He had to scan his card again and punch in a series of program codes before the elevator agreed to move. He pretended to be interested in staring at his shoes, avoiding my eyes as if he already regretted being friendly. But I wouldn't give up so easily.

"Looks like I won't be breaking out of here in this thing," I noted of the elevator space.

"Not likely," he said.

I tapped my chin thoughtfully. "Well, there aren't any windows in this place, as far as I can see. There's a stairwell. That might be the best plan to escape at this point. Or maybe the air vents, that's how they always do it in the movies."

He gazed at me with a poker face. "You think I'm going to give you pointers on how to break out of here?" He stared at me for a few seconds to determine if I was serious or insane. I didn't know where I was getting the nerve to talk to the DC staff like this.

"Sorry," I said. I told him I was just tired of being ordered around all day. "I have a low tolerance for following rules."

"Look where that got you," he observed.

I shrugged. At this point, I'd sunk as low as a person could. I was officially the world's biggest loser. The positive side about crashing to the bottom is that you can only rise up.

"What's your name?" I tested him.

"Only the doctors are allowed to share their names," he told me. "They don't encourage conversation in here."

"That's too bad," I said, and looked at the elevator doors. "You must get lonely."

I could feel him watching me.

"I mean, I've known you only a few minutes, but you seem like a people person."

He cleared his throat again and his tone shifted to professional. "We always escort people to their first counseling sessions. Show you how this place breathes," he said. The doors slid open and we entered a brightly lit hallway. It looked exactly like the fourth floor: a narrow corridor with rooms spaced at equal intervals.

"Do people live down here?" I asked, and he shook his head.

"Most of these are counseling rooms," he told me. Our shoes brushed against the shiny linoleum floor. He stopped next to a door with a sign on it that said IMAGINE YOUR WAY. He opened the door for me but I hesitated to walk through.

"You'll be fine," he assured me. I stepped inside the room. It was completely empty, nothing but bare white walls. As soon as the door clicked shut behind me the screens snapped on. I gasped at the sight. The world around me—the walls, ceiling, and floor—

had turned into a forest. Tall pines waved thick arms of needles around me and their branches climbed like ladders until they disappeared into the sky. A cool wind brushed my face. Bright green ferns blanketed the ground, and rocks and fallen logs were covered in thick green moss that looked as soft as fur. A blue sky was visible above, through the shade of branches. It looked like I'd walked inside a fairy tale.

I followed a dirt trail that felt soft and real under my feet. The gravel crunched under my sandals. A slow stream rippled alongside the trail and I bent down to watch the water glide over rocks and sand. I started to relax. Maybe people were wrong about detention centers. Maybe the point wasn't to scare kids into accepting the digital world but to seduce them into it.

I wondered which emotion was more powerful in the human mind: fear or desire.

I reached my hand down to touch the bubbling stream, and the water was ice-cold and refreshing on my fingers. I brought my fingers to my mouth as if I could taste it but my dream was interrupted when the door buzzed open.

I stood up and a tall woman walked in. She had straight red hair that hung over her shoulders and she wore a long white lab coat. She carried a flipscreen tucked under one arm. She looked around at the rainforest and grinned.

"Interesting choice," she said, and her voice echoed inside the empty room.

"Choice?" I asked.

I looked around at the scene but when she shut the door the image changed. The lush forest landscape turned into muted brown paint. The floor turned into beige tiles and the ceiling into white plaster and harsh lights. My senses shriveled in response. It was like someone offering you a plate filled with bars of milk chocolate and then taking it away and handing over plain toast.

"How did you do that?" I asked.

"This is an imagery screen," she told me, and raised a hand to point at one of the walls. "It depicts whatever you desire. You were trying to relax when you walked in, so the computer programmed a scene to settle your mood." I blinked at the walls, stunned that seconds ago the place had looked like a rainforest. She crossed the room, and her high heels clicked loudly on the bare floors.

"I'm Dr. Stevenson," she told me. She pressed her finger on a panel in the wall and a square, cushioned area, the size of a chair seat, rotated down and formed a right angle with the wall.

"Have a seat," she said. I walked across the room, my sandals dragging with each step, and sat down. She asked for my hand and I hesitantly offered it to her. Her grip was cold on my skin as she ran my fingerprint along a scanner. She looked over at the wall screen and my name instantly appeared in neon yellow.

"Madeline Freeman," she stated. Images popped up around me. My entire life was depicted in words, graphs, and pictures. There were profile pictures and yearly school photos. There were images of my family and some of my online friends. There was even a shot of my parents' wedding picture. My health records were all there, my family tree sprouting up from the ground and billowing out like branches and leaves. There were graphs and charts showing how I stacked up against my peers academically and socially. There were lists of all my grades, my social groups, and my interest groups. All my contacts were noted. It showed where I shopped online. It listed the current classes I was taking—only nine credits to finish and then I could take my DS graduation exams.

She clasped her hands behind her back and studied the information. Her eyes fell on one particular spot and I followed her gaze and saw her reading my criminal record. It showed that I had assisted with a DC interception a few months before and that I was a suspect in what had happened at Club Nino, as well as guilty of aiding in an interception that same night. But the worst crime, the one I committed when I was fifteen years old, wasn't even listed. My dad was still managing to cover it up.

"Looks like you've been running with the wrong crowd," Dr. Stevenson said. "The digital-school dropouts, as they're referred to."

She unraveled a white cord attached to a MindReader and told me to put it on. I did as she asked and pressed the cold metal to my temples until it stuck into place. I felt a tingling sensation from the reader vibrating against my skin.

"To be honest, I'm not interested in your criminal record," she told me. "This is why you're here," she said, and pointed to a chart on the opposite wall. Looking closer, I realized it wasn't a chart; it was the outline of a human brain. *My* brain. It was split up into two sections, one red and one blue. The blue side was markedly larger. One word next to a percentage labeled each area of my brain:

POSITIVE: 11%

NEGATIVE: 89%

I looked from her to the screen and back, waiting for her to explain.

"Our minds are like energy fields, Madeline," she said. "They're controlled by our emotions, which is what I'm measuring right now. As you can see, you harbor mostly negative emotions like fear, anger, anxiety, and hostility. Very unhealthy. These kinds of feelings are toxic. They're like viruses infecting your mind. If you don't fight them off, they'll eventually take over."

I blinked at the screen. "How can you tell what I'm *feeling?*"

She pointed to the MindReader I wore. "This MR is the center's own design. The electrodes can analyze emotional activity in your brain, and our modeling system categorizes it."

"How convenient," I mumbled.

She studied me. "What was that?"

"Why don't you *ask* me how I'm feeling? I thought that was the way counseling worked. You ask the questions and I answer them." I looked back at the screen and wondered what my brain activity for rebellion looked like. It was probably off the charts.

She nodded like she was used to this kind of response. "Technology's come a long way," she informed me. "This instrument can measure your brain waves, your blood pressure, and your hormone levels. The neuroscope," she said, pointing to the electrode, "is one hundred percent accurate. No human being, no matter how intelligent, can compete with that kind of perfection.

"Some psychiatrists," she continued, "prefer to counsel the old-fashioned way and ask questions, but humans are confusing creatures to understand. They lie, they doubt. They say one thing and mean another. They repress some emotions, they obsess over others. It can take years of work to draw any kind of conclusions. This system can do it in a matter of seconds," she said with a smile.

You're right, I thought. *Why ask me questions when you can plug me in and categorize my brain? Saves lots of time.* She studied my eyes for a few seconds and then pointed at the screen, which was still recording my apparently angry brain waves.

"This number is what concerns me," she said. "Negative energy is like a disease in the body. It weakens you. It festers. It wears you down. It can make you self-destructive, even violent. It's unhealthy to internalize these emotions for very long."

"At least I'm feeling something," I pointed out.

"You feel very strong emotions, Madeline," she agreed. "But my goal at the DC is to help you find a positive outlook on life. What we aim to work on here is your animosity toward your life, *toward DS,* which is breeding your hostility. We want you to be happy. We want to show you, day by day, why this system is right and is best for everyone. Why you should trust it, not fight it. Life is too short to be this angry. Our goal is to increase this number," she said, and pointed her finger at the red, positive area of my brain.

I stared at the numbers, not convinced they reflected what she claimed.

"And we have six months to do it," she added, and reached into the front pocket of her lab coat. I blinked at her words.

"Six months?"

"That's a normal DC sentence. Sometimes it's shorter if you're open to the treatment." In her hand, she held a small compact. She flipped it open and there was a square tablet inside. I immediately shook my head.

"It's just a relaxant," she said. "It dissolves on your tongue. It's the only way to guarantee we're getting the facts out of you during these meetings. Although we might not need that with you," she added with a tight grin. "You seem more than eager to speak your mind."

I looked at the orange tablet with apprehension. "If I'm already being honest, I don't need it," I pointed out. "Besides, can't the reader tell if I'm lying?"

She nodded. "It can tell me if you're lying, but unfortunately it can't tell me what the truth is. A lot of students think if they cooperate, if they say what we want to hear, then we'll let them go. But that's not the way it works. This medicine helps us open up your mind so we can see everything inside. So we can help you."

She held out the drug, but I still didn't take it. My mind was all I had left, the only weapon I had in here, which, I realized, was why they wanted it. My mind was the last weapon they needed to confiscate.

"What if I refuse?" I asked.

She raised her eyebrows. "It's mandatory. You can take this willingly or we can administer the drug through a syringe, with force if necessary. Most people prefer this way to the needle." She continued to hold out the compact and waited. "You can't fight what's inevitable, Maddie."

I grabbed the tablet and put it in my mouth and it dissolved quickly on my tongue. It fizzled and tasted like the cough medicine my mom gave me when I was little and had a cold. Dr. Stevenson closed the compact and slid it into her pocket.

She smiled. "Now we can begin the session," she told me.

I nodded but my head felt heavy, like weights were inside it, pressing it down. The room was fuzzy and all the sharp angles turned soft. I looked up at the ceiling and tried to focus, but a foggy halo framed the lights above me. They dimmed, going from white to yellow to gold.

"The Cure's starting to work," I heard her say, and her voice echoed against the walls.

I started to fall forward but a hand guided me back, and then I was sinking.

I closed my eyes and when I opened them I was sitting in a desk in an old-fashioned classroom. It was a face-to-face high school, like my mom used to describe, with desks aligned in rows, all facing the front of the room, where a middle-aged man in a dark beard and glasses was lecturing. He was animated and used his hands while he talked. A student sat in front of me, someone I didn't recognize, and I watched the teacher's lecture form paragraphs on his computer screen while he typed his own notes in the margins. It was archaic, like I'd time-traveled back thirty years.

I looked to my side and froze. Justin was sitting at a desk in the next aisle. I glanced around and saw that Clare, Noah, Pat, Scott, and Molly were all in the room. I recognized Erin from soccer and some of my old digital contacts. I even recognized Jake and Riley, two of Justin's friends I'd met back in Oregon. There was a poster on the wall of the periodic table and illustrations of how to identify types of plants and flowers. What was I doing in a science class? I studied Justin's profile while he took notes. He wrote longhand, the way he preferred. He was the only one writing.

I could feel the energy I always sensed in his presence but I still didn't accept he was real. I reached out to touch his arm and felt his skin warm under mine. It was so natural to have my hand there. He looked at me and grinned.

He leaned in close. "Stop staring at my lips," he whispered.

I could hear his shoe moving across the ground. I could feel his body heat. I was so relieved to see him I wanted to cry. I curled my fingers around his arm tight, until my knuckles raised out white through my skin.

"What's wrong?" he asked.

"Justin, what are we doing here?" I whispered. "Where are we?"

His grin disappeared. "Are you all right?"

That's when the explosion hit. We felt it before we heard it, a shudder, like a tsunami had slammed against the walls of the school. Then the windows blew out from a gust so strong it ripped me out of my seat. My body was thrown forward and I felt a searing heat rip through my leg. I flew, pushed through the air in a wave of heat, until a concrete wall caught my shoulder with a cracking punch.

The next thing I heard were screams. A chorus of them, high and shrieked. They were worse than the explosion. Screams circled in the air followed by thunder as wood and concrete and steel shifted out of balance with a crash. I covered my head as I was attacked in all directions from the ceiling dropping around me, piles of splintering wood and crumbling concrete.

Then, just as quickly as all the noise had erupted, it suddenly stopped and there was a silence. I tried to lift my head but it was too heavy. The ground around me was warm and wet. Someone was mewling close by. I blinked my eyes open and stared at blue sky above, sunlight streaming in through a cloud of dust. How did I get outside?

People coughed and gasped around me. Standing pillars of concrete buckled and fell, sending up more clouds of ash. I tried to move but I was stuck. I attempted to lift myself up and pain shot through my leg and made me gasp. I grabbed my leg, and my jeans were ripped and my skin was wet. There was a hole where my knee used to be and my fingers touched soft, swollen flesh that was so painful I started to heave. I couldn't tell if my leg was completely severed from the knee down; there was too much blood. Acid burned my throat and poured out of my mouth. I tried to roll on my side but my leg was stuck under slabs of glass. I screamed for someone to help me but no one answered.

I lifted my head and looked around. I could see Clare. She lay motionless a few feet away. I called out to her. Fallen beams and rubble separated us. I could smell smoke now. Flames crackled like laughter. I coughed on the fumes and tried to free my leg. I screamed for Justin. I screamed because it was the only thing I could do.

My eyes searched the devastated yard that used to be a school. The pain in my leg caught my breath in my throat. It stole my voice. I swallowed back tears. The smoke was getting thick, like a pillow pressed hard against my face to suffocate me. The heat was unbearable. Fire crackled and snorted. I closed my eyes against the burning air and started to choke. Then a hand reached out and started to lift me free.

❁

"Justin!" I screamed, and this time the shout woke me up. I bolted straight up in bed, shaking and sweat soaked. The blackness around me was as thick and gritty as coal. I instinctively grabbed my leg and exhaled in relief to feel it underneath my pants, sweaty and soaked through, but all in one piece. I lifted my leg and bent my knee back and forth. I touched my shirt and felt something warm and thick and realized I had thrown up. I pulled the shirt off and winced at the acidic smell. I threw it down on the floor and hugged myself to keep warm.

"On," I mumbled, and squinted as light flooded down from the ceiling like fluorescent rain. I half expected to be in a hospital room, but I was back in my dorm room, lying on the narrow cot. I shivered and looked around fearfully, expecting someone to be lurking. I listened closely at the walls to hear the ticking of a bomb or a distant scream. Silence answered me and it was secretive and cold.

I tried to remember how I'd gotten back to my room. The last memory I had was the counseling session. I wiped sweat off my forehead and realized I had soaked through all my clothes. My pants clung to me like a second skin, and the sweat was turning cold and making my body shake in response.

"It was just a nightmare," I whispered out loud to console myself. I rested my forehead on my knees and took deep, slow breaths. I wrapped my arms around myself and rocked.

"It was just a nightmare."

I wanted to see one person. The one person who could assure me everything would be all right. The one person I believed in more than myself. I knew he was close. I knew he was fighting to get me out. I stared at the emptiness surrounding me. I couldn't see him with my eyes but I could find him with my mind. I curled my mind around him and held on as tight as I could.

CHAPTER ten

The clock on the wall read 6:00 a.m. The door unlocked with a smooth hum. I stood up too fast and a head rush nearly made me topple over. I balanced myself with a hand on the edge of my desk. My temples were pounding. I groaned and rubbed my fingers over my forehead. My body felt like it had been through a marathon. I peeled off the rest of my sweaty clothes and put on a fresh pair of underwear.

The details of the nightmare were already starting to fade. I couldn't remember who specifically was in my dream or where we had been. I just remembered feelings: terror, pain, heartbreak, and despair.

I sat down and tried to think, but my mind was heavy and muddled. I turned on the wall screen to find what I wrote yesterday, but the document was gone. I sighed and assumed the detention center had erased it. Obviously, they didn't want us to record our memories here.

I stood up and paced as I tried to recall what happened last night, but my thoughts were fragmented. They shifted and slipped through my consciousness before I could grasp hold of them. I could scarcely remember a face from yesterday, let alone details. Even Dr. Stevenson was a blur, like a picture out of focus.

I opened a new document, thinking that if I began again, the words might help me remember. I needed to try.

"A woman gave me a tour," I said out loud. Wait, was *tour* the right word? "She helped me settle in," I said. "I met with Dr. Stevenson. She wants to help me. She said I'm sick." I stopped pacing and considered this. "Maybe she's right. Maybe they're not trying to punish me in here. They're trying to save me. Maybe there is something wrong with me."

I blinked at the wall in front of me, at my own words, and wondered who had spoken them. Emotions churned through my mind, but they were distant and shattered; they weren't my own. I couldn't separate real from imaginary. What was real?

I pulled my fingers through my sweaty hair and it made my head ache. I wanted to be angry but I was only empty. I wanted to think but I could hardly feel. I was numb.

I tugged on a clean pair of scrubs and headed for the door. My room was pressing in on me. Maybe walking around would help me think. I opened the door but stopped when I heard the elevator at the end of the hall. I looked down the corridor and saw a girl in a wheelchair. Her head leaned to one side like she was asleep, and straight brown hair fell over her face so I couldn't see her features. I didn't recognize the woman escorting her—she had gray hair pulled back in a bun and wore a white lab coat like Dr. Stevenson. I stepped toward them and was about to call out, desperate to talk to someone, but the doctor looked at me and pressed a finger over her mouth. Her narrowed eyes warned me to keep back. I obediently stayed in place until they turned the corner, moving out of my sight.

I sighed and shuffled down to the food station and ordered a cup of coffee. The machine dispensed steaming black liquid and I looked at the coffee with a faint smile. It was something familiar, and at that moment, I needed to be reminded there was a world outside of this place. It reminded me I still existed. I sat down on the cold metal seat and breathed in the warm, rich steam, already feeling revived.

I heard footsteps and looked up to see the boy who had escorted me to the counseling session. He came around the corner carrying a box and when he saw me he stopped so quickly his shoes squeaked against the floor. We stared at each other for a few seconds, the room quiet except for a few trickles and hums from the food station. He looked at me like he'd never seen a human being before.

"What are you doing out of your room?" he asked.

I kicked into defense mode. "The doors unlock at six. I thought I could use this whenever I wanted." I pointed to the machine with my thumb. "My one little luxury?" My voice came out hoarse, and my throat hurt as if I'd been screaming for hours.

He set the box down on a table next to a storage closet and his eyes locked on mine. He didn't look angry to see me out of my room. All I could see was surprise.

"I know you can leave your room, but why did you want to?" he asked.

"What are you talking about?" I asked. I winced at another piercing pain in my temple and started rubbing my forehead, which only made it worse. It felt like my head was caught in a mousetrap.

"You're dehydrated," he said. "That's why your head hurts."

"How do you know my head hurts?" I asked.

"Everybody's does the first couple of months. It's part of the transition process." He ordered a bottle of water from the machine, uncapped it, and handed it to me. I put the coffee down. My lips were parched, and staring at the water made me realize how thirsty I was. I took it and slammed the bottle down in a few gulps. The water was so cold and refreshing, I could feel it slide down my dry throat, all the way to my stomach. The pressure in my head was already starting to lift. I stood up and ordered another bottle and grabbed my coffee.

"Thanks," I said, and hugged the cold water to my chest. My throat felt a little better.

"No problem."

"What's your official job here?" I asked. "The detention-center know-it-all?"

He grinned. "Something like that. I'm just a privileged veteran." He watched me carefully, like he was waiting for me to do something. He took a step closer while I uncapped the second bottle of water and inhaled it in five easy gulps. I wiped my mouth and when I looked back at him, he was right next to me, close enough for us to touch.

"What are you staring at?" I asked.

"You're not afraid of me, are you?"

I wanted to laugh at the suspicion on his face. He'd just helped me out. "Why would I be afraid of you?"

"Because I'm standing so close to you. Doesn't it freak you out?"

"I haven't showered yet," I said. "Maybe you should be the one freaking out."

He didn't smile, and I studied him seriously this time. He was a head taller than me and his eyes were intense on mine, but he was hardly intimidating. His eyes gave him away. They were compassionate. If I felt anything, it was that he was genuine.

"No," I answered. "I'm not afraid of you. Should I be?"

He seemed puzzled by my response. "You should get back to your room. People aren't supposed to hang around out here," he reminded me. "If you leave your room for more than ten minutes, the Eye starts to wonder."

My headache was starting to lift. Before I walked away I managed a weak smile.

"How long have you worked here?" I asked.

"How long is your sentence?" he asked, ignoring my question.

"Six months."

He nodded. "That's pretty standard."

I shook my head. "I can't wait that long," I said.

"You'll adjust," he said, and turned to unlock the storage closet.

"I'm getting out of here," I announced. He stopped and turned back, probably to see if I was serious. "I can't wait six months," I said, to remove any doubt. "I'll find a way out, or my friends will break in. Whichever happens first."

He frowned. "I'm going to pretend I didn't hear that. You know it's my job to report those kinds of remarks."

"Sorry," I said. "I'm not thinking straight. I guess it's that tablet they gave me. The Cure, right?" I stopped when this memory came back to me. For a split second I had clarity. I could see the compact in Dr. Stevenson's hand. I could taste the tablet in my mouth. Just as quickly, the image disappeared, covered in a fog. But I knew what I saw.

He froze suddenly and stared at me.

"So, they are drugging us in here, aren't they," I said. It wasn't a question. It was a fact.

"How do you know about that?"

"I remember," I said. Judging from his look of disbelief, I wasn't supposed to remember. *Anything.*

He backed up slowly, opened the storage closet without another word, and disappeared inside.

I turned the corner, walked down the hall to my room, and shut the door. I leaned against it and regretted being so outspoken. I hadn't even been here twenty-four hours and I was already getting written up. My father would be so proud.

CHAPTER *eleven*

I expected the routine of a detention center to be tough, disciplined, and militant. I imagined people shouting orders at us, waking us before dawn to march us in line, forcing us to adhere to a strict schedule. But after spending a few weeks at the DC, I'd come to discover that their idea of structure was a life of chronic isolation.

My days fell into a mundane routine. The detention center limited the use of computer programs. I had access to the three DS classes I needed to finish and was restricted from socializing or entertainment sites. My only social contacts were a few DS professors and tutors. Movies, music, and books were limited and censored. I was allowed to use only two programs: one to design the wall screens of my personal prison cell (how liberating) and the other to fill out countless questionnaires meant to help me find myself (and lasso all that negative energy with a rope and pull it free).

My counseling sessions still ended in nightmares; they became expected villains that infiltrated my mind, invaders trying to break into my consciousness and rob me of my sanity. Sleep came in sporadic waves and was usually plagued with dreams that were so real I woke up screaming but that I forgot within a few seconds. The few times I tried to make sense of them, the memories were blocked, as if they were behind a gate in my mind that I couldn't lift. All I could remember were my feelings.

You can't control your thoughts when you sleep. I was learning my mind had a mind of its own—and I had a feeling that was what the DC was determined to manipulate.

I tried to distract myself. I designed two digital windows in my room because the walls were suffocating. I could display any climate I was in the mood for: clear and sunny weather, overcast, heavy rain, light mists, a blizzard. I could even place a tornado along my path, and speakers brought it all to life with the sound of hail and wind and the clap of thunder. I liked the idea there was a force outside the detention center stronger than the force inside. A tornado could take out this entire place in one gust. It could pulverize anything in its path. It made me think something could set me free.

I knew I was weaker. Skinnier. Tired. I knew my walls were starting to crumble. But I refused to accept it. Sometimes denial can be your greatest ally.

❂

One morning a message blinked on my screen informing me I had a counseling session in twenty minutes. I checked the box indicating that I'd received the notice. I went to the session alone. I did everything alone. When I opened my door that morning, there was another inmate coming out of the bathroom at the end of the hall. My first instinct was to avoid her, but that was quickly replaced by desperation. I needed to talk to someone, to remind myself there were human beings living on the other side of my walls.

"Hey," I called out to her. I shuffled toward her and her spine tensed as if I'd jolted her with a Taser gun. She froze with her back to me and I stopped halfway down the hall. Her arms went rigid and her back was stiff and straight. Her hands shook next to her sides and I could have sworn I heard a whimper.

"Sorry if I scared you," I said to her back. "You're just the first kid I've seen in here. You don't have to talk to me." She lowered her head, pivoted slowly on one foot, and took a quiet step toward what I assumed was her room. She moved so carefully you would have thought someone was holding a gun to her head and threatening to shoot if she made a sound. Her hair was mangy and fell past her shoulders. I took another step down the hall and she peeked at me through stringy clumps of hair. This time I was the one who froze. The skin on her face was pale and gaunt and her eyes were sunken. She looked like she was fighting a disease and the disease was winning. But more than any of that, what stopped me was the terror in her eyes, the way she looked at me like I was about to attack her. There was hate there too, a territorial warning to leave her alone.

She slid inside her room and shut the door. I realized I wasn't breathing and suddenly my lungs kicked in, clawing for oxygen. I stumbled forward and the elevator doors opened and I ducked inside, grateful to escape that hallway and that girl and that stare, that awful, hateful stare.

Dr. Stevenson was waiting for me when I walked in, the seat already pulled down. She moved quickly to unwind the cord around a MindReader.

"Lucky for you I had an open session today." She handed me the MindReader and told me to put it on.

"Did I do something wrong?" I asked.

"What do you define as wrong?" she asked me.

Great, I thought. *Mind games, just what I need.* "I haven't broken any rules," I said. Then I remembered what I'd said to that staff worker. He probably ratted me out.

"Students normally have only one counseling session a week, but the Eye has informed us you've been leaving your room several times a day. You even addressed another girl in the hallway on your way down here." She opened up a compact, revealing the orange tablet. I took it and placed it on my tongue.

"Didn't the staff tell you, no talking to other students?" she asked.

"I'm sorry," I said honestly. But I couldn't argue anymore. My mind started to float out of my head and toward the ceiling. My thoughts were light and I didn't have the energy to reach out for them and yank them back. I could see the screens and then I was standing in the hallway on my floor. I recognized it because all the room numbers were in the 400s. I looked around, confused, wondering what the point of the session had been if she'd kept me only a few minutes. That was supposed to be a punishment?

I heard something rattle, and a wheelchair turned the corner and came toward me. I recognized the same gray-haired doctor pushing the same girl I'd seen a few weeks ago, with her head down and her hair falling over half her face. I walked toward them and as the wheelchair approached, the girl suddenly stirred and sat up straighter. She reached her pale arms out like she needed my help. I leaned down, and just as I did, she sprang out of the wheelchair and leaped at me, like a jumping spider.

The hair was swept away from her face to reveal skin that was so thin and tight it was translucent. I could see the outline of a skull underneath. Her eyes were black holes. I screamed and backed against the wall as her fingers reached for my neck; she opened her mouth, and the skull's teeth came at me. I shoved her shoulders away, but all I felt were bones. I tried to run but my feet slid and slipped and I fell to my knees. The girl was behind me, clambering after me. Her nails clicked against the hard ground. I crawled and scrambled toward my room, screaming for someone to help.

Something chased after me, hissing and pulling at my ankles. Pointy skeletal fingers clawed at my skin, gashing my legs. I heard an animal behind me growling and snapping its teeth, and I kicked and jabbed my way to my room. I slammed the door shut with my foot, panting and whimpering on the cold floor. The animal hissed and cried behind the door, clawing at the metal. I leaned back on my shaking arms, trying to catch my breath. My heart was thrashing. I pressed my hand against my chest and focused on my breaths and that's when I caught movement out of the corner of my eye. I heard something flutter. I turned and there was a girl standing in my room, next to my bed. I recognized her. It was the girl I'd tried to talk to in the hallway.

"It's you," I said, my voice shaky. "What are you doing in here?" She smiled at me. But it was a maddening smile. Her sunken eyes were black. She started to laugh and the laugh turned into a snarl as she lunged at me, her arms raised above her head and a silver blade clenched between her hands. I reached up and caught her skinny wrists and the blade stopped an inch from my forehead.

❖

I shot straight up in my bed and barely caught the scream in my throat. I panted for air in the blackness. I instinctively grabbed at my chest to feel my drumming pulse, to remind myself I was alive. I wiped sweaty hair out of my eyes and rolled up into a tight ball and started to cry. I cried because the images were still there; they were real, as if I were living someone else's memory. I curled up as small as I could. Maybe if I made myself tiny enough I'd disappear completely. Maybe then I'd be left alone.

I turned my wall screen on and looked for a program to design rain. I turned my ceiling into a thick gray storm front. My speakers sprinkled the patter of drops around my ears. It sounded like a chorus of tears. I let it drown me. I rolled up again and felt freezing cold, but the cold was not outside or around me. The cold was inside. I was chilled to my core, like my chest was an icebox. My thoughts hung like jagged icicles.

CHAPTER twelve

When I couldn't stand the headache any longer, I forced myself out of bed and changed into clean scrubs. I put my hand on the metal door handle and was about to push down when an image flashed in my mind. A girl's skeletal face. A knife diving at my head. I snapped my hand away from the handle like it had burned my fingers. I pressed my hand to my heart and felt it hammering as if it were right there directly underneath my skin, as if it had escaped its cocoon of ribs. Then, as quickly as the image had seized me, it dissolved, leaving me feeling merely scared and vulnerable. I rested my forehead on the door and tried to kick the feeling out of my mind.

"What the hell is happening to me?" I whispered, my palms flat against the door. In my mind, buried deep inside, I knew that wasn't a memory. I knew it was just a nightmare, just fiction. I couldn't let my fears run my life. I forced myself to move. I forced myself to fight back.

I opened the door a crack and listened for any unusual noise but heard only the humming of the lights and the churning of the food station around the corner. I remembered the hot coffee, and it made me think of my mom and Baley, my chocolate Lab, and home. I clung to that memory of love and support and let it swallow me. For a moment I felt brave. I wanted more of that feeling—maybe it was hope, or love. I followed it and held on to it like a rope and let it guide me.

I moved down the hall with as much life as a zombie. I dragged my feet to the food machine and ordered three waters and slammed one of them in a few desperate gulps. Already, the details of my dream were blurred. Mentally, it was fading. But my body was still jolted by the shock. My shoulders were tense with panic.

I heard steps approaching and fear made me jump. My half-closed eyes flew open and my pulse hammered. I grabbed the counter. My first instinct was to hide. I recognized the tall, gangly staff worker as he came around the corner, but when he saw me he kept his distance, as if he knew better than to approach me too fast. He gave me a few seconds to calm down. It looked like he was used to this kind of reaction.

"Out of your room again?" he asked.

I let go of my grip on the counter, and my heart relaxed. "I'm catching on it's not very common around here," I said, my throat raw.

"You don't look very good," he said.

I laughed darkly. I hadn't looked at myself in days. I could only guess how disheveled I'd become. It's hard to care about your body when you're losing your mind. I rubbed my head and shook it back and forth. The small movement made me nauseated.

"Come on," he said to me. I grabbed the water bottles and followed him wordlessly. Instead of escorting me back to my room, as I'd assumed he would, he opened the storage closet next to the food machine. A light switched on, and when the door shut behind us, he scanned his finger to open another door in the back of the small room. A blinding streak of light filled the doorway.

I held my hand over my eyes to shield them from its intensity. I winced as my eyes adjusted and then I followed him onto a small wrought-iron balcony, crudely constructed, as if it had been an afterthought once the building was completed. It was a narrow space that looked out to a desolate shipping yard on the other side of the electric fence. The view was nothing spectacular, just the abandoned dockyard, dusty and brown and sprouting weeds. I slowly raised my hand into the air to feel the warmth of the sunshine. The air smelled dry and it moved and circulated like a breeze.

"What program is this?" I asked, and gulped in a breath of fresh air.

"It's not a program," he said. "We're outside."

I smiled my first smile in weeks. It felt strange to wear the expression. I was using muscles I'd forgotten I had. We sat down on the metal grating.

"Aren't you worried someone will see us?" I asked.

He shook his head. "I've haven't seen a person on this side of the grounds for as long as I've worked here. I think staff used to smoke out here, but no one uses it anymore." He rested his elbows on his folded knees. "My name's Gabe, by the way."

I lifted my head to the sunshine and took a long drink of water. I listened to the breeze, the way it stirred the air, and I reached out one of my hands so it could tickle my fingertips. I could feel Gabe watching me, but I hesitated, unsure what to say to him. I wanted to confide in someone. My mom used to tell me you should trust people until they give you a reason not to. But I stopped believing that because the people I should have been able to trust let me down. I was starting to think I could only trust myself.

I decided to test Gabe. To see if *he* trusted *me*.

"Gabe," I said, "can the Eye see that we left?"

He shook his head and looked right at me, his eyes focused on mine. His eyes were light blue, with a darker ring around the iris. They were deep and calm, like water. He seemed to be studying my eyes as well, probably because it was just as rare for him to make eye contact with people as it was for me. "It only monitors the hallway; it can't see the storage closet, around the corner. Not that I should be telling you this." It was a relief to hear honesty. I took a chance.

"I've been having nightmares," I said. I assumed he already knew this; I wasn't telling him anything new. I was just opening up a window in my mind and giving him a little peek inside.

He nodded. "It's just a stage. They'll go away after a while, once you adjust to being here."

I thought about the word *adjust*. He made it sound so simple, but to me the word meant giving in. Breaking down. Losing the fight.

"Does this happen to everybody?" I asked him.

He nodded. "It's part of the transition process. It's a normal reaction to the detention center."

"Normal?" I repeated.

"Sure," he said. "Think of all the changes you're going through. Your life's been completely uprooted and thrown off balance. You were separated from your family, from your past, from everything. Change is a huge stress on the body. That's what causes the nightmares. It's like posttraumatic stress disorder."

I took another sip of water. "You know, if I wanted to hear a load of psychological bullshit, I would have just asked Dr. Stevenson."

Gabe shifted next to me. "You have a lot of nerve, you know that?" he said.

I nodded because my nerve was all I had left and it was hanging on by a shaky fuse, ready to disconnect. "I've never had nightmares in my life," I said stubbornly. "Why would I suddenly start having vivid nightmares that I instantly forget when I wake up?"

His mouth tightened. "I don't know. I'm not a psychiatrist."

We were both quiet for a few seconds. I knew Gabe was holding something back. He knew more than he let on. He didn't trust me yet.

"What's your theory?" he asked. "About the nightmares?"

I sighed and rubbed my forehead.

"I can't think straight long enough to have any definite theories. It's like my brain's asleep half the time. But I know they're giving me some kind of a drug. And I know I'm hallucinating. Except my mind thinks it's real. I can feel the pain in my nightmares. I physically and mentally experience it. I can't draw the line between dreaming and reality anymore. It's like they're force-feeding memories into my head. Then, when I wake up, a switch turns off in my mind. I can't remember any details."

"Why would they force you to have nightmares only to have you wake up and instantly forget? What would be the point of that?" he asked, as if he'd been wondering this for years but had never had anyone to talk to about it.

"I don't know," I said. "But my friends could help figure out what's going on." I met Gabe's eyes and took a chance. He didn't look away.

"What could your friends do?" he asked.

"They could study me, take blood tests. Give us some answers. Something isn't right in here and you know it."

I was taking a huge risk. Gabe could be working at the DC to spy on students, to draw out anyone still trying to rebel. But I had a decision to make and I decided to put my faith in someone I barely knew. I was gambling with my life but at this point I had nothing to lose. My life didn't belong to me inside here.

He hesitated and it gave me hope.

"Gabe, I know you can help me. You must be allowed out of here once in a while? You can contact my friends. They're going to try and break in here anyway, even if you don't help," I added, because I never stopped believing Justin was looking for me.

He raised his eyebrows. "Oh, really? Who are your friends? The leaders of the digital-school protesters?" His tone was sarcastic but I nodded.

"Yes," I said.

He looked out at the dusty gravel yard. "If you try to break out of here and it comes back to me . . ." His voice trailed off.

"I won't run away, I promise. I need to get outside the gates, just for a couple hours." I leaned forward. "Please, help me. You don't agree with this place. I know you don't, or you wouldn't be sitting here with me right now."

He looked conflicted. He stared down at his hands and slowly nodded.

I told him he needed to contact Justin Solvi. "He has to know I'm okay."

Gabe perked up when the words came out of my mouth. "You're friends with Justin Solvi?"

I nodded. "You've heard of him?"

"You could say he's a household name around here. You know how much the government would love to arrest that guy?"

I smiled. "They haven't had much luck."

He shook his head. "Somehow his record is always clean. There's rumors and stories but no trail. It's like trying to track a ghost."

"He exists, believe me," I said. "You'll never find him. He has no online identities. These days that does make you a ghost."

"I've been following news stories about him," Gabe said. "I know he inspires a lot of people to fight digital school, but look where it gets them. Right here," he said.

"He's trying to intercept people before they make it this far," I said, defending him. "He's trying to help."

He was quiet for a few seconds. "You should get back to your room," he said. "The Eye keeps track of how long you're gone."

CHAPTER thirteen

"Time for some more brain-busting?" I asked Dr. Stevenson at my next appointment. I was so exhausted I could have curled up on the cushion and fallen asleep, but I did my best to look energetic. I couldn't accept the idea that she was winning.

"How have you been feeling?" she asked as she read my pulse.

I wondered why she bothered asking. Couldn't she plug me in and see for herself? Wasn't that the point of her convenient technology?

"I'm fine," I said simply.

"Any questions for me?"

I shook my head.

"Any concerns?" she pressed.

I focused my eyes on hers. She had small, narrow eyes the color of wet sand. She tried to use them to make me buckle, to spill my mind. But I'd grown up with a father whose eyes were like bullets. I was trained to deflect the blow.

We watched each other. I had hundreds of questions but was certain she'd give me phony answers. *Why do I have these nightmares that seem like you're planting a mechanism in my brain to ac-*

tivate fear? Why do I wake up drenched in sweat? More absurdly, why can't I remember details once I wake up? Where are my memories going? Why are you filling my mind with experiences that aren't my own, with memories I would never want?

I decided to answer her with something she didn't expect.

"There is one thing that's bothering me," I said. She nodded like she knew what was coming. She was waiting for me to mention the nightmares.

"I miss being around people," I said. "I miss my friends. I wish we could at least interact with other inmates."

She opened her mouth to say something, but then hesitated and instead of speaking nodded slowly. I knew what the hesitation was. She was surprised.

"In a few months you'll be able to socialize again. You can make new contacts and chat all you want."

I shook my head. "I miss being face-to-face with people. It's so much more intimate." I paused and had to fight a smile in response to the deep frown on her face. This, she didn't expect. "And I miss being outside," I added. "I miss the sun."

Her eyebrows pulled together. "Well, we have programs to simulate sunshine. There's virtual tanning or weather programs you can download. Sunexposure.com is a good one. Sunstreaks .com is another popular choice."

I shook my head again. "It doesn't compare to the real thing."

She thought about this for a second. "You're right," she said. "It's much better than the real thing."

My mouth fell open. Did she seriously think programs that mimicked nature were superior to nature itself?

"How do you see it that way?" I asked. I felt like our roles were reversed. Now I was doing the counseling, as if she needed the therapy more than I did.

She leaned her back against the wall and looked out across the room. "It's one of our greatest human flaws, Madeline," she said. "We desire the very things that harm us. We don't know how to discipline our desires. We never know our limits until we hurt ourselves. It's what leads to our downfall—the things we want the most ultimately destroy us."

I asked her how the sun was dangerous.

"The sun is necessary. We need it to sustain life. But we're also drawn to it. We're mystified by it, we bask in it, but the sun is just a ball of radiation. It's poison to our skin, and people don't know how to limit themselves. We expose ourselves to it until we're burned, until we get cancer. It's the same with eating. We need food to nourish us, but we'll eat until we make ourselves sick. People need to be prescribed the right dose of their desires in order to live. Humans need guidelines and parameters or our desires become our own suicides."

Looking at Dr. Stevenson, I doubted her milky skin had ever been exposed to the sun. She could be thirty years old, she could be fifty. It was hard to tell because there were no laugh lines around her eyes or her mouth. She didn't have any wrinkles, but she also didn't have any signs of living. There was something empty and dull about her pale skin.

"People don't like to be forced," I said.

"Look at it as being guided," she said simply. "Humans think they're invincible. They feel entitled to overindulge in anything they want. They think everything on this earth was put here for their enjoyment. Even the sun. And humans are inherently selfish. We overindulge until someone cuts us off, until we learn how to pace our desires. We are a dangerous species to let loose, Madeline. This planet won't thrive unless we're contained."

She took the compact out of her lab-coat pocket and handed it to me. I took the tablet obediently. I couldn't tell what stung more, the pill in my mouth or the anger pulsing through my spine that this shortsighted scientist was controlling my mind and I was powerless to fight back.

Or was I powerless? Was that merely what they wanted me to believe?

I folded in on myself. They wanted to open up my mind in here, so that's what I was determined to fight. I imagined my brain was a house and I locked all the doors and boarded up the windows. *I won't let you inside,* I thought. *I won't look at you. You are not real. You cannot find me in here; you can't break in. I'm not yours. This is just my body. Just a layer of me, one piece. You can't begin to contain me.*

I closed my eyes and when I opened them, they immediately started to burn. I was standing inside of a thick cloud of smoke. I inhaled and my lungs rejected the contaminated air and left me choking. Screams pelted my ears. People shouted for me to run. The world was camouflaged in white ash.

Panic took over and pushed my legs forward. I couldn't see anything; my eyes burned with tears and I tried to breathe again but the smoke scratched against my lungs like sandpaper. People pushed past me. Footsteps stomped and dragged and tripped. Something crashed nearby and I instinctively covered my head as the ground rumbled. Glass shattered around me like high-pitched screams, and the white sheet of ash blew against me with a hot gust. I heard a child crying next to me. I reached my hand out to find her but all I felt was heat. I could smell blood around me; it had a metallic odor, like hot iron.

I fell over something on the ground and when I felt around for what had tripped me, I touched cold fingers. I held on to them and squeezed, then bent my head down closer and realized I was holding a severed arm, blown off and lying in the street. I lifted myself up before fear could hold me down. My hands were covered in blood.

Sirens wailed around me. Debris was falling from above, as if the sky were splintering into pieces. I kept running but I didn't know if I was running into danger or away from it. Faces flooded through my mind: Justin's, my parents', my friends'. I screamed out for them, for anyone to help. I could taste acid in my mouth. A body fell from the sky and landed so close to me that the ground under my feet shook and I heard a slap as blood splattered into my eyes.

❋

I woke up screaming in my bed. I had kicked off all the sheets. My body was damp with sweat. I thought someone was in the room and I instinctively wrapped my arms over my head.

"On," I cried, and the lights snapped on and I covered my face with my hands, but I still peered through slits between my fingers. The room was completely bare. There was no sign of blood or any kind of struggle. Tears ran freely down my face and into my fingers. My sweat turned cold and I started to shiver. I needed to go to the bathroom, but there was no way I was going outside. I glared at the door like it was my enemy. Fear pulled on every corner of my mind, but I mentally pushed back. I forced myself to think about something real, so I imagined Justin. I let his fingers play through my hair. I let his words rain over me. The idea warmed me up, starting inside and slowly working its way out. I knew he was out there, right now, looking for me. I wrapped my mind around that and held on to it like a lifeline. Already, my nightmare was starting to fade. I kept my mind on Justin. I refused to let any other thought seep in. I stared at him like he was staring right back at me.

❋

There was a knock at my door and the sound made me jump in my bed. I bolted up and looked around at my wall screens, at the safe boundaries of my life, and sucked in a shaky breath. The door eased open and I could smell strong coffee. I lay back down and pulled the sheets up to my chin as Gabe walked in my room. He perched himself on the side of my desk and held the coffee out to me, waiting for me to take it. I looked at the white ceramic mug. There was steam slowly curling above it. The smell made my stomach knot.

I yanked the covers over my face. I'd barely slept the last few nights, my mind always tormented with nightmares.

"What are you doing in here?" I mumbled through the sheet.

"I haven't seen you in a few days," Gabe said. "That isn't like you." I peeked out at him. He held the cup out to me again. "Time to get up."

I curled away from him. "Leave me alone," I grumbled.

"You should eat something," Gabe noted.

I groaned in response. In the three weeks I'd been here I'd yet to order a meal. I forced down a few sandwich bars and fruit when I could stomach it. I rarely felt hungry. Eating sustains life and lately I hadn't felt very alive. I didn't have to look in the mirror to see I was losing weight. My scrubs were already feeling looser.

I buried my head in the pillow because it felt strangely normal to want to suffocate.

I heard Gabe stand up and I instinctively pulled the blanket tighter around me, like I needed to protect myself. I was getting jumpier every day. Any noise or sudden movement made my heart skip and my stomach clench.

"You'll feel better if you shower," he said.

I grunted in reply.

"Tonight's a big night," I heard him say. "I don't think you want to miss it."

I pulled the sheets down past my chest and blinked at him. Something small took root in my heart, like a seed of hope.

"Why?" I asked.

He grinned. "Don't you want to see your friends?"

I managed to sit up. I asked him if he was serious. I dared to smile.

"One hour," he told me. "Midnight. Be ready to go." With that, he turned and walked out of the room.

CHAPTER fourteen

I paced back and forth, my sandals swishing against the floor of my room. I had finally climbed out of bed and Gabe left my door unlocked so I could shower and change. I wore my scrubs and a hooded sweatshirt. I ate a cereal bar but I had to force it down. My heart was pounding with nerves. A little before midnight, I heard a light tap at the door. I opened it and Gabe motioned for me to follow him.

He walked ahead of me down the hall and I was careful to keep a few steps behind him. I needed the distance. Close human contact was starting to scare me. In the past few weeks, all I'd experienced around people was pain. When people were face-to-face, tragedy struck. A look felt like a bee sting. It started to seem natural to be separated from people. I craved being alone. No one could hurt me inside my wall screens. They were slowly becoming a comfort, a cushion between me and the harsh world outside. I was stepping out of it less and less.

I had passed a girl in the hall twice this week on my way to the bathroom and each time we both kept our eyes averted and leaned toward opposite walls, staying far away from each other, as if we carried contagious disease. I didn't even see people as people. I saw only shadows and movements that could hurt me. I saw violence dressed in green scrubs. I didn't look in the mirror anymore. The wall screen could project a mirror if I wanted to use it. I imagined myself instead—the hair I wished I had, the curves and the clothes. I fixed my mind on that image because it was easier than accepting my reflection.

We walked to the elevator and Gabe opened it with his key-card. Inside, he punched in a code and the elevator slowly descended. Neither of us spoke. When the doors opened, we stepped out into a long corridor that looked more like a cement tunnel than a hallway. The floor and walls were light gray and the narrow space was lit by old-fashioned bulbs that cast spidery shadows across the ceiling.

"We're on the basement floor." Gabe finally spoke up. "We don't have to whisper anymore. No one comes down here. No Eyes."

"What about upstairs?" I asked. "Didn't it see us leave?"

"The Eyes turn off at night," Gabe said, "when all the doors are bolted. Not that you need to know that. It's pointless to have them on; no one can leave the room at night without being escorted, and we haven't had an emergency call in years. Kids are too well trained."

"Or too terrified," I pointed out.

"Maybe," Gabe agreed.

I zipped my hoodie up against the dank, heavy air.

"What do they use this for?" I asked. "The DC morgue?" As soon as the words left my mouth I felt fear wrap a cold arm around me because it might be true.

"They hardly use it at all," Gabe assured me. "It's mostly for storage. This floor survived the Big Quake, but when they built the dormitory they didn't have any use for it. The rest of the staff's afraid to come down here. They say it's haunted."

I followed him down the long hallway and asked him how he discovered it.

"The electrical generator's down here," he told me and opened a door at the end of the hall. We walked inside a wide space lit with so many blinking computer monitors we didn't have to turn on the overhead lights. He explained the DC was run on solar energy distributed through an energy grid. "This is where I discovered a way out."

We walked around a generator that occupied most of the space in the room and emitted a low rumble. Metal pipes grew out of the machine like branches and climbed toward vents in the ceiling. It coughed to life as we passed and the sound made me jump.

"In an earthquake last year, the power grid shut off. Some electricians came in to fix it and they brought me down here for security. That's when I found this." He pushed away a pile of metal bed frames stacked on a roller. There was a steel door behind it, almost impossible to see, since it blended in with the gray basement walls.

"There's no handle," Gabe pointed out. "I think that's why no one noticed it before. But then I accidentally stepped on this." He pressed the toe of his tennis shoe down on a small, metal square in the floor, and it released a lock on the door. The heavy door eased open with a sigh and Gabe swung it back all the way. A sheet of darkness welcomed us.

"What's out there?" I asked. "A sewer?" My adventurous side was definitely lacking these days. The last thing I could handle was a dark, rat-infested tunnel.

Gabe gave me an encouraging smile but I shook my head and stepped back. "I'm not in any condition for cave exploring."

He raised his hands and told me it was the only way out of the DC. "It's fine," he assured me. "It's an old underground subway line they don't use anymore." He reminded me that since the Big Quake, all of the trains and ZipLines in L.A. had been built aboveground. "It leads to an opening a block from the ocean."

I leaned forward and stuck my head into the deserted tunnel. All I could hear was my own breathing. All I could feel was cool, pitch-black air.

"Does anyone ever go in it?" I asked.

"I've seen kids messing around on bikes down here," he said. "I heard someone driving through on a motorcycle a few days ago. That's why everyone in the DC thinks this floor is haunted. They've probably heard people in the tunnel."

He stepped out and turned on a flashlight. The wide beam of light illuminated two subway lines that ran through the middle of the tunnel. I stalled at the door.

He pulled lightly on my sleeve, but I jerked my arm away from the touch, nearly slapping him.

"Sorry," I mumbled. "Natural reflex."

"I hope it's an unnatural reflex," Gabe said. "It's kind of sad when every woman you interact with wants to deck you." He waited for me to move on my own. "It's safe," he promised. "I use this all the time."

"Why do *you* use it?" I asked.

He shrugged like it was obvious. "Everybody needs a break from this place," he pointed out.

"But you work here. Can't you leave out the front gate? Don't you get time off?"

Instead of answering me, he motioned for me to follow him. "We better find your friends," he said.

I walked behind him on a concrete ledge built high above the tracks. Distant voices echoed softly ahead of us, and bobbing flashlights floated our way. I started to see the outline of tall shadows behind them.

"Maddie?" I recognized Clare's voice.

"Clare," I said, and my voice echoed.

"Maddie!" I could hear her footsteps running toward me, gaining ground. The beam of a flashlight grew until it was blinding, like something was crashing in my direction. Warning lights went on in my mind and told me to do one thing: run. My heart jumped and I pushed past Gabe to get back to the DC. He caught my arm to hold me still. I turned and swung my fist at him, but he blocked my swing with his other arm, and the flashlight was knocked out of his hand.

More voices shouted in the distance.

"Slow down!" Gabe yelled at Clare, but it was too late. She was nearly on top of us and I sucked in a deep breath. Gabe knew what was coming. He grabbed me around the waist and pressed his hand so tight against my mouth it pushed my lips against my teeth and muffled the scream that ripped through my throat. I hadn't expected Gabe to be strong, but he pinned me so hard against him I couldn't move my arms. I kicked my legs out and screamed but he easily held me down. His lips were close to my ear.

"It's okay, it's okay," he whispered. I could sense other people crowding around us, too close.

"Back off!" Gabe shouted at them.

Panic took over. I tried to scream again but his hand was still pressed over my mouth. I squeezed my eyes shut and waited for the explosion. For the tunnel to fall in around us. For my friends to die. We'd be buried alive down here. It would be all my fault.

Fear rushed through my veins like ice water and my body went limp. It was hopeless. Maybe my dreams were some kind of a prophecy. I could smell smoke around us and it made me choke.

I gasped for breath and tried to scream again, to warn everyone to run.

"What's wrong with her?" I recognized Justin's voice.

"Something triggered a memory," I heard Gabe say.

My knees gave out and Gabe lowered me to the ground. My lungs strained for breath through air that was too thick to breathe. I focused on my dorm room, where it was safe, where I could control the elements. Gabe rubbed his hand lightly on my back, but it didn't help. His fingers left trails of chills. What was the point in consoling me when we were all going to die?

The sweat was back, covering my body and seeping through my clothes. I gasped and coughed for air. I was shaking and whimpering on all fours, like a wounded animal. And then the air felt weighted, so heavy it pulled me down until I was buried in darkness.

CHAPTER *fifteen*

I woke up to a murmur of voices swirling around me, but the voices weren't shouting or ordering me to run. They were calm and fell around me like a soft rain shower. For once it wasn't a nightmare. It sounded like music and I kept my eyes closed and listened for a few minutes, enjoying the lyrics.

"I'm so sorry," I heard Clare say, her voice sagging with concern.

"Stop apologizing, it's not your fault. I should have warned you guys about this," I heard Gabe explain. "No sudden movements. And don't try to touch her. She can't handle contact right now. She'll just associate it with the nightmares."

"What nightmares?" I recognized Molly's voice in the mix. She'd hardly said two words to me in my life; what was she doing here?

"It was too soon to bring her out," Gabe said. "The first six weeks are the worst. I thought she might be able to handle it."

"What the hell are you talking about?"

Justin's voice made my blood start to move and something inside of me that had been severed became connected. I rolled onto my back and blinked my eyes open to a dim ceiling light. I was in a bed. I glanced around the room, which was small, the size of my dorm room, and with metal closets filling the wall space. Everyone around me took several steps back. I weakly propped myself up on my elbows and squinted at a sea of anxious faces. I could feel my pulse pounding in my temples.

"She should be all right now, just keep your distance," Gabe said, as if I were a mountain lion that had a broken leg but was still capable of biting.

Clare stood next to Gabe, at the foot of the bed, her eyes red and puffy. She studied me like she didn't recognize me anymore. I looked around and slowly registered the other faces. Pat was there, watching me with a mixture of anger and worry. Molly stood the closest to my side, and Justin leaned against the wall, the farthest away from me. His gray baseball cap was pulled low on his face, but I could still see his eyes fixed on mine like they wanted to grab hold of me. His arms were crossed over his chest.

"Where am I?" I asked, my throat parched and scratchy.

"We're back in the basement," Gabe said. "You're safe in here, don't worry."

I nodded slowly. More silence followed. Everyone was staring at me with nervous eyes. They were waiting for me to do something crazy.

"Would you guys please stop looking at me like I just woke up from the dead?" I pleaded, even though that summed up how I felt. My fingers went to my forehead and I winced at my throbbing headache. I reached for a bottle of water sitting on a chair next to the bed and stacked a few pillows behind my back so I could sit up. Molly took a step forward to help me, but the movement caused me to panic and I held an arm out to block her.

"Don't come near me," I warned her; it sounded more heated than I'd meant it to, but I was still scared. I took a drink of water and glanced at Justin. I could see so many questions on his face. I could see worry lines around his mouth. There were dark circles under his eyes, like he hadn't slept in weeks. I wanted to tell him everything would be fine. I wanted to tell him I wasn't afraid. But I couldn't lie to him. So I just looked away.

"How much longer do we have?" Molly asked.

"I need to get her back soon," Gabe said. He looked unsettled. I wondered what would happen to Gabe if he got caught. I wondered why he was risking so much for me, for a stranger he hardly knew.

Molly nodded. "Well, the good news is I can't find any evidence of physical harm. No sign of needles, and your bloodwork is clean." She told me she'd done a physical exam while I was asleep and had sedated me, taken a blood sample, and done a bioassay to test for chemicals. She sat down on a metal chair and pulled her blond hair back with concentration.

"No offense, but what are you doing here?" I asked her.

"I'm working on a PhD in neuroscience," she said. "When Clare said what was going on, I volunteered to come down here. I'm a year away from taking my preliminary exams," she added proudly.

I remembered Clare told me this once, that Molly was some kind of child prodigy. "You must be loving me right now," I said dryly. "I'm your dream research subject. And they *are* drugging me," I informed her.

"I can't find any traces," she said.

I told her it was some kind of tablet. "They call it the Cure."

"What are your symptoms? Side effects?" she asked.

It hurt to think. I didn't want to think. "I can't remember," I mumbled. "I black out after every session."

"Gabe says you have nightmares?" Molly asked.

I nodded. "But as soon as I wake up I completely forget them.

Only feelings stay with me. Panic and fear and I'm scared of any human contact. But I can't remember any specific details."

She nodded thoughtfully. "Well, I'll need to run some more tests when I can get to a lab."

"No. You're not running any more tests because she's coming with us tonight," Clare insisted. I looked over at Gabe, and he slowly mouthed *No way.* I knew he was right. I couldn't leave here tonight because I knew the reality. I wouldn't be free.

I shook my head. "I'm not going anywhere."

"We're not leaving you in here," she said, and looked at Justin. "Right?" she asked him. "We can't—"

"I'd be a fugitive again," I interrupted Clare. "With a lifetime prison sentence hanging over my head." And I'd be a risk to all of them, I thought, especially Gabe.

Clare shook her head. "We'll figure it out. You're not staying in here. That's not an option. You look like you're being tortured."

I blinked sadly back at her. I didn't want my life to be one lie after another. I got myself in here. Looking around the room, at my closest friends, I had my answer. I made my decision.

"I'm staying," I told Clare.

"You *want* to stay here?" Pat asked.

"I'm trying to look on the positive side," I said, and imagined how proud those words would make Dr. Stevenson.

All of them raised their eyebrows and stared at me. Like I was nuts. Maybe I was.

"You see a positive side to this?" Pat inquired.

"This could be our shot at bringing down DS," I offered. I glanced at Justin, and his eyes narrowed. I knew he guessed what I was thinking.

"You've got the publicity you want," I said. "You just saw what happened to me. If you can prove what's going on in these detention centers, that they're torturing kids to keep them addicted to a digital life, do you know what kind of trouble that would start? It would finally show how corrupt this system is. People would have to admit it's gone too far. They would have to be open to changing it."

Pat shook his head. "The media will just twist the facts. I'm sure they've already thought of it. They probably have the news story ready to broadcast if any of the truth leaks out."

"The media doesn't know this is happening," I argued. "No one knows. That's why they're getting away with it."

"I don't think we should do anything until we know exactly what's going on in here," Molly said. "We don't have enough evidence yet to prove anything." She appeared to be the only person in the room on my side. I saw *Nobel Prize in Medicine* written all over her face.

"Exactly," I agreed. "Use me to find the evidence. Let me be the experiment."

Justin's mouth was hard. I knew his mind was racing for any possible alternative. But he couldn't question it. This plan was foolproof. Besides, I was exhausted with running away.

"It might work," Molly said.

"It has to work," I said. "I'm staying in here until we figure out a way to get everybody out."

"No, you're not staying," Clare argued. She took a step toward me and Gabe had to grab her arm and pull her back.

"It makes sense," I told her. "I can be your guinea pig. It's like Molly said, we need to understand what's going on before we can help anyone."

I waited for Justin to step in and agree, but he didn't say anything. His eyes were focused on the ground in front of him.

"We can't do anything until we know what we're up against," I said.

"I'm not letting you do this," Clare said. "They're torturing kids inside here. Emotionally, mentally, physically. It sounds like they're turning you into a blue screen and then reprogramming you." She glared at Justin. "Aren't you going to say anything? I love her, and I know you love her too. Tell her not to do this."

I watched him and wondered if what Clare said was true. He didn't admit it. He didn't deny it either.

He blew out a slow breath and looked at me. "This is your call," he said.

"You could tell her what you *think* she should do," Pat said with an irritated frown. "You know she listens to you."

Justin kicked himself away from the wall. "I'm not going to tell you what to do," he said to me. I nodded and his eyes focused on Pat's. "And if you try to tell Madeline not to do something, it just encourages her to turn right around and do it. So fighting her isn't going to help." He looked back at me. "I think her mind's made up."

I smiled because he was right. He didn't smile back. He didn't look the least bit happy with my decision.

"I think it's crazy," Justin said. "I think it's going to get a lot worse before it gets any better. But"—he paused—"I think you're strong enough to get through it."

"You're all insane," Clare said, her voice breaking. "She's our friend. You don't encourage your friends to go on a suicide mission. Madeline, you don't have to do this. You don't need to prove anything."

"We're wasting time arguing about it," I said. I stood up and planted my feet firmly because if I didn't hold my ground I was going to sink in. "I need you all to support me in this," I told everyone. "If there's anything you've taught me, it's to stop talking and get up and *do* something. Look at a problem and see an opportunity. That's what I want to do. For once in my life I want to help solve a problem, not be the cause of it. So, from this moment on, support me," I said. "That's all I ask. I can't handle any doubt right now."

"What can we do to help?" Justin asked Gabe.

Gabe shrugged and said meeting face-to-face would be good for me. "The DC forces isolation, so the more human interaction she gets, the better, even if it scares her. It might keep her mind strong. And then you can do the research you need to."

"He's right," Molly agreed. "Direct communication helps strengthen the amygdala and it might stimulate a positive cognitive unconscious."

Gabe wrinkled his eyebrows. "I have no idea what you just said, but sure."

"You think human contact helps?" Pat asked, and reminded us what happened in the tunnel.

Gabe nodded. "In small doses. We just have to remember to give her distance. No touching, no hugging, no running up to her in dark tunnels," he said, to Clare, specifically.

Justin looked over at me thoughtfully. I could see he had a different theory, but he kept his distance. "I want all of us to meet here one night a week," he said. "Molly can observe her and test for anything she can find. And one night a week, I meet with Maddie. Alone. Can you arrange for that?" he asked, and Gabe nodded.

Justin took careful steps toward me. He reached for something in his back pocket and the gesture made me wince. I leaned away from him, but when I looked down I realized he was holding my journal.

"I thought you might want this," he told me.

I looked down at the worn red leather. "How did you get it?" I asked, and Clare spoke up.

"I convinced Joe to let me have it," she said. "Let's just say I had a few words with him after we realized he ratted you out."

"You can keep it down here," Gabe said. "There's nowhere to hide it in your room."

I took the journal, careful to avoid touching Justin's hand, and rubbed my fingers over the soft cover. I flipped through some of the pages. I'd missed the feel of the thick real paper and its earthy smell. There was a pen stuck inside.

"Thanks."

"Three days," Justin told me. "I'll see you then?"

I nodded and he studied my face for a few more seconds.

"I won't let anything happen to you," he promised me. Then he turned and headed out the door without another word. The rest of the group slowly followed him. Clare frowned over her shoulder at me, and Pat had to nudge her out the door. I watched Justin leave and, despite how calm he was acting, I knew it was a front. I knew because when I'd taken the journal from him, his hand had been shaking.

October 2060

Tonight I don't have any doubts. For the first time in my life, I'm taking steps that are completely my choice. For the first time I'm striving for something I believe in. I don't know how things are going to turn out and maybe that's the purpose of life. I don't want to be handed the answers. I want to learn the answers for myself, because that's the only way I'll believe them.

Confidence grows when you know what you want, when you don't have to be told who you are. You know it on the inside so you don't have to force it on the outside. It just radiates. And your steps become effortless.

For once I believe in something. And it's like a map showing what direction I should go. There's only one certainty in life: how you come into the world. Where you go from there is up to you.

CHAPTER *sixteen*

"I can't believe you are dating the leader of the DS rebels," Gabe told me. "No wonder your dad locked you up."

We sat outside on the balcony, and warm sunlight heated the air around us. I was feeling better today. Maybe because I knew I was seeing Justin that night. I sipped my coffee and it was hot and bitter and warmed my stomach. I lifted my head to the sun. I felt like a snake, arching my neck and looking for the heat. I allowed myself to sneak outside with Gabe for about ten minutes once a week. The Eye knew how long I was out of my room, but as far as I could tell, I wasn't being punished for it. The Eye watched to see if I was interacting with people; it didn't seem interested when I chose to be alone.

"What I'd like to know," Gabe said, "is how you can date someone who supposedly doesn't exist."

He seemed fascinated with my life, almost as if he'd never been outside the walls of the DC, but every time I asked him about his past, he changed the subject. I didn't press the topic. Apparently every male figure in my life preferred to be distant and taciturn.

Gabe sat on one end of the balcony and I sat on the other. It was about as close and intimate as I could get.

I pulled the legs of my sweatpants up to let the sun touch my skin. "I wouldn't call it dating. Justin's a little more closed off than the average person."

"You can't really blame him, considering."

I raised my eyebrows at the last word. "Considering what?"

"You know. What happened with his last girlfriend, Kristin Locke?"

The word *girlfriend* almost knocked me over. I set my coffee cup down and stared at him. "Who's Kristin Locke?" *And how do you know more about Justin's dating past than I do?*

He looked at me with surprise. "Come on, you've never heard about her? No one's told you anything?"

There was shock on his face, like he saw I was missing a huge piece of a puzzle. Like this entire time, I never knew Justin. I sat up straighter and fixed my eyes on him.

"Told me what?" I waited for him to explain while thoughts flooded my head until they spilled over. Kristin Locke was the love of his life? She broke his heart? She's the mother of their illegitimate love child? "What are you talking about, Gabe?" I demanded.

"Maybe it isn't true," he offered, and looked away, pretending to be fascinated with something in the distance.

I crossed my arms over my chest. "Spill it."

He took a deep breath. "Kristin Locke died in a riot a few years ago. Justin was training her. People said they were dating, but I don't know for sure."

"She died?" I asked. "What happened?"

"It was a demonstration in Boise, Idaho. Protesters were there to fight a vote to build a detention center in the city. They were just trying to stir up some media attention and get people to sign a petition. It wasn't supposed to be a huge event. But a bomb went off in front of the courthouse. She was the only one who was killed."

Gabe said he remembered watching it on the news. "Someone rigged an explosive under the steps. The police figured out it was an assassination attempt on Richard Vaughn, the designer of detention centers. He was going to speak there that afternoon.

"The bomb was on a timer that short-circuited," he said. "The only reason I remember is that after that, the DS rebels put a ban on bringing any weapons to protests. They've been completely outlawed since her death. They called it the Locke Down. No weapons. Fight with words, not bullets."

I nodded. I remember hearing about the Locke Down. It was a peace movement among protesters. It was a way to avoid violence: never carry the weapons to start it. I remember my father bringing it up. I just never knew the story behind it. But almost every story begins with another story's end.

So many pieces slid into place. Why Justin worked so hard to avoid violence. Why he was so protective of me. Why he never planned too far into the future. Why he was so determined to live in the moment. He claimed it was his parents and his upbringing, but I was suspicious there was something more. Fighting DS had always been so personal to him, more like a vendetta than a passion. Now I knew why.

I realized my hands were clenched. Why hadn't Justin ever told me about this? Didn't he confide in anyone? He always told me never to hold things in because thoughts eventually make you crack. Did he think he needed to be a warrior all the time, that he was too selfless to feel grief?

"I'm sure he was going to tell you eventually," Gabe assured me.

I nodded but my head was weary. My heart was tight. I wanted to be there for Justin. But how can you be there for someone who doesn't need you? It's like trying to scale a wall without anyone on the top throwing you a rope. You just keep sliding down and eventually your muscles give out, and your energy and your will and your heart.

❁

Gabe and I took the elevator down to the basement at midnight. I had showered and put on fresh clothes but I still looked battered and tired. I was barely sleeping and there were purple shadows under my eyes. My hair was tied in a ratty ponytail, and my clothes hung loose on my scrawny limbs. A part of me didn't want to see Justin. I was exhausted and anxious and the fact that I looked like a recovering meth addict didn't help my self-esteem.

Gabe opened the tunnel entrance and handed me a flashlight. "Want me to walk you the rest of the way?"

I told him I'd be fine. He said he programmed the elevator to take me back to my floor. He shut the door behind me and I looked down the mouth of the tunnel. Another light hovered in the distance, still and constant. I followed it and my steps echoed around the curved walls. Justin waited for me with an extra coat hanging over his arm. He had on a black stocking cap and wore a down vest over his sweatshirt. I stopped when we were several feet apart. He handed me the coat.

"It's Clare's," he said. "It's a little cold out."

I put my arms through the sleeves. I didn't meet his eyes.

He took a step closer to me to see how I'd react. I expected a rush of nerves, but instead I felt a warm energy press against my chest. I still craved him. He reached out and brushed his fingers across my hand, but carefully, to see if I'd snap them away. We were both relieved when I didn't. I finally looked up at him. We stood a foot apart for a few seconds, watching each other.

"Don't worry," I assured him. "I'm not going to pass out this time. Although I'm sure you've had that effect on women before."

He smirked. "Glad to see your sarcasm is still intact."

He looked down at my hand and laced his fingers with mine. His skin was so warm. I let my mind fixate on the energy of his touch. He leaned closer and lifted my hand to examine it in the dim glow of his flashlight. I really saw him now, his hair sticking out from under the cap and around his ears, his eyes that were aware of everything, his solid hand. I was starting to wake up. The rough skin on his fingers traced over my knuckles and he kissed each of my fingertips, one at a time. All the panic I'd felt since I'd been in the detention center evaporated like steam off my skin. He dropped my hand from his lips and his eyes relaxed.

"Come on," he said. "Let's get you out of here for a little while."

I asked him where we were going.

He nodded ahead of us. "You'll see."

My thoughts traveled to Kristin Locke. Her story felt like footsteps following behind us. I couldn't ignore her presence. I hated that Justin held it back from me, that he would keep something so pivotal buried inside. I knew I'd have to bring Kristin up eventually. But not tonight. Tonight I just wanted to feel light again. I wanted to float.

The tunnel slowly rose and gave way to ground and the ceiling gave way to sky. The air moved and I lifted my hand to feel it brushing my fingertips. It felt like a curtain, like soft petals, like time. It was alive. My lungs kicked in like a car engine revving to life. The air was my ignition. The sky was my fuel. I took a deep breath and looked up.

A single streetlight lit the entrance around the tunnel, but beyond that, blackness stretched in the sky. Black is my favorite color. It's limitless. It's indefinable. It keeps you guessing. When there's nothing to see, you're forced to imagine. It makes every shape, every person more mysterious because you can't see all the details.

I forgot who I was in the detention center. I didn't have to ask Justin why he pressed to meet with me alone. He'd brought me out here to help me get reacquainted. Darkness opened her arms and wrapped them tightly around me to welcome me home. It felt good to be in her strong embrace. Darkness doesn't judge. Darkness can't even see. She only feels. She flies and flows through the night like an angel with giant wings.

Justin led me down to the beach. We heard the wave generators churning water for energy. They occupied parts of the coast from Santa Barbara all the way to San Diego to power the cities packed in between. White lights illuminated huge propellers cutting through the water to create some of the city's energy. They were all in sync and cartwheeled through the waves like a tumbling performance.

We sat down in the soft sand, just at the edge of the tide. The waves ran up to greet us, narrowly missing our feet, only to skitter shyly away. I grinned at the water, like it was playing with me, like it was going out of its way to make me smile.

"I'm surprised you didn't fight me about staying in the DC," I told Justin. It was getting strange to hear my voice out loud. Gabe and I talked like we were tiptoeing around in the dark, afraid of getting caught. The DC forced us to think that talking face-to-face was unhealthy and subversive. I used my voice less and less every day. Sometimes, I wondered why I even had one.

He admitted he almost had. "It makes me sick to think you're going through with this." His eyes met mine and silver light cut across them.

"Then why did you let me?" I asked. I was starting to wish he hadn't. I was tired of trying to be brave.

He sighed as if he regretted it too. "Because if I were in your shoes, I would have done the same thing. And I know you can handle it."

"How do you know that?" I asked, because I needed to be reminded that I was strong. I was starting to forget.

"Because I think you're right. You can make a difference." He told me experiences were kind of like fate, and fate usually came in the form of a test. He told me fate liked to be worshiped. It liked to see us fall on our knees before it offered to help us up. I wondered if he was referring to what happened to Kristin.

He stretched his long legs out and sat back on his hands. "I think what you're doing is the fastest way to motivate a change. If we can free all these detention centers, people will have to start listening."

I pressed my hand into the cold sand and felt as small as the grains that stuck to my fingers.

"I'm starting to doubt if I can do this," I admitted.

"You have to block it. Doubt just corners you. It steers you into a dead end if you follow it. Don't doubt what you're doing, Maddie. It's the right thing, I promise."

He turned so he was facing me and he reached out slowly and turned my body so our legs were entwined. He held both of my hands in his. "I know you'll be fine. *You will be fine.*"

I frowned at him. "I don't know anymore," I said.

"I won't let anything happen to you. I'm not leaving this city without you. And I've always believed that what doesn't kill you makes you stronger."

I looked in his dark eyes. I heard my dad say that line all the time but I never trusted it. I dropped his hands and leaned back.

"Why do people say that? What does that expression mean anyway?"

"I think it's true. The most difficult experiences define us."

I shook my head. "I think the opposite's true."

He studied me curiously. I didn't expect Justin to understand. Our ideas of survival were black and white.

"When your time is up, what are your last thoughts going to be?" I asked. "All of your miserable memories? When you were lonely or scared or heartbroken? The things that almost kill you don't make you stronger. If anything, they make you bitter and closed off and broken."

Justin considered this. "I've never looked at it that way."

That doesn't surprise me, I wanted to say. But I needed to be careful with this conversation.

"I think what you have to live for makes you stronger," I said. "When I have these nightmares, when I feel like I'm about to break, I focus on you. I focus on the memories I have with the people I love. The places I love. The memories that make this life worth it in the first place. If I was about to die, I wouldn't dwell on the things that didn't kill me. I'd think about the people I'd want to see one last time so I could tell them how much they mean to me. Love makes you stronger. It's our strongest weapon. It's the only weapon the DC hasn't taken from me. It's the only reason they haven't broken me yet."

He was quiet next to me. Our time was slowly winding down. I wanted to hold the time, to widen it, to lengthen it. I wanted to wade in slow movements of time.

CHAPTER seventeen

Over the next few weeks, life limped and crawled by. The DC fought to take over my mind, and I worked to preserve it. They tried to smash down my hope and my confidence, so I gave myself daily exercises to focus on things that lifted me up, things that I loved. I tried to marinate in those thoughts, to put them on and wear them around. I meditated on people and places and experiences that inspired me. I made daily lists of ten things I loved. I listed them in my journal, or sometimes in the privacy of my mind. It was my own secret therapy. My ten favorite foods. Ten most influential people. Ten greatest moments. Ten strengths. Each list made me think and reflect. It exercised a side of my brain the DC wanted to paralyze. It was a small way to fight back.

I hadn't gone out of my room except to use the bathroom. Every time I looked at my door handle I felt nauseated. I couldn't place what was triggering the panic — it was just a reaction, like a reflex. Outside of my walls was a world I couldn't control and that idea was immobilizing.

Every week I met with Molly so she could study me like I was a medical experiment. She gave me a physical exam and took blood, which I needed to be sedated for since I couldn't handle contact with anyone except Justin. I started to panic if someone was within ten feet of me. Even Justin could only hold my hand, and he touched it as delicately as paper. Molly attached electrodes to my forehead so she could study my brain activity while we went through countless questionnaires and examinations. She took pages of notes. Usually Pat and Clare were there, sometimes Scott, and always Justin.

After a month of meetings, Molly was still struggling to pinpoint the reason for my nightmares and subsequent amnesia. My physical exams and bloodwork came up clean every time. Other than my loss of weight, the only serious ailment I suffered from was fatigue. Unfortunately, the lack of sleep would make it harder to fight the DC. Sleep deprivation can cause depression, a loss of appetite, stress, anxiety—even hallucinations. The DC could claim that was the reason for the inmates' paranoia.

Pat sat on a chair in the basement and sighed when Molly announced, once again, that my bloodwork didn't show a trace of drugs. I sat on a cot and chewed at my nails. I knew what Pat was thinking. These meetings were draining everyone and so far we had nothing to show for them. But we were all too stubborn to admit defeat.

"So," Pat said. "Let's go over what we know. She's being psychologically tortured. She's losing weight. They're frying her brain with drugs we can't detect. We knew this since day one. Are we making any progress here? Or is this a waste of all our time and Maddie's health?"

Molly shifted in her seat. "This isn't a waste, Pat," she said. "And a defeatist attitude isn't going to help anyone."

"You mean a realistic attitude," he argued.

Molly looked back at her flipscreen that held charts of my brain activity. "What we need is evidence. We're trying to shut down a correctional facility, not a chatroom. We can't go on a hunch. We need hard facts."

"Why don't we discuss how we're going to get Maddie out of here," Pat said angrily.

I smiled at Pat to try to calm him down. I appreciated he was looking out for me. But I knew Molly was right. We couldn't stop now. I hid the fact that these group meetings were getting harder for me to sit through. Being around so many people was giving me anxiety. People carried energy, like batteries, and it was starting to feel like radiation pressing on me.

We were all quiet for a few minutes. I thought about what happened at Club Nino and the attention it generated.

"What if we caused a mass exit?" I spoke up. "Let the whole school loose and get national news coverage. Expose what Vaughn's doing. I bet the government doesn't have an explanation ready for why hundreds of drugged teenagers in hospital scrubs are running loose on the streets of L.A."

Molly shook her head. "If all these kids are drugged, who knows how they'll react. If we try to break them out now, they could all have nervous breakdowns. Remember how you reacted the first time you saw us," she said. She took a MindReader out of her bag and started to explain why she was using it, but I cut her off.

"I'm used to these," I told her quickly and slipped it on.

"What?" Molly asked. "You never told me they use Mind-Readers in here. You just mentioned imagery screens." She raised her hands in the air. "How did you forget to tell me this?"

"I'm sorry," I said. "It's not like I'm very detail oriented these days."

"What's the big deal?" Gabe asked.

"They could be downloading memories into your brain," Molly told me.

"They can do that?" Clare asked.

"It's illegal, but technically, yes, they've been able to do it for years. Doctors used to try it with Alzheimer's and amnesia cases. They used MindReaders to install memories. But it was risky, and the memories were never completely accurate. And it was too easy to brainwash people. Way too many ethical issues."

"Is there any way to test your theory?" Justin asked. Molly nodded.

"I can run a simulation. But without knowing what the drug's doing, it won't be a hundred percent accurate."

"I can try and get you the drug." Gabe suddenly spoke up. "Pat's right, you'll never find anything in Maddie's blood. The DC sees to that. I'd like to know what's in it myself," he said.

Molly asked how he could get it.

"Some of the doctors leave extras out on their desks. They used to keep documented records of each tablet, but it's gotten lax the last few years. Since I clean out their offices . . ." He didn't have to finish the sentence for all of us to understand.

"What if they notice it's gone?" I asked. "What if you get caught?"

"Hopefully you'll figure out a way to free this place so it won't matter," he said.

"Why are you helping us?" Clare suddenly asked. Her voice wasn't accusing; Clare couldn't sound threatening if she tried. She sounded grateful. Everyone watched Gabe, all equally interested in his answer. His cheeks flushed with embarrassment at the attention.

"It's no big deal," he mumbled, and sat back in his seat.

Clare pressed him. "Out of almost a thousand kids you decided to help Maddie. Why?"

He lifted his hands in the air like it was obvious. "Because out of all the kids locked up in here, only three have ever made eye contact with me after the first counseling session. Maddie's one of them. You guys don't understand how rare it is to have people look at you in here, let alone have the nerve to talk." He pointed at me. "Usually that drug works so fast, people go into hibernation. One hit, and they're brain-dead. Some kids don't even leave their rooms to use the bathroom. It's that bad."

We all winced at his last detail.

"Everybody who comes through this place vanishes. It's like they surrender the second they walk in the gate. They have no fight at all. But you acted like it was just an inconvenience," he said to me. "Not many people announce they plan to break out of a detention center to a staff member."

"You said that?" Molly asked.

I glanced at Justin and he just rolled his eyes. "What did I have to lose? I've been censoring myself for seventeen years. I didn't feel like I was living until six months ago, when I stopped caring what people thought. When you hold back you don't do this world any favors. You don't make any impression."

"You definitely made an impression," Gabe said. "I almost reported you."

Justin asked Gabe how long he had been working at the DC. He paused for a second, considering whether or not to open up, but he gave in. He realized we were all on the same side.

"Six years," he said. "I've been here since I was eleven. I'm what people like to call a purebred."

"Nice," Justin said with admiration.

"What's a purebred?" I asked.

"People that grow up without computers," Justin answered for him.

Gabe nodded and said his parents were farmers. He grew up in northern California, east of the Cascades, in a small town made up of families living on sustainable farms. They grew just enough food to support themselves.

"We didn't use money," he said. "We lived without technology as much as we could. We used solar power for electricity; that's it. We didn't have phones or computers or televisions. There was only one computer in my town, at our community building, but I never used it."

"That's impossible. How can you live like that?" Pat asked. "You were completely cut off."

"I never felt like I was cut off," Gabe said. "It's all I knew. I grew up working outside, using my hands, getting exercise, living off the land. We listened to the news on the radio sometimes, but it was like listening to a sci-fi movie. Everything was about being digital or virtual or plugging in or tuning in. I couldn't understand it. It sounded like they were talking about machines, not humans."

Justin and I shared a smile. Gabe wasn't far off.

Clare asked Gabe how he ended up in the detention center and he explained the government had discovered their community and broke it up. "It's illegal to deny your kids access to digital school," he told us. "We didn't even have the option to attend DS. So they relocated us.

"My parents were arrested," he continued, "and so were half the people in my town. I doubt it exists anymore." His words came out slower as he recalled the memory. "Younger kids were sent to live with other relatives. I didn't have any living relatives so I stayed with a foster family in San Francisco, but I ran away after a few months. When the police caught me, they sent me here."

"Did the DC even know what to do with you?" I asked.

He shook his head. "I can read, I can write, but I've never

touched a computer. No one bothered to teach me. So they started putting me to work. They realized I could fix anything. I've done every job in this place, from maintenance to laundry. Even security. They handed me a staff shirt three years ago and gave me a room in the employee suites." Gabe smiled to himself. "I don't care if I live my whole life without touching a computer. It's my goal not to."

"Can't you just leave?" Molly asked him.

"I thought about it," Gabe said. "But my foster parents signed a contract that I'd work here until I was eighteen, for room and board. I have less than a year left. I figure I can hold out." He checked the time and looked over at me.

"We need to head back," he said.

When we stood up to go, I said I needed to talk to Clare. Alone. Everyone nodded and they all said goodbye as they filtered out.

When Gabe shut the door, Clare turned to me, her face worried. "What's wrong?" she asked.

I picked at a piece of loose thread on my scrubs. I didn't know how to transition, so I decided to be blunt.

"Why didn't anyone tell me about Kristin Locke?"

Her mouth fell open when the name left my lips. A flush of regret traveled over her face. "Maddie—"

"You should have told me, Clare. At least you." She sat down at the edge of the bed, and I pulled my legs away from her and curled my arm protectively around them. I sat up straighter on the cot and balled up the sheets in my other hand.

"Justin told you?" Her question only made me more upset.

"He never got around to it. Gabe brought it up—he assumed I already knew, since friends usually confide in each other."

She nodded slowly. "I'm sorry. I wanted to tell you, but we're not supposed to bring it up. Ever. Justin never talks about it. We just don't go there with him. I needed to respect that. But I honestly thought he'd tell you."

"Yeah, well, I guess that's just too personal for him." I leaned my head against the wall and breathed out a long sigh. My thoughts felt heavy and it took effort to push them through my lips. "Why is he trying to keep me in the dark?"

She told me it was the way he coped with what happened.

"Doesn't he let anyone in?" I asked.

Clare shook her head and smiled sadly. "I told you, you picked a challenging guy to love."

"It's easy to love Justin," I pointed out. "Anyone can do that. He's amazing."

She thought about this. "Okay, it's easy to love him. It's getting *him* to love that's the problem."

"How did he handle Kristin's death?" I asked.

"It was pretty bad," she said. "He cut himself off from everyone. He disappeared. We didn't hear from him for months. It's like he fell into a black hole."

"He thinks it's his fault," I said, not knowing the situation but knowing Justin.

Clare nodded. "I know he feels responsible. He's the one who organized the protest and signed her up to volunteer. He had to find her body after the explosion. He had to tell her parents."

Hot tears burned my eyes. I pressed my hands over my face.

"Maddie? That happened years ago. I think he's made his peace with it. I haven't seen him happier than he is now, when he's with you. If anything, he's just scared to get close to anyone again. He's not afraid of getting hurt, but *he doesn't want to hurt you.* The people he's closest to have been killed or arrested or exiled. It's not a great track record. That's why I was so shocked to see him let his guard down with you. He never has before."

I wiped my eyes with my sleeve. It felt good to cry. It was a release. It expelled energy I didn't want to carry inside of me, energy that was weighing down my heart. The heaviness started to dissolve.

"I used to think he was too good for me," I admitted. "When we first met, he had traveled and done things I couldn't imagine. I felt like he had lived five lives and I was barely living one."

"That's not true," Clare said.

"I know. That's what I needed to realize. At first I thought he could teach me so much, and I had nothing to give back to him. But he doesn't have life figured out any more than I do. He's naive in so many ways."

"You should talk to him about it," she said. "Maybe you're right, maybe he needs to vent to someone. I just never had the guts to bring it up with him. If anyone's brave enough, it's you."

CHAPTER eighteen

"You've been here for four months," Dr. Stevenson informed me in the imagery room. It was my first counseling session in weeks. The nightmares had nearly ended. I hadn't been given a dose of the Cure in weeks. I was starting to get my appetite back.

"Time for you to get back on your feet," she told me. I sat down on the cushioned seat and she turned on the wall screens. I expected her to hand me a MindReader, but a computer program popped up on the screen. It read LADC SETUP in blinking orange letters.

She explained that the program took about two hours to complete. "Once you're registered, you can continue using it from your dorm room. It's designed to help you reconnect with society. Don't worry," she assured me. "It's only a simulated version. Think of it as a steppingstone. You can practice socializing and communicating again before you do the real thing."

"You think I'm ready?" I asked her with fake dread in my voice. The detention center hadn't broken me and I assumed Dr. Stevenson was perceptive enough to see that. I was surprised they were letting me move on to this stage.

"Remember, our chief goal at the DC is to prepare you for society. We want to know you'll go out into the world and be a responsible, law-abiding citizen. That you'll make a positive impact."

Dr. Stevenson told me she would be back in two hours to check on me, or I could hit the Complete button if I was done sooner. She walked out of the room and I concentrated on the screen.

A single white sentence wrapped around the room, and a deep male voice boomed through the speakers with an ominous force.

"The world is yours to shape," the man said, and I jumped in my seat from the sound. A photograph of the planet Earth appeared on the screen and two floating hands cupped it.

A man's image walked around from behind Earth, as if humans could be as large as a planet. He walked across the wall screens of the room in slow, confident strides.

I was waiting for him to say, *This planet has been brought to you by technology.com. Your life has been granted to you by Digital School, Inc. Any questions?*

"It's time to design your perfect life!" he exclaimed. He wore a dark, tailored suit and a red tie. He had a chiseled jaw and a deep cleft in his chin. He looked like a cologne model waiting to be discovered who was doing infomercials in the meantime to pay the bills. He was middle-aged, and his black hair was shiny and slicked back with gel to expose a sharp widow's peak.

He clapped his hands together and his eyes shined. "Welcome to your LADC itinerary setup," he said. "We'll begin by helping you establish a routine. Life needs to be predictable in order to be functional. The schedule I'm about to show you is merely a suggestion. Use it as a jumping-off point. Feel free to organize the timing and activities to fit your individual needs. We want to help you structure your ideal day.

"Remember," he added with a grin, like we were in on a secret together, "life rests in the palm of your hand. It is yours to create and re-create. It is your garden to plant, your blueprint to design, your picture to sketch. Life is a program. Enjoy the facilitating."

"Inspiring," I mumbled. I stared at a mock schedule the LADC so kindly offered:

8:00 a.m.	News updates, mail, and messages from DS
9:00 a.m.	Virtual exercise teams
10:00 a.m.	DS classes
12:00 p.m.	Contact chatting/profile managing
1:00 p.m.	Video/music/entertainment streaming
2:00 p.m.	DS classes
4:00 p.m.	Gaming
5:00 p.m.	DS classes
6:00 p.m.	Contact chatting/profile managing
8:00 p.m.	DS homework
10:00 p.m.	Video/music/entertainment streaming

I shook my head at the computer schedule considered a life. "I don't think so," I stated. I stood up and paced around the room. I brainstormed my own schedule out loud, and the wall screen illuminated my words.

8:00 a.m.	Walk my dog outside in the fresh air
9:00 a.m.	Make breakfast, preferably chocolate chip pancakes, stop at a coffee shop before I catch the train downtown
10:00 a.m.	Attend face-to-face classes with my friends
5:00 p.m.	Play sports, invite my friends over, ride a train just to see where it goes, talk to strangers, travel, plant a garden, cook dinner, laugh, talk, live

| 8:00 p.m. | Attempt to concentrate on homework but mostly obsess over boys, one boy in particular |
| 10:00 p.m. | Write, draw, read, watch live music, go out to a movie—do something that inspires me, that lets me go to bed feeling like I made the most out of the day |

I told the computer program I was done, and a small hour-glass filled the screen. I drummed my fingers on my sides and waited.

My host snapped back on, his perfect features looking befuddled, his mouth in a frown. "I'm sorry," he said. "None of your requests meets the program options. Please try again. Or consider the following revised version with our suggestions."

8:00 a.m.	Take a chatwalk
9:00 a.m.	Take vitamins, browse a virtual coffee shop
10:00 a.m.	Attend digital school with your contacts
5:00 p.m.	Chat with contacts, view movies, play virtual sports, take a virtual train ride, purchase a synthetic garden
8:00 p.m.	DS homework
10:00 p.m.	Write on your flipscreen, draw on your ceiling canvas, listen to your books, listen to streamed music, watch movies online, go to bed satisfied, like you viewed the most out of the day

I declined the schedule option. I skipped ahead to the second step of the program. Maybe I'd have better luck with this one.

A new host greeted me, this time a girl about my age with long black hair that fell to her waist. She had red glitter highlights and waved her hands while she talked. Her neon-rainbow nail polish made me dizzy.

"Welcome to the LADC Rebrand Yourself section of the program," she said with a wide smile. "The following steps will allow you to create the life that you want. You were sent here because you were confused about your identity. We can help with that!" She said this easily, like helping me find my true identity, my soul's purpose in this world, was as simple as measuring my feet to find my shoe size.

She tossed her hair to one side and waved her hand over the screen. The Earth appeared again, floating far away from her outstretched arm.

"This system is meant to help you re-acclimate yourself to the real world," she said, pointing to the distant blue and green planet. The screen zoomed in on the image slowly, and the Earth drew closer and its continents came into view. The screen continued to zoom until all I could see was the United States, and the image kept narrowing in until it fell on a single house and, finally, on a single girl sitting behind a wall screen.

The host looked at me and clasped her hands behind her back. "First, who are you? What do you enjoy doing? What defines you? How do you want others to perceive you? We've made it easy to discover yourself in the following four steps. When you're ready, say 'Begin' to start the process!"

Words popped up on the screen. *Step One: Re-create Yourself!*

"Begin," I said.

"Fill out the following questionnaire," the girl instructed me. "Your answers will be pooled with other contacts' to help recommend your future friends."

Her doe eyes peered into mine like she could really see me. "This is your moment to shine. Who do you want to be? Close your eyes and visualize that person. Are you edgy, clean-cut, professional, alternative? Now build yourself one step at a time. You are the architect of your own destiny. Draw your outline and step inside."

"That was very moving," I said.

I began the questionnaire. There were only twenty-nine questions. I stared at the document before I started. That was it? Answering twenty-nine questions could define me? I wondered if the answers to twenty-nine questions could even describe this room, let alone the complexity of a person. Or maybe people weren't that complex anymore. Maybe technology was making us so full we were empty.

I hurried through the questions and submitted the list.

"Good," the girl said. "Now go to the About Me step and fill out the ten profile-building questions. You will be able to finish your online identity in just a few minutes. Remember, you can go back and edit your identity at any time. Try it out!"

I opened the About Me file and filled out ten basic profile questions. I played with responses. I said I was Amish. I said I was sexually confused. I said I was four foot eleven, I was a harpist, and I enjoyed dog grooming. I said my favorite food was raw eggs over mushrooms, and what I looked for in a friend was someone who could drive a dirt bike and fight like a ninja. I said I was interested in communism and free love. I hit Submit.

"Perfect!" she congratulated me. "Now we can move on to step two."

"Fantastic," I replied.

Words illuminated the screen. *Step Two: Reconnect!*

"Instantly make lifelong contacts that meet your interests. Are you ready to begin socializing?" she asked with an adventurous grin.

"Absolutely," I said to the screen. I blinked and within two seconds my host was back with a report.

She informed me she'd found 4,682 contacts that matched my profile answers. "Would you like to meet them?" she asked.

"Yes," I said. A list filled the room. It spanned every inch of wall space. Letters, words, and names climbed around me. It looked like a sequence code, like a bizarre strand of digital DNA. But there was nothing human about it.

These were my new friends.

"Show," I said. The list disappeared and in its place popped up thousands of profile pictures. It was a stadium of faces blinking back at me, some smiling, some laughing, and some straight-faced and serious. I could enlarge any photo I wanted by pointing at it. I could read up on people's profile answers, their background and histories. I surveyed the room. The contacts were mostly young, about my age. They covered every style, ethnicity, and culture. I instantly had a wide range of friends. It was a virtual melting pot of diversity.

"Continue to step three?" she asked.

I was starting to lose my sense of humor. My lips pressed together. I'd been put through months of brainwashing to prepare me for this? They'd dumbed me down so I was clueless enough to think this was living?

"Begin," I said.

Step Three: Advertise the New You!

"It's time to market yourself," my host informed me. "People are like products. You need to put yourself on the shelf if you want others to see you. But first, make yourself stand out. Advertise! Build a slogan of the new you to attract friends, colleagues, contacts, and partners."

This was the design portion of the registration process. Time to build my image. I used FacePaint, a program that allowed you to digitally enhance your features. I chose a picture from my records taken about a year and a half ago, me sitting in the backyard with Baley. I cropped the photo and enlarged myself. I added blemishes to my skin and fat rolls to my neck and arms. I gave my hair streaks of gray. I squeezed my body down until I was half my height. I moved my eyes closer together and added an inch of length to my nose. I stained a few of my teeth brown and added blotches of dirt stains to my shirt. I turned my smile into a snarl. I tattooed a smashed beer can on my biceps. I played with Baley's image until it looked like I had my arm around a pig squatting next to me. When I finished I added the picture to my registration and let out a satisfied laugh.

Step Four: Get Connected!

A giant Submit button flashed on the screen. Now that I was rebranded, it was time to get back into the digital world. Time to hang up the advertisement.

"Submit," I said. I was plugged back in. Instantly, I was bombarded with invites, advertisements, chat requests, parties, study groups, volunteer opportunities, internships, and workout classes. This simulated version even told me I had a date request. How thoughtful.

I blinked at the screen and couldn't believe it. It would take me a week to respond to all this feedback. And, I figured, that was the point. It could take a lifetime to weed through all of the people and contacts I was making, the videos to watch, the music to listen to, the movies to catch up on, the online shopping to try. I could dedicate all my time to this life. No one could hurt me in this existence. I was another girl in the bubble.

It was a utopia. So why did it feel so hollow?

The door buzzed open and my heart knocked against my chest. Only an hour had passed, and I hadn't hit the Complete button. I tried deleting the screen, but it wouldn't clear any of my comments. Dr. Stevenson's heels clicked loudly through the door. Then the shoes stopped. I turned and saw her staring at the screen.

Her eyes scanned my schedule glumly. She glared at my interview questions and tightened her lips at my design photo. There wasn't a trace of humor in her face.

She looked at me for an explanation.

"I thought this was just a practice run," I told her, and started to chew my nails.

"Do you find our methods funny?"

I didn't answer her. Instead, I looked back at the wall screen, where my answer was obvious. Her eyes flashed with anger, and my confidence was kicked down. I realized what a huge mistake I'd made. The past hour had been more of a test than a registration process.

"It was just a joke," I said. "Is it a crime to have a sense of humor?"

"Why do you go out of your way to mock the system?"

I shot her a look. "Why do you go out of your way to brainwash anyone that disagrees with the system? People aren't programmable. Someone will always fight back," I said.

"There's no point, Madeline. You're shooting at a bulletproof target. What's right and what's best wins in the end."

I nodded because this was the one point we agreed on.

She looked at the screen and back to me. "I'm scheduling you for two treatment sessions a week for four more weeks. We'll also suspend your online programs. You obviously aren't ready for society yet."

My body tensed from my neck all the way to my toes. "I've been here for months. I thought I was done with the treatment."

"You like to think you give the orders around here. Obviously, we haven't gotten through to you. Yet. But don't worry, Madeline. We have a hundred percent success rate at the LADC. No one gets out of here without being cured. I'll simply have to make you my personal case study."

CHAPTER nineteen

I woke up and could feel my thoughts traveling through my head. They moved like water down a riverbed. They lingered in some spots and sped quickly past others. They played in circles at my temples. They flooded over the banks of my brain.

My eyes fluttered and started to open. Something was different. I felt like I was lying inside a cloud, warm and soft and weightless. There were no nightmares. No cold sweats. But still, there was friction. An energy field surrounded me, pulling me in and holding me tight. A touch as warm as sunlight traced my eyebrows. And then there was a voice.

"It's me," he said. Then I realized the movement I felt was his fingers lightly tracing across my forehead. They were his fingers orchestrating my jagged mind into a calm canyon. We sat at the opening of the subway tunnel. He had his back against the wall, and I was using his body like a deep armchair.

"How long have we been here?" I asked.

"You fell asleep and it started raining so I moved us in here," he said. I nodded lazily. Justin knew I was going through more treatments and it was starting to drain me. He tucked me tighter in his arms. I could feel his chest rising and sinking. He whispered in my ear. "I probably should have brought you back to the basement, but I wasn't ready to give you up."

His voice was so solid, I could lean on it. I wanted to turn him on at night and listen to him while I fell asleep. I wanted to sit him next to my bed so I had his face to wake up to every morning. I imagined someday I'd have that. We'd be together. Life could be different. Sometimes the only way to get through the present is to focus on the future.

It was pouring rain outside. Rain dripped off the mouth of the tunnel and dove into the ground. Drops caught the reflection of streetlights in the background and pulled light down like golden ribbons. Water pooled in a tiny lake in front of us. Rain punched the lake into a thousand tiny potholes. Everything tapped and splashed like drummers on parade. Justin held my hand and I limply held his back. I stared at the symphony outside. It was liquid fireworks.

I took a long, contented breath. "It's beautiful," I said.

He buried his lips in my hair and I didn't flinch from the contact. My thoughts felt like clouds, slowly gathering up only to drift away. I had to train my thoughts and force them to connect. He squeezed my hand and it brought me back. I told Justin I used to think water had magical powers.

"My grandma used to take me on walks when I was little," I said. My voice felt far away but I followed after it, determined to keep up with it. "We hiked along the Willamette River. I used to spend hours looking at rocks. I was amazed how beautiful they looked underwater; all their colors were magnified and polished. I spent whole afternoons collecting them. But as soon as they dried, they lost their luster. They just looked drab and dusty and pale. After that, I always thought water was magical, that it could make anything beautiful. I believed water could bring out the best in people. It's hard for me not to be happy around it. Anything that can make a dull rock look like a jewel has to be pretty powerful."

Justin nodded and told me he knew what I meant.

"I collected those rocks for years," I said. "I still have a jar in my room. Even if they do turn pale when they dry, I wanted something to remind me to believe in magic." I let out a long sigh and watched the rain. "I just want the ocean to reach out and wipe away this life. Wipe away the DC and my memories and make me new again. Water has the power to do that."

"So do you," he said.

I smiled at the curtain of raindrops. "Why does it feel so good to be outside?" I asked.

"It doesn't feel good to everyone," he reminded me.

"I don't understand that," I said. "It's an escape. It's the only place you can be where nothing's expected of you. You don't have to perform or conform. You don't have to impress anybody. You don't have to act out a role. You can finally relax."

His fingers played in mine.

"Nature reminds you who you are," Justin said, "and most of us don't want to be reminded. People don't know who they are anymore. They're being told who to be so much of the time they don't get the chance to figure it out for themselves."

"Maybe we're always changing."

"Maybe we're always performing."

"Then who are we really?" I wondered. "At the end of the day, with the lights off, all alone, which of those personalities that we take on and off are real?"

"I don't think we know anymore. Besides, we never have to be alone, so we can avoid thinking about it."

"So what are you saying?" I asked. "We all need to find ourselves?"

"I'm saying maybe we all need to be okay with who we are ten minutes longer every day. Maybe we need to stop worrying so much about being accepted and caring what people think about us. But we need to accept ourselves first. Maybe we need to plug back into this," he said, and nodded to the world outside.

I thought about calling nature an escape. It's strange because nature was the real world. It was always there, free, right outside people's doors. The real world was always waiting. Yet people called it an escape. You shouldn't have to escape in order to be real.

CHAPTER *twenty*

I stayed in bed all day, staring with eyes that didn't see. I felt like I was being erased. The nightmares were endless. My counseling sessions were twice a week now. Gabe promised me it would only last a few more weeks. I had been in the DC over four months. My body was exhausted. My mind, what I used to value most, had become my worst enemy. It lived inside my skin but my thoughts didn't belong to me anymore.

I was tired of fighting my dreams. I was losing the solid line between dream and reality. The system was wearing me down.

My wall screens turned into constant sheets of rain. I heard a knock on my door and mumbled to come in. I didn't have to shift my eyes to know it was Gabe. He checked in on me every night, when the Eye turned off. He was becoming more of a nurse than a friend. He tried to force food and water into me. He reminded me to shower and get out of bed and take care of myself. He forced me to talk, to move, to breathe. I was starting to resent him for it. I just wanted to fade.

He set a sandwich bar and juice box on my desk. I smelled turkey and cheese and garlic but it just made me queasy.

"You should eat something."

I blinked up at the rain. The clouds hung lazily over me. His words slid around me like water around oil. They fell to the ground and disappeared. I was too numb to nod. I was giving up. The visits with Molly weren't working. I slept through half my nights with Justin. Seeing people just made me more depressed. They showed me a mirror and I couldn't stand the person in the reflection.

"You'll feel better if you get up, Maddie," he said. "Take a shower."

I rubbed my hand over my hollow stomach. "What's the point?"

"No offense, but you look terrible. You need to clean up."

"No, I mean of this life," I said. "What's the point of this life?"

Gabe sat down in the chair next to me. "It's the only one we've got," he said. "So we shouldn't waste it. Come on, Maddie. Remember what you're trying to do in here."

He reached out to give me the sandwich but his movement was too sudden and I flinched and swatted his hand away.

"Sorry," he said, and scooted the chair back until it hit the desk frame. Silver rain fell behind him.

Gabe glanced at his watch. "We need to get going. It's midnight."

"I'm not going," I said. "I don't feel good."

"People are counting on you," he reminded me.

I told him there was nothing I could do. I felt like I was withering. I couldn't stop shaking. Everywhere; my teeth, my shoulders, my arms. I wrapped my blanket tighter around me.

"Don't you want to get out of here?"

I shook my head. "It's not safe out there."

"It's not safe *in here.* Being around people will help."

"You can't trust people. We're all twisted. We're all waiting to snap. We all work better alone."

"That's not true," he said. "We all care about you. We're depending on you. You need to have hope."

"Hope's dead," I mumbled to the sky.

Gabe told me he didn't believe it. He said I was the strongest person he knew.

I laughed weakly. I felt as strong as a blade of grass.

"It's just your nightmares," he said. "Don't let this place break you."

"I want this to go away. I want to feel normal again. Something's in my head, Gabe. They planted something in my head." I started to cry. My shoulders shook, and my chest and my ribs. It felt like the rain had seeped inside of me and was pouring out. Tears replaced my blood with water, my heart with a river. They ran down my face and it was so strange to act human at a time when I felt as lifeless as a machine.

"Justin's waiting downstairs. Don't you want to see him?"

A tiny wing fluttered inside of me at the sound of his name. A spark lit up, like a match striking a rough surface and catching fire. Before my mind could cave in, my heart convinced my legs to move.

✻

Justin took me to the beach again. The air was humid and heavy but the sky was clear. The moon was full with a hazy layer wrapped around it, like a gold halo. There was a scattering of stars in the sky. We sat down in the soft sand and listened to the waves. I was still groggy; my thoughts came out slowly, like they were being filtered through a sieve.

I looked out at the sky. "I almost forgot stars exist," I said flatly. Justin held my limp hand in his. His fingers were laced with mine but I hardly felt the contact, as if something were disconnected.

"I know," he said. "You're slipping, Maddie."

I nodded. "Mm-hm," I said with a knowing smile. A small laugh climbed up my throat. It was the hopeless laugh of surrender.

"It feels good to slip," I said. It was easier to give in than to fight back. There was sweetness to letting go. Falling is freeing. The farther you drop the lighter you feel until you're weightless. A permanent fog settled around my mind and it wrapped me up in a warm blanket. Trying to think was like pulling off the blanket only to feel the cold drafts. Why shiver when you can stay warm like this forever?

"I think it's really amazing what you're doing," he said. He was trying to catch me and pull me back but I wasn't fooled. I didn't want a parachute this time. I was enjoying the free fall.

"I'm not *doing* anything," I said. "I'm being undone. My whole life. I've been undone." My voice came out monotone. "Every time I put myself back together it happens again. It's pointless."

He was quiet for a few seconds. He squeezed my hand. Justin was still the only person who could touch me. His eyes were on my profile and then they met mine and there was a crease there, this worried concentration. His eyes were full of emotion, which was unsettling. It broke his calm surface. It was like pulling a single thread and watching something solid and colorful and perfect unravel. The warm blanket around my mind started to slip. Maybe it was guilt or sadness creeping in, but I didn't like the feeling, so I tried to kick it away and reach for the blanket instead.

"I need to tell you something," he said, "and you're not going to like what I'm about to say. But I think you need to hear it." He sucked in a long breath. "You need to stop thinking so much about yourself. It doesn't do any good to dwell on yourself. Trust me, it only makes things worse."

My fingers suddenly flexed inside his hand but he squeezed my hand harder before I could yank it away. "Excuse me?" I glared at him.

He told me I needed to take a step back and refocus. "Right now you're just focusing on yourself. You're too shortsighted. That's how they're beating you."

Something kicked in my chest and it jarred my eyes open wider. It took me a second to place what I was feeling. It was anger. I stared at him with shock. "I can't believe you're saying this to me right now."

His eyes were tight and unforgiving. As vigilant as my father's. "Believe it."

"Aren't I entitled to feel a little self-pity?"

"No," he said. "Pity's a waste of time." He held my gaze and there was no apology on his face. His dark eyes were relentless. I twisted my hand free from his and my impulsive reaction made amusement swim over his eyes, like he was happy to get a rise out of me.

"You forget—I'm in a *detention center,*" I yelled. "You forget—I'm being psychologically tortured. Sorry if I'm not fully embracing my situation with a positive outlook."

His mouth curled up at the corner. "There's the Maddie I know," he said, and his grin welcomed me back.

I picked myself up off the ground but Justin caught me before I could walk away. He held my shoulders so I had to face him. I tried to wriggle myself free, not because his physical touch bothered me but because his words hurt.

"*You* forget something," he said. "This whole thing, it isn't about you. Don't you get it? Take yourself out of the equation. What you're doing is bigger than this, it's bigger than you," he said and pressed his hands tighter on my shoulders. "People are depending on you. You're responsible now because you know what's going on in there. You've committed yourself because you believe in something. Don't lose sight of that."

I shook his hands off me and backed up a few steps. "It's not that easy. They're controlling my mind in there," I said, and pointed back at the tunnel, at the dark hole waiting to swallow me up again like the mouth of a snake.

"Only if you let them. Only if you stop seeing a way out. Don't let them beat you down. Stop focusing so much on the problem. It's only going to make the struggle feel worse. Focus on the answer. Put your energy in that."

"I can't do anything!" I shouted. "I'm not on a mission to save the world, Justin. Don't mistake your goals for mine. I'm just trying to survive. I'm just one person."

I expected him to get angry at this, but his voice stayed calm.

"That's not true," he argued. "There are a lot of people backing you up on this. You're only one person if that's the way you choose to see it. Don't let yourself feel that small. That's how the system beats you. You're thousands of people. You're not alone."

I turned and marched down the beach. "I'm not in the mood for one of your leadership speeches right now," I yelled over my shoulder.

"So what are you going to do? Quit?" he yelled after me. "Shrivel up and die?"

"I can't do anything," I repeated. I wanted him to let me give up. Didn't he ever give up? "They censor all of my words," I said through tears. "They're monitoring everything I do."

"That never stopped you before," he reminded me. He reached out for me but I pulled my hand back. I exhaled a bitter sigh. My breath felt stale and tired. My lungs felt black.

"Maybe this is all pointless," I said.

Justin shook his head. "Maddie." He paused for a second to pick his words. "You've always been monitored—by your dad, by Damon, by school. You know how to be bigger than what's trying to confine you. Don't stop now."

Tears ran down my cheeks. "So what am I supposed to do?"

"You're in there to help us figure out what's going on. We need you to be stronger than them or this whole thing is useless. You can't let them beat you down. You're going to become consumed and you'll just turn into another one of the sleepwalkers." He spoke the words slowly to make sure they sank in. "Look at what they're trying to steal. They're not trying to hold your body hostage. It's your mind they want. So, see out of it mentally. Attack back with your mind."

I knew he was trying to help. But I still wanted to fail. "Maybe you shouldn't count on me."

"If anyone can do this it's you. I have more faith in you than anyone I've ever met."

I pressed my lips together and thought about his words. He was right. I was breaking down, and if I let myself give in, I wouldn't be any use to anyone.

"I'm sorry," he said. "I'm just trying to help you realize you're not alone."

"You're right," I admitted. I narrowed my eyes at him. "But maybe you need to realize the same thing."

"Me?" he asked, his face puzzled.

I told him he had more faith in people than anyone I'd ever met. He grew up being tossed around, living out of a suitcase, never knowing what to expect. "I grew up pampered and spoiled and you have more faith in your heart than all the people I know combined. But you don't know how to love anyone," I said.

"Give me a break," he said, and took a few steps back. "This again?"

"Have you ever opened up about your past?" I demanded.

"Where is all this coming from?" Then he knew before I had to tell him. His eyes narrowed. He kicked his foot in the dirt and sent a spray of sand sailing through the air. After all the times I'd envied him for staying calm and being patient, I'd finally found a place where he couldn't control his anger. It's when he allowed himself to care.

"Clare," he said. "I should have guessed. So Kristin's death has been turned into gossip?"

"Gabe told me, and it's not like that. He honestly thought I knew. I *should* have known."

Justin shook his head and stuffed his hands in his pockets. "No. It's got nothing to do with you." His eyes were open but the shields were in full force. "I don't talk about it. To anybody."

"Maybe you should."

"There's nothing to say." His face was unreadable.

I wanted so badly to be easy on Justin. But I couldn't stand there and watch him hold all of those memories and feel responsible.

"How am I supposed to know you if you keep something like that from me? How is anyone supposed to *know* you?"

He inhaled a slow breath. I could hear the anger seething off his body. It sounded like steam. "It's my mistake," he said, and pressed his fingers hard against his chest. "My burden to carry. I don't need to put it on anybody else. I'm not like that. So leave it alone," he warned me.

Tears welled up in my eyes at the hurt on Justin's face. Maybe I was trying to bring him down. Maybe I wanted someone to feel as miserable as me. Now I could see why no one had had the courage to bring it up with him before. They didn't want to see him break.

"I just want to help you," I said, mirroring what he'd said to me minutes before.

"I don't want anyone to help me." His eyes were burning. "You want to know how I deal? I take the shit that happens in life and I use it as a catalyst for change."

The tears spilled down my face. I wanted to reach out to Justin but his eyes were scorched.

"Most of what I do today all stems from that experience. That's how I use tragedy. It's a wake-up call. It reminds me to make the most of my life. To never waste a second of it. It reminds me why this world has to change. That's how I deal with the shitty things life hands you. I don't sit around and talk about it and dwell on it. I don't feel sorry for myself and ask why things happen. You'll go crazy if you sit around dwelling on *why*. Because there are no answers. You can't change the past." He took a deep breath. "I'd like to think Kristin's death was a wake-up call. And I take steps every day to make sure it doesn't happen to someone else's daughter or best friend or girlfriend."

He turned and headed down the beach.

"I'm sorry," I yelled after him. "I love you. That's all. And I hate that I love you, you know that? I really hate it."

He stopped walking and stood there, his head down.

"You're a hypocrite," I said. "You're the one saying everyone needs a middle ground. You need to learn to accept that. You let the system break you too."

I didn't know what else to say. Dark energy passed between us, something I had never felt before, and it scared me. Beating down Justin only beat me down lower. I couldn't handle his presence, angry and hurt and turned away from me like it was all my fault.

I didn't want to make the moment any worse so I backed up, but before I could turn away Justin was right there. He grabbed my face in his hands and leaned his head down.

My mind told me to scream but something made me stop. My muscles flexed and jumped under my skin, urging me to run. But something else was stronger inside of me. Something kept my feet standing in place.

His lips touched mine and it melted a layer of ice that had formed around my heart. I grabbed his jacket and pulled him closer and I wrapped my arms around him because I realized this was what I needed more than anything. He folded me inside his arms and pressed his lips harder against mine.

He let me drain him.

It was selfish because I was taking every piece of happiness he could give me. I sucked the lightness out of him and I felt hopelessness drift out of my soul like a black cloud of ash. I was going to suck him dry—I emptied all the light out of him. There was more in that kiss than love; it was necessity, it was pain and fear that I was pushing into him so I could steal his strength. I needed to store it away so I could live off it. I could feel Justin's heart hammering against mine and I slowly felt a hole inside me start to fill with something real. Something warm.

I finally let go and Justin looked down at me. He took a deep breath, something like relief, and pressed his forehead against mine. Neither of us spoke. He let go of my eyes and dropped his hands. He turned and walked away.

January 2061

Mother whispered, "Jump.
And don't be afraid to fall.
Your wings will catch you."

It's a haiku I memorized when I was young, from a picture book
my mom handed down to me. I remember tracing my fingers over the
bird's wings on the page. Every time I read it, it means something different to me, depending on where I'm at in my life. I try to live by
these words, to have courage and faith, but it's so hard to use my wings
in this life.
Maybe it's about being happy.
The real world is becoming warped and dirty and there's lead in
my feet. I'm not getting any lucky breaks in here. I don't want to be
here. I want to be there. Sometimes there is no bright side so it forces
your eyes to adjust to the dark.
Where is happy?
Will I one day be able to put my feet up and toast to the sun? Will
I be happy? Or is happiness just this fleeting moment you spend your
life chasing after only to feel it slip through your fingers and leave you
wanting more? Is happiness just bait used to move us through life?

CHAPTER twenty-one

"Okay, Maddie," Molly said. "I have a test for you." She held a MindReader in one hand and the Cure in the other. It wasn't a full dose of the drug, just a quarter piece. Gabe had gotten us a sample, as promised. She motioned to a flipscreen in front of me and explained she'd play the video at the same time it was downloaded through the reader.

"I'll study how you react," she said. Clare, Gabe, Justin, and Pat sat around us in a half circle. I picked up the MindReader and hesitated.

"Don't worry," she said. "It's not a nightmare. You'll enjoy this dream, I promise."

I was intrigued. I dropped the tablet in my mouth and slid on the MindReader. The fog was already setting in.

I closed my eyes and when I opened them I was standing on the summit of a sandy hill, looking down over the edge. The hill rippled below and around me like it was moving and its brown slope flowed all the way down to a wide river below.

"You ready?" Justin asked. I turned and he was standing a few

feet away, wearing a hooded sweatshirt and jeans and this enor-
mous smile I'd seen on him only a few times, when he was at his
best, when he was about to fly. Clare and Gabe stood on the other
side of him. The sun beat down on us and the air was dry; the
wind was a hot gust.

Soft, sandy hills stretched out beneath me, spread out for
miles. Gabe dropped down and the steep incline swallowed him.
I watched him propel a board underneath his feet down the sand
dune, like he was snowboarding. Clare followed behind him.
They slalomed down the hill, cutting switchbacks through the
slope and leaving shallow ridges in the soft ground. They kicked
up waves of sand behind them.

"Put those on," Justin reminded me, and nudged my arm. I
reached up and touched thick plastic goggles wrapped around my
head. I pulled them over my face, and the hillsides and water were
tinted orange. I looked down and realized my feet were strapped
to a board. Justin didn't need to encourage me to go. It all came
naturally. I leaned forward, shifted my weight, and gravity did the
rest. My knees bent into a squat and my arms were held out for
balance but my legs and hips felt like they'd done this before. I
rode down the giant sand dune like I was surfing a wave.

The gradient steepened and I picked up speed, turning easily
by pushing on one foot or the other. The ground was so smooth I
felt like I was riding on water. The wind pushed against my face
and my hands and roared in my ears as if I were flying through it.
I squatted lower to the ground so I could go faster. Gabe was fifty
yards in front of me and I watched him catch a jump, flying off a
rock ledge through the air and landing gracefully on the padded
ground. I turned my board and headed for the same ledge. I
reached my arms out wide to keep steady and flew off the jump
and felt weightless. The water moved and glistened below in the

sun and I screamed down at the valley as I landed perfectly in the soft, smooth sand. I dug my board in, cutting through the ground and sending sand up in a long spray.

The golden hillside was starting to fade to darker brown and then black. The water turned blurry. I realized I wasn't standing, I was lying down. I opened my eyes, and the scene disappeared, replaced by ceiling lights. My heart was pounding, and I could still feel the adrenaline shooting through my legs. I blinked at Molly and she was holding the MindReader, staring down at me. I frowned at her for cutting the dream short. Justin, Clare, Gabe, and Pat stared at me, fascinated. Justin bit his nails like he was trying to hide a smile.

"Whatever that was, give me more of it," I said with a grin.

"You were laughing the entire time," Justin informed me.

I pressed my hands on my stomach and it was tight and sore from working muscles I hadn't used in months.

"Do you remember anything?" Molly asked.

I opened my mouth to answer her, but I was already forgetting. I could remember a rush, I told her, this feeling of flying. "I remember sun, and people were there. Justin and Gabe, I think."

Molly nodded.

"That's all?" she asked, and I nodded. She looked down at the flipscreen that had recorded the descriptions I was telling her during the dream: the people, the wide river, the endless miles of rolling dunes, and the last jump I took off the rock ledge. I read over the descriptions and I couldn't remember a single detail.

"I said all that?" I asked.

"When you weren't laughing," she told me. She played the video back for me again, on the flipscreen. It was a roughly edited documentary of a single guy sandboarding.

"Scott watched this a few weeks ago and now sandboarding is all he talks about," Molly said. We all watched the documentary.

The man filming it had a camera strapped to his head, so the viewers felt like they were surfing the dune with him. But the dune he was on had a gentle gradient and he was by himself. There wasn't any water visible anywhere, and no endless miles of dunes like I described in my experience.

"It's interesting," Molly said. "We played the video for ten minutes, but you've been out for an hour. My guess is if you take the full dose, it knocks you out for about six to eight hours."

"So what is the drug doing?" I asked her.

"It makes you hallucinate, obviously," she said. "It actually shocks your mind and encourages your brain to create proteins that are necessary for memory building. At the same time, it acts as a relaxant. So while it slows down some neural pathways, it opens up others. It takes what you see and what's being downloaded and mixes it with your own memories. That's how it's personalized. You cast the roles and change the scenery. Have you been to the Columbia River Gorge?" she asked me.

I nodded. I told her my father grew up in The Dalles, in northern Oregon, and we used to take trips up there as a family in the summer.

"The steep, rolling hills and that river you described, it sounds like the program mixed with your memory of the gorge to make it authentic."

"But when I wake up, why can't I remember anything?"

"It's called an amnesia blackout," she told me. "It's similar to a blackout people get from drinking too much. Your salient short-term memories don't make it into your long-term memory so you can never remember specific details. The drug lets you hang on to just the smallest details and emotions, until something triggers the memory. But it gets buried so deep in your subconscious you don't even realize it's a memory. Instead, it just becomes a reaction."

"So, let me get this straight," Justin said. "The DC's planting memories disguised as nightmares in people's minds?"

Molly nodded. "Once the memories are downloaded, your mind can't help but run off of those files. You're taught to fear society. You're taught to think being around people is just a tragedy waiting to happen, like in the real world violence is lurking around every corner. Anything can trigger it. They can condition you to fear hallways, door handles, windows. Anything leading to the outside world. So you go out of your way to avoid those feelings. You live in digital school. The system becomes a cure. They're trapping you with your own mind. You're mentally building your own walls."

"That's why they don't need much security in here," Gabe added. "Kids are too afraid to leave their rooms, let alone to try to escape the building."

"What's in the drug, exactly?" I asked.

"I'm still running some tests on it," she said. She used her flip-screen to diagram a barrage of charts and graphs while she explained. "One of the ingredients is salvia. It's a natural herb that stays in the bloodstream for only a few hours, which is why I couldn't detect it. The drug activates your prefrontal cortex."

We all blinked back at her and Gabe raised his hand and asked Molly to speak in English.

She sighed and projected an image of the brain. "It's the part of the brain that controls emotions," she said. "Think of your mind as a computer. This is my theory: the detention center is downloading memories, like the school bombings that happened on M-Twenty-Eight, school shootings, and terrorist attacks, and they use your memories to cast the roles—all the people closest to you, your friends and family. That's why it's believable. It becomes personal."

"But it feels real," I told Molly. "How do you explain that? I can feel pain. I can smell smoke. I can feel my leg getting shot off."

"The drug makes it real," Molly said. "It blurs the line between the conscious and subconscious."

"Okay," Pat said. "Now we know what the DC's trying to do. What's the next step?"

Molly sighed and sat back in her seat. "First, we need to find a counter-drug. Something to separate the dreams from the reality so the students realize those nightmares aren't real memories. And now we have the evidence we need to prove what's going on."

"Hopefully you can find a counter-drug before they completely fry my brain," I said, and took a sip of water.

Pat suddenly stood up and pushed his chair back with a screech. "That's it," he said. "She's not going back in there." He glared around the room and his eyes stopped on Justin. "Haven't you all seen enough?" he asked him, as if this entire detention center were his creation. Justin's eyes stayed on Pat's but he didn't argue.

"Madeline will be fine," Molly assured us. "I really think this is temporary—"

"You don't know that," Pat interrupted. "You don't know the long-term effects this place has. You said it yourself—you have your evidence. So let's get her out of here. *Now.*"

Pat glared at Justin, daring him to disagree.

"I can't tell her what to do," Justin said calmly.

"Tell her what's best for her. Do you think you're the only person in this room who cares about her?"

Justin raised his eyebrows. "Are we really going to get into this right now?"

Pat took a step closer to Justin. "Since you've met her, all you've done is mess with her life."

"You mean save her life," Clare argued.

"What is wrong with you people?" Pat said. "Don't you care about anything other than your precious mission?" He looked from Molly to Justin. "You guys don't even see people. You just use them for your own purpose, for your own experiments and connections. But I'm not going to let you use Maddie."

"They're not using me, Pat," I cut in.

"Oh yeah?" He glared back at Justin. "Where were you when she moved to L.A.? I know you never called her. You're not involved in her life. You're only down here now because you see her as a way to fight DS."

"That's not true—" I began but Pat interrupted me.

"You're too blind to see anything but your job. You don't care about anyone except yourself."

I widened my eyes at Pat. Did he honestly believe that? I'd never heard anyone cut Justin down before, especially by calling him selfish. He never thought about himself.

"I care more than you think," Justin said, his mouth tight. He was losing his cool and his eyes bore into Pat's.

"What classes is she taking? What color did she paint her bedroom? What's her favorite TV show? You don't know the day-to-day things."

"Don't ever assume what I know," Justin answered him, his voice fighting to stay calm. Pat's hands balled up into fists and the muscles in his arms flexed. I stood up before a fight broke out.

"Would you guys stop talking about me like I'm not in the room? I'm staying. I'm not giving up and I don't care what any of you think. It's my decision. No one's making it for me." I turned to face Pat. "Justin doesn't want me in here any more than you do. But I made a commitment. I'm not leaving until we know how to get everyone in this building out, until we have a plan in place. I'm your eyes and ears right now. You guys need me in here."

"You've been through enough," Pat said. He glared at Molly. "Take your tests. Do your little psychological experiments. But I'm not going to sit here and watch you do it anymore," he said, and he opened the basement door and stalked out. We were all quiet for a few moments. Justin's face was flushed. He refused to meet my eyes.

"You're right, Maddie," Molly said. "I think we need to let you carry this out."

"Maybe we should listen to Pat," Clare grumbled. She slumped into her seat and rested her head in her hands. "We're your friends. We need to keep you out of harm's way, not throw you in it. We'll figure out something else."

I crossed my arms over my chest. "I'm staying in here until my sentence is up or until we find a way to break every kid out of here. I have less than two months left." I forced my voice to steady. "Besides, I've survived the worst part. They haven't broken me yet."

CHAPTER twenty-two

"Her funeral was online," he said.

Justin and I sat on a rock, perched above the beach. There was a soft wind blowing. The air was humid and it smelled like rain was close. No stars were visible. The sky was stained black.

He pulled his baseball cap low so the brim shaded his eyes. I stared straight ahead because I didn't want him to stop. You can puncture a moment with the wrong words. So I stayed silent.

"Kristin's funeral," he said. "It was a virtual service." He spoke slowly, and for the first time I realized he struggled with words only when they were ones he'd never said before.

"I'd never been to a funeral before. I didn't know what to expect. They set up a website to host the memorial service. You could log on and add comments and feedback and post pictures and share stories. There was a slide show and a forum. There were advertisements. They turned her life into a commercialized website."

His body was rigid. Tense. He tried to keep his voice calm but

190

I could hear it tainted with bitterness, like something toxic was coming out of it.

"It's pretty easy to build a website for funerals," he said. "I checked it out after Kristin's death. It's laid out in ten steps. It takes about a half an hour."

I nodded as I listened.

"It made me so sick. That's all people are worth these days, a half an hour of our time. No one travels to funerals. No one's expected to make the sacrifice anymore. We can't be inconvenienced." He paused for a few seconds and his face tightened. I didn't know what to say so I just squeezed his hand.

"That's how desensitized we've become," he said. "I'm scared of only one thing. One. That we don't value people anymore. I can't accept that. Because if it's true, if we don't value human life, what's the point? What are we living for?" He pushed out a heavy breath. "Her funeral was a wake-up call on so many levels. People don't appreciate each other when they're alive. Why would they go out of their way for someone who's dead?"

When my grandmother passed away, we organized an online memorial; that way, more people could attend. It was convenient because family didn't have to travel across the country. It made sense, economically. People didn't have to buy expensive airplane tickets and take leave from work. Kids didn't have to miss school. People didn't have to miss out on their own plans. It was practical. I never thought of it being less intimate. Until now.

"It wasn't your fault," I told him.

"I placed her there. I stationed her at the protest. On the steps, right on top of that bomb."

"You told me once it can take lives to prove a point," I said.

He took a long, haggard breath.

191

"It's not your fault," I repeated. "Justin, you can't save everyone."

He nodded like he was finally willing to accept it.

"I can see why fighting DS is so personal to you now," I said. "Is that the only way to discover what you want to do with your life? When it becomes personal?"

He lay on his back and looked up at the sky and laced his fingers over his chest.

"You like to get deep," he said, and looked over at me.

"If it isn't deep, what's the point?" I asked, and I smiled to myself after I said the words. A year ago, I would have thought the opposite was true.

"I've always been against DS," he told me. "I dropped out when I was fourteen. I never liked being on a computer all day, it's just a world I didn't fit into. It always felt like I was outside of life, looking in but never living it. I was always on the cusp of knowing people. But I knew I was missing something and I hated that feeling. It's like staring at a photograph full of holes. I wanted to see the full picture.

"And then Kristin died." He swallowed. "Okay. This might sound strange, but I don't think you ever know completely what you want until you get hurt. It takes pain. And I'm not talking about getting a bad grade, or missing people, or getting in a fight with somebody. I'm talking about the kind of hurt that feels like torture. It twists your mind until it feels like it's bleeding. It's like a part of you dies. It gives you a new set of eyes. Life slows down so much you can hear all your thoughts and that's when you start to question things. You start to wonder what the point of life is and why you're in it, who you wish was in your life, or out of it. And then you figure it out. You dig your way through all that pain so you never have to experience it again."

He told me that's how he figured out what he wanted to do with his life. He told me he was convinced most people were motivated not by what they wanted but by what they wanted to avoid.

He looked at me. "That's the strangest thing about hitting rock bottom," he said. "It makes you start over again. It sets you free."

The LADC trained me to be a programmed machine during the day. At night, the rules were optional and shoved aside like curtains. Life became a different kind of production—one without directions or scripts or dress rehearsals. Meeting people face-to-face was the only antidote I needed. It pumped life back into my veins.

One night, Gabe and I walked down to the basement hallway where I was meeting Molly for my weekly series of tests. When we rounded the corner of the generator room, I froze. A group was waiting for me, gathered around glittering light on a folding table. I took a few steps closer and realized the lights were candles—real candles flickering on top of a cake. Justin was there, Clare, Molly, Scott; even Pat showed up. I walked over and read the icing. *Happy Eighteenth: Convict, Felon, and Friend.* It was fitting.

I smiled at my friends. They didn't keep track of dates in the DC. I'd had no way of knowing it was my eighteenth birthday.

My birthday celebration usually consisted of a frozen cake my mom ordered online and thousands of birthday wishes from my contacts with happy one-liners. My wall screen flashed all day with messages I could never keep up with. I felt so popular scrolling down a list of thousands of names. I didn't recognize any of the faces, but I still called them my friends because we were matched with similar profiles and interests.

I never went out, of course, but sometimes I'd have a virtual dress-up party or my parents would pay for me to get into an exclusive gossip club (VIP online parties where you could chat with a celebrity for a steep cover charge). I would dress my profile picture up in makeup and glitter and glamour, all in the comfort of my pajamas. I watched my avatar smile. My cartoon was so happy. I even had a happiness meter on the side of my profile in the shape of a cart. It filled up with yellow bubbles according to how many friends I had, how well I was doing in school, and how many clubs I joined. On my birthday, my cart was always full to the top, overflowing with yellow joy.

I used to look at that yellow meter and feel happy. But I was always feeling happy for someone else. I was only playing dolls.

Tonight, we played card games around the table, and the noise of the generators and the thick walls of the basement kept our voices from being heard outside the room. In a strange way, it was the best birthday I ever had. Even though I had lost nearly everything, I'd gained so much. I saw so much love and support around me. It fed me like food.

We played games for hours; we talked about freeing people in the DC; and we talked about change. I watched Justin and Scott joke back and forth and I watched people smile and I watched real eyes shine, and the energy was better than any drug. When you know you're breaking the rules, it fires you up. It's a rush to know you're bending something solid. It's a high to see how far you can twist your fate. We all glowed that night.

I thanked my friends and told all of them I loved them, because I did. This was my family. Gabe was like a brother. I was closer to him than to Joe because Gabe actually saw me, not the idea of me. He accepted me, he encouraged me. Most important, he took the time to know me. Relationships can be built only if you invest time in people, whether they're your family or not. I was beginning to believe friends could replace family. When it comes down to it, you want to be around people who appreciate you.

Molly handed me my birthday present, a small blue box wrapped in a red bow. I opened it and found a clear vial inside, but it was empty.

I turned the glass in my fingers. "Thanks?" I asked. I looked up at her and she smiled.

"It's the counter-drug," she said. "It's ready." I looked from the vial to her and she explained it was a gas form. "That's the only way we can administer it to the entire dorm," she said. She pointed to the air ducts and said that the gas could be pumped from the basement into the ducts three times a day on a timer. Gabe said he could help set it up. The drug was odorless, and Molly said there weren't any side effects.

"It acts as a shield," she said. "It attacks the drug before it can shock you. We hope to bring back your insanity soon," she said with a smile.

"What about the other students?" I asked.

"The ones that are still in here should be fine," she said. "The ones that have already been released can get rehabilitation, if they're open to it. Memories can be erased as easily as they're inserted. It would just take some time and willingness for them to get help. I think when they find out what's been going on in here, they'll be willing to get the treatment."

We passed a bottle of champagne and everyone took a sip. It was Justin's idea. He said champagne was the liveliest drink. It was used to toast life's accomplishments: weddings, graduations, wins, milestones. We toasted to our future success.

I looked around the basement and thought it was strange that in the darkest places you could find the most light. Hope works like that. It hides and blends in, only to pop out when you least expect it. It's always a surprise, something you step on, trip over, or stumble on by accident. It hides in the divots of our lives, in the loneliest valleys. It's like a child, always playing hide-and-seek to keep our lives unpredictable. Just when we're about to give up, hope turns on, like light, to guide our way.

CHAPTER *twenty-four*

I heard a knock at my door and yelled, "Come in." I had my stereo on and was nodding along to the music while I finished a paper for DS.

"What's up?" I asked. I turned in my seat with a smile, expecting to see Gabe. Connie stood in the doorway, the woman who'd escorted me into the DC and given me the tour. She studied my appearance with a frown.

"You're awfully perky these days," she noted, as if looking alive and healthy were unattractive traits. I reminded myself to be careful. We were close to freeing the detention center's inmates and I didn't want to raise suspicion. I was supposed to cower from people, not welcome them.

"It must be the coffee," I explained; mistake number two. I wasn't supposed to want to leave my room, especially for something as frivolous as coffee. I shut off my music and scooted back my desk chair, then jumped out of my seat with a little too much energy. I stopped midway through the room and winced at my wall screens.

That morning I'd painted them. I drew a yellow sun on the ceiling, like a golden lantern shining happiness around me. I turned two of my wall screens into a front yard and drew homes on either side of me. One of the homes was made out of coarse red brick and it reminded me of the home in Bayview I'd stayed in with Justin. I drew a yellow house on the other side that reminded me of Eden. I felt like I was surrounded by friends. I built a Ferris wheel on one of the front lawns. I painted my other wall screens blue so I wouldn't know the difference between walls and air. I built a train track through the center of my room to remind me to move. I wrote poems on the sidewalks with red and yellow chalk, and the words connected the houses. I wrote poems all the way up to each front door. I took cold, empty walls and gave them life.

Connie looked around with awe at the Ferris wheel, the neighborhood I'd created, the sunlight and train tracks, as if she'd forgotten a world existed outside the DC. I wanted to kick myself for being so careless.

"Come with me" was all she said.

I nodded slowly. I hadn't had a counseling session in a few weeks and was optimistic they were finally over. I had gotten my appetite back. I had gone weeks without waking up sweating and soaking through my clothes from nightmares.

I followed her into the hallway and reminded myself to keep my distance.

"Is this about my room?" I asked. "I have a right to design my wall screens. I read the DC rules."

She scanned her keycard next to the elevator. "Young lady," she said, "I'm familiar with the rules. This isn't a discipline issue. You have a visitor," she informed me as we stepped inside the elevator.

"Detention centers allow visitors?" I asked with disbelief.

She chuckled to herself. "More VIP treatment, it seems."

"Who is it?" I asked.

"That will be enough questions," she said, and tightened her lips to show she meant it.

We stood silently until we hit the ground floor and then she escorted me out the dorm entrance. It was the first time I'd been permitted outside the building since I was registered here, five months ago. We walked out into the dusty courtyard. I followed her down a concrete path to the office building on the other side of the lot. The courtyard was quiet except for loose rocks crunching under our shoes. The metal doors buzzed open and Connie ushered me inside. All the windows and blinds were tightly closed even though it was a sunny, mild day. The air in the lobby was cold, and the light inside was a dim bluish gray.

Connie pointed down the hall.

"Last office on the right," she informed me. I nodded and took a few steps but I was distracted. Wall screens on both sides of me lit up facts, statistics, and accomplishments of detention centers. It was like walking through a neon shrine. Most of the acknowledgments were of Richard Vaughn and his advances in neuroscience and psychology. I stopped, captivated by a diagram of the United States. Red dots on the screen represented all the existing detention centers. The size of the dot indicated the size of the center. There were centers in nearly every state. Most of the dots were small; the largest was the center in Iowa. The third largest, I noticed, was the LADC.

I approached an open office door and voices seeped into the hallway, men's voices. The sound of one voice, strong and powerful, practically knocked me over with surprise.

"I have every right to tour these facilities," I heard my father announce, and I froze in midstep.

"Not without an appointment," another voice responded. "This is not your area to oversee, Kevin. You have no authority inside my centers. You don't have the training or background to question my practices."

I pressed my back flat against the wall, as if they could see me from around the corner. The panic and fear I battled for months to control was rising up again.

"I'm not trying to step on your toes, Richard," my father said, his voice calm. "I'm just interested in seeing the facility since it contains my students, and my daughter."

"Write a proposal, let me look over your concerns, and we'll set up a time in the future. We don't do drop-ins around here."

"Don't you think we should collaborate?" my father asked. "Shouldn't your mission coincide with mine? If we work together, it can only improve the system."

I narrowed my eyes at this. My father rarely collaborated with anyone. He had to have other motives.

"All we do here is try to help young adults, just like you do. Isn't that collaborating? This facility is a safe haven. I'm helping them feel secure. This is a damn paradise. That's why you designed DS, isn't it, Kevin? To create a perfect, peaceful coexistence? A place where people can live free of fear? Free of violence and discrimination?"

"That was my intention," my dad said.

"Well, that's why I funded your *intention*. And my centers encourage that. Unless the board sees a problem with my performance, I'd prefer to keep my studies at the DC confidential. Just as I'm sure you have matters of your own you'd like to keep *confidential*."

I couldn't believe what I was hearing. Richard Vaughn was blackmailing my dad, and he was using me as the bargaining chip.

"My concern is how exactly you're going about *encouraging* the students," my dad retorted.

"Neuroscience is my field," Richard stated. "Education is yours. I don't look over your shoulder. I'd appreciate it if you'd back off mine. Remember who is boss here. If you don't like my rules I can replace you with someone who does."

"This center is not what I established," I heard my father say.

"You wanted to create a peaceful society. You recruit the orchestra. You conduct them. I make sure they stay in tune. People leave each other alone, thanks to me. Isn't that what you want? For people to be left alone? That's what society prefers."

"There's still the issue of my daughter," my father said.

"Don't blame me that you have no control over her. I've given you chances. I even agreed to let the paperwork show she was in here while she was living with your son."

"And now I'm thinking you were only helping me so you could help yourself," my father argued. "You didn't want me to come down here and sniff around."

"You would find nothing," Richard assured him.

"Hey," Connie whispered, and scaring me so bad that I nearly jumped out of my sandals. "What are you doing standing here?" she barked at me. "Go on," she said, and shoved me toward the door.

Connie had to push me all the way in since my feet refused to cooperate. We turned in to a large office. The screens inside were filled with more maps and awards and articles featuring the detention centers.

Richard sat behind a black desk and my father stood on the other side of it. I had seen photographs of Richard. He had thick, white hair that stood up in a messy heap on his head. He was lean and his blue eyes studied me suspiciously. There were deep wrinkles in his forehead and around his mouth, which was pinched into a frown.

My dad whirled around when he heard us, and his eyes found mine. For a few seconds, he just stared at me. My father could mask his emotions better than any actor. But for a moment I saw complete shock, as if he were seeing a ghost, just a rough approximation of who his daughter used to be.

"Madeline?" He said my name as if he were asking, as if he didn't recognize his own daughter. I hadn't looked in a mirror in weeks. I rarely did these days because I was disgusted with the girl who looked back at me.

"Hi, Dad," I said.

Richard studied me from head to foot and scrunched his eyes at my disheveled appearance. I hadn't showered in a few days. My hair was a ratty mess, snarled and stringy and falling limp around my shoulders, past my chest. I knew my face looked gaunt from my meager diet. Dark shadows hugged my eyes from lack of sleep. My skin was pale from a diet that consisted mostly of coffee. The scrubs hung on me like my shoulders were as wiry as a clothes hanger.

I crossed my arms over my chest and arched my back. I was the product of Richard's prodigious accomplishments. I was his poster child. I wanted him to take a good, long look at me. What did he think of his program now?

Richard glared at Connie. "Next time, when I ask for a student, see that they show up looking a little more presentable," he said, as if my appearance were a grooming accident and not due to months of torture.

"Yes, sir," she said.

My dad took in my appearance, my sullen face, my weak frame. I met his gaze, our eyes crashing together like trains on the same track. I wanted him to see me like this. I wanted him to get a firsthand look at what was happening inside here.

"I have appointments, so if there isn't anything further to discuss?" Richard asked.

"I think we're done here," my dad said. He shifted his eyes to Richard. "I'd like to talk to my daughter for a few minutes. Alone."

"We don't usually allow visitors."

"I think in this case you can make an exception."

My dad pressed his gaze, and I saw Richard back down.

"Connie, see that Madeline returns to her room when they're finished. You've got ten minutes."

Connie nodded, and my dad led me out of the office, down the hall. He pressed his hand against my lower back while we walked, which made me stiffen, and informed Connie we'd be outside. He opened the front door and we were met by the bright sun. I squinted underneath it but the heat was appreciated after the sterile office building. We walked until we were in the center of the courtyard, and my dad turned to stare at me.

He dropped his cool composure. He looked horrified.

"Are you all right?"

"I'm fine," I stated.

"How are you fine? You look emaciated. What's going on, Maddie?"

I studied my dad. He was the person I'd grown up admiring. He used to be such a hero in my eyes. A national celebrity. Someone so brave and strong. Sometimes I liked to believe I inherited a few of those traits. And staring at him, I knew I still loved my father. I couldn't help it. Love was ingrained in my skin, in my fibers. And love pushes you to open up. It encourages you to trust. I didn't want to fight him anymore. I didn't have the heart. I only wanted to tell him the truth.

"I need to tell you something," I said, and he nodded quickly. I knew I didn't have much time. I told him the highlights—that the detention center was brainwashing kids, that they were planting fear in our minds to control us, that we were all being drugged and emotionally tortured.

"I don't believe it," he said. "We test kids the moment they're released from these centers. We've never found any evidence of abuse, mental or physical. There's never been one incident of drugs reported."

I groaned at his comments. "Dad, stop looking at people like we're just some points on a graph. I'm not a statistic. Look at me. Look at what they're turning us into. They're killing us. They're poisoning us. There isn't time to argue about it. Look around and see it for yourself. It's gone too far, can't you see that now? I'm living proof of it. We're not the enemy. We're the victims."

My dad blew out an angry sigh. "If you had stopped associating with people like Justin Solvi, none of this would have happened. Those people are bringing you down, Madeline. They're recruiting you to be in a radical cult, nothing more. Maybe now you'll start to agree with me."

I glared at him for assuming this. "It isn't Justin's fault. He's the reason why I'm surviving this hellhole," I argued. "My friends are the ones helping me get through this. I could have broken out of here months ago if I wanted. I'm in here because I choose to be in here."

He shook his head. "Some friends, to encourage you to stay in here and rot."

"Don't you get it? You know me better than that. I made the decision to stay. They didn't encourage me. And don't forget that you willingly put me in here," I reminded him.

"I had no choice, Maddie. Paul recognized you. It was all over the news. I had to let it happen."

"To make yourself look good," I pointed out.

He inhaled a deep breath. His eyes blinked hard. "One day, I hope you'll forgive me," he said. "One day you'll understand."

I hated that expression. Adults always said "One day you'll understand," but what they really meant was they didn't want to take the time to understand us.

He stared at me with disbelief, as if he'd only just heard what I'd said. "You're telling me you could escape, but you're willingly staying in here? Why?"

"I'd rather be miserable in here, fighting for the life I want, than out there, being forced to live half a life. At least I know what I want. Not very many people can claim that." I tightened my lips, and my eyes mirrored the stubbornness in his. I lowered my voice. I took a huge risk, because for the first time, he looked scared. A door was open, a passage that my dad rarely welcomed me through. It was his vulnerable side. It was a tunnel that passed the thick walls of his mind and went straight to his heart. It was a passage I thought he had closed on me, but I could see it was open. He still loved me, and when you love someone, it's your instinct to help them.

"My friends are out there, working twenty-four hours a day. We're figuring out a way to free all of these kids before it's too late. The only reason I'm not a vegetable right now is that they're risking their freedom for me. They're meeting with me every week to help me get through this. That's why the DC hasn't broken me yet."

He ran a hand through his hair. "Madeline, I'm begging you to be rational. What you're talking about is impossible. You could be executed for something like this."

"Not if you're willing to help."

He told me there was nothing he could do. "I have no authority here."

"You can use your voice. Speak out against the DCs when we expose what's really going on. We have the evidence; we can prove it. You can't be blind anymore to what's happening in here. You see it with your own eyes now. So, back us up." My eyes pleaded with him to agree. "You know how much weight your words carry."

He studied my face. He was wavering. "Do you realize how that would make me look?"

I nodded. He could go to jail. He would most likely be linked to what was happening at the DC. The crime would be on his shoulders as well.

"Dad, I know you started something with the best intentions. I know you did it out of love. But the system is broken. Remember the reason you started DS—to save lives. But look at me. There are thousands of kids like me in these centers. And it's all covered up. Richard is covering it up. And you have the power to stop it. Please, support us. That's all I ask. Be honest."

He narrowed his eyes. "Do you think we're ever going to be at a point where we can trust each other, Madeline?" he asked.

I nodded. "Maybe we can start to try."

The office door opened and Connie stalked out. I backed away from my dad and followed her to the dorms. I looked over at him before I went inside and even in the direct sunlight his face was shadowed in anger. Anger can unravel you. It can give you the fuel you need to make a change. I could only hope it would work on my father.

CHAPTER twenty-five

Over the next month, the stifling air inside the dormitory started to move. Doors began to open. The atmosphere was spiked with life.

The changes would have been invisible to the average person, but they jumped out at me like flashing lights. The first time I noticed something different, I was on my way to the bathroom. I passed a girl in the hall. Usually, if we saw another person in the hall, we bolted. We avoided one another like we carried contagious diseases that could be transferred by any connection, even eye contact.

But this time in the hall, neither the girl nor I cowered. We didn't hug opposite sides of the hall. We looked right at each other. Our eyes locked. She was skinny, like me. She had red hair and freckles. Her eyes were light brown. Her mouth curved into a shy smile. She said "Hey" when she passed, and it nearly made my heart stop with surprise.

"Hey," I said back to her and returned the smile. I was beaming. My body was flushed with so much energy I wanted to sprint through the halls and scream. By the time I made it to the bathroom, my eyes had filled with tears. I closed the door and slid down the wall to the floor and basked in that simple moment. I'd forgotten how desperate I was to feel hope, to see some kind of acknowledgment that this struggle was worth it. I wiped the tears off my face. I hadn't realized I was walking such a fine line, so close to the edge of despair. I'd been avoiding it the past few months. My friends helped me avoid it. They helped me to only see courage and strength and love. And that's what got me through. I'd never looked down into that giant abyss of despair because my friends had forced me to keep looking up.

That girl, that stranger, had looked at me; she smiled; she spoke. The counter-drug was starting to work. We had a chance, a real chance, to free these people. It wasn't a dream anymore.

The more I looked for signs of life, the more I saw. People were leaving their doors open. Voices flooded out. Music filtered out. Girls started hanging around the food machine like it was a coffee shop. Conversations spilled into the air. The Eyes reported us and extra counseling sessions were called, but the MindReaders didn't work anymore.

The DC fought to contain us. They added extra security. Doors were locked permanently and we all had to have escorts every time we left our rooms. The Eye reported all our movements. But it didn't matter. We were winning.

❀

I settled into my desk chair with a cup of coffee. Only three more weeks until my six-month sentence was up. I could taste freedom. The nightmares had stopped completely. I hadn't met with Dr. Stevenson in over a month. I'd behaved since then; I stayed in my room and focused my energy on getting out of here. I dedicated my time to finishing my DS classes. I paid my dues and served my time. Now I just needed to coast through, blend in, and stay out of trouble. Then I could shut the whole place down.

I turned on my wall screen to finish a research assignment for Computer Ethics, the final project for my last DS class. My screen suddenly locked and I set my coffee cup on the desk with a frown.

"Hey," I mumbled out loud and tried to restart the computer. A blinking yellow light alerted me I had a message. I touched the light and there was a note informing me I had a mandatory counseling appointment.

I sighed at the screen. It must be my last session, maybe to discuss how the release works. Would someone be allowed to pick me up? I checked off that I'd received the message, and the screen brought me back to my DS assignment.

❖

After eating dinner and sliding my food tray through the slot, I headed for the elevator. My scrubs still hung on me, but I had gained enough weight that my face had some color, and my cheeks were filling out again. I rode the elevator downstairs to my assigned counseling room, but when I walked inside, it wasn't Dr. Stevenson waiting to greet me. Standing next to the wall seat was Richard Vaughn. I stopped at the edge of the room. I started to back up, as if I'd walked in on someone else's counseling appointment.

"Madeline," he said with a smile that was too friendly to trust. He waved me in. "Come in," he said, and motioned to the chair next to him. He was taller than I'd imagined, taller than Justin. He pressed his hands down into the pockets of his long white lab coat, which reached almost to his ankles.

When the door shut behind me, the wall screens snapped on. Classical music filtered through the surround speakers, long dramatic chords of violins and cellos. It was graceful and melancholy, like music convincing you to move on after a tragedy. I looked around the wall screens and my eyes absorbed the most picturesque landscape I'd ever seen. The sky above was deep blue, cloudless, and stretched over us like a canopy. The room was no longer a detention center. Richard and I were on top of a hill looking down at a green valley below us. We stood on an old asphalt road that curved down a gentle slope. Green hills rolled through the distance like frozen waves of land. They looked as soft as velvet to touch. The hills dipped toward a crystal blue lake in the center. The still water reflected the sky and the hills. There wasn't a single person or building in sight. Just wilderness and sunshine. The classical music seemed to flow out of the ground and down from the sky, and the wind and the trees moved to the rhythm.

"It's paradise," I said, like I was in a trance. I didn't want to walk out of it. My feet floated like I was caught in a spell, like I could join the flock of white birds passing overhead. "Does this place actually exist?"

Richard walked in a circle around me. He smiled out at the valley and nodded. "Of course it exists, Madeline. It's my favorite program," he said. "Anything we want exists. That's the beauty of technology."

I watched him carefully. *Beauty or power?* I wanted to ask. I made my way across the room and sat down on the seat. He approached me and the landscape snapped off. I reached my hand out and wanted to pull it back. I could get lost in that valley and down those warm, inviting hills. The landscape turned into pale flesh-colored walls. Richard walked over to me and rested his hand on my shoulder. My body tensed under his touch.

"When I'm in town I like to meet with a few of the patients personally," he said. "I'm the DC director, but I used to be a psychiatrist myself."

I politely shrugged his hand off my shoulder. There was no point in pretending to cower in front of Richard.

"I know your background," I said. "You specialized in neuroscience at UCLA. You won awards for discovering hallucinogenic herbs. Then you specialized in memory-recovery treatments. You helped people with Alzheimer's regain memory by using shock therapy. You made millions in the drug market and sponsored digital school." I was quoting information Molly had dug up on him—details I never would have been able to find in the DC.

He tilted his head to the side. "That's right," he said, clearly impressed. "I've dedicated my life to the study of the human brain. It's the most complicated computer ever created. It's a beautiful machine."

"Organ," I mumbled, to clarify that it was *not* a machine. I wished Justin were here right now. This was a topic he would love to debate.

Richard took a cord out of his pocket that was attached to the same MindReader Dr. Stevenson used with me, and I obediently slipped it on. I felt the familiar tingling sensation in my head. I wasn't scared. I knew any memory he tried to download would be blocked.

"Dr. Stevenson told me you were reluctant to cooperate with our program."

"Reluctant?" I asked, and my mouth fell open at this accusation. I had experienced everything every other student had faced. I'd had just as many nightmares. I didn't cut any corners. The only difference was I fought back.

"It's as if you're immune to our therapy," he said, "which is very rare." He pointed at the wall screen. An image of my brain appeared, its tunnels and ridges and canals wrapped in a tight bundle. It was the same picture I'd seen at my first counseling session. Once again, the blue and red colors were drastically unbalanced.

POSITIVE: 3%

NEGATIVE: 97%

I couldn't help but smile. I had managed to build even more defiance against their system. Then, staring at the image, it hit me what these numbers actually represented. It was another trick. The DC switched around the emotions. The 97 percent didn't stand for anger and panic and anxiety and negative energy. That number was the positive reading; it stood for hope and courage and optimism and strength.

"In all the years my program has thrived, I've never seen a student actually become more hostile from our procedures. You certainly have a lot of your father in you, don't you? A very strong character. Mentally incorrigible."

I looked back at him and nodded. "You mean unbreakable?"

"Defiance has its limits," he said, and paused for a few seconds. "That's why I'm scheduling you for a second round of treatment, one counseling session a week," he said, and smiled at me. "With a slightly different drug. I think you'll come around this time."

"What?" I said. My hands clamped down on the sides of my seat and squeezed the plastic cushion. I looked back at the screen and the numbers were already changing as panic started to take over. "You can't do that."

He raised an eyebrow at me. "I run every DC in the country," he stated. "I assure you I can. I'm lengthening your sentence to another six months, since your last sentence appeared to be such a joke to you. You don't waste our time inside of here, Madeline." His wrinkled mouth formed a thin line. "You only waste yours."

I took a deep breath. This wasn't happening. I'd come this far. I'd endured months of torture. But I couldn't do it again. I knew I couldn't physically or mentally go through the nightmares again. I was getting nauseated just thinking about it.

"We're also going to freeze your computer use for the time being. I don't think you're ready to be involved with digital school or socializing yet."

"Dr. Vaughn," I said, and tried to keep my voice steady, as if he would bargain with me. "My sentence is almost over."

"We have the right to extend it if we feel you aren't ready."

"Why?" I asked. "Why do I need more counseling sessions?"

His pale blue eyes were hard on mine. "Because you're a threat, Madeline. You're dangerous to society. We can't let you out knowing you'll just cause problems again. People are happy now, don't you see? They like to be entertained; they feel entitled to have everything they want handed to them. The world you are fighting for simply cannot happen."

He leaned in closer until his face was inches from mine. "And I'm not about to let one teenage girl jeopardize my entire program."

My walls of self-assurance crumbled. Richard had found my pillar of confidence and ignited an explosive at the base of it. I'd be worthless if I went through another round of nightmares. I'd take up all of Justin's time again, making him hold my hand through another taxing round of treatment. I'd risk my friends' lives to keep them meeting with me. This whole thing had been pointless. I felt tears prick the back of my eyes and blinked them away. I pressed my lips together to keep them from shaking.

Richard walked into the center of the room and pointed up at the screen, at the image of my brain still suspended there. He reached his hand around it like he was holding it. It made my stomach clench.

"Let me tell you why the brain fascinates me," he said. "Our entire lives, we're educated. Logic is painstakingly drilled into us. If we were smart, we would be more logical. But for how large our brains are, humans defy logic. They only want to make decisions with their emotions. Logic is wasted on us." He looked over at me. "That's what makes us dangerous. We're the smartest, yet the most unpredictable force on this planet."

"Emotions aren't always bad," I pointed out.

He raised his arms up helplessly. "We can't control them. When something is out of our control, it needs to be monitored. We're irrational creatures. We make self-indulgent decisions, not wise ones. How can you trust such an unpredictable species?"

"Our emotions protect us," I argued. I was desperate to prove a point. "We've existed for thousands of years for a reason. We wouldn't be here today without our emotions. Fear makes us smarter. It forces our senses awake. Anger makes us change. Love makes us compassionate. Maybe you're focusing your counseling sessions on the *wrong* emotions."

He shook his head. "Humans refuse to learn. We make the same circular mistakes over and over in life because we always let our emotions get in the way and do the thinking for us. Our own minds are our weakest link. Someone needs to put us in our place."

"We don't belong in a cage."

He frowned. "Metaphorically speaking, yes we do. Wouldn't you agree that you've always lived within boundaries? Schedules? Rules? You've always been guided. It's the only way we can survive. We think we're the smartest, most superior species on the planet, Madeline, yet we're the only species that is destroying it."

He took a vial out of his lab coat and uncapped it. "I remember your father told me, about three years ago, what a disappointment you were to him. How you never seemed to learn. Now I can see why."

"I'm not taking that," I said.

"Relax," he said, and the wall screen snapped back to that perfect hillside. A velvet green valley surrounded us, and soft cotton clouds swelled in the blue sky. Classical music filled the air but now the stringed instruments sounded like a cry. A violin wailed out a lonely monologue. A breeze stirred the room. I knew I couldn't fight him. I downed the liquid in the vial and waited to black out.

I squeezed my eyes shut, expecting the dark curtain to fall over my mind. But this time it was different. Seconds after I swallowed the drug my mind jerked, like someone had slammed my head against a wall. My temples pushed against my eyes. The valley and sky pressed together into a spinning swirl. He bent closer to me and I reached out for him. I couldn't breathe.

"Do you want to know why I showed you my favorite program?" he asked. His words pierced my mind like knives. He was in my head, his fingers clawing at my brain. My head throbbed, and screams circled around me, high, desperate cries for help. I was too stunned to answer. Too paralyzed to move. My heart beat so fast it ached. I withered like a plant dying under a blazing desert sun.

"I showed it to you because I want the last thing you see to be beautiful," he whispered. "I think it's the best way to die."

When I could finally open my eyes, I was standing in an empty hallway. I wasn't in the dormitory anymore. This hallway was bright, lit by a stream of fluorescent lights. To my right was a row of glass panes that separated the hall from an office. A handful of people sat inside behind desks separated by beige cubicle walls. MAIN OFFICE read a sign posted over the door. Across the hall were closed doors; a sign on one said ATTENDANCE, and the other said GUIDANCE COUNSELOR.

Three short bells rang in quick succession, and the noise was answered by doors opening and a swarm of voices and footsteps flooding into the air. Students shuffled through the hallway carrying books, all of them shouting as if they were competing for who could talk the loudest. They looked about my age, and that's when it dawned on me.

I was in a high school.

The office door swung open, nearly grazing my side. I backed up a few feet, and a man in a suit and tie walked out. He was tall, and his dark hair was combed neatly back on his head. He glanced quickly in my direction and waved down the hall to a teacher. My father was hard to miss, with his confident stride and arrogant energy. But he was nearly twenty years younger. He was skinnier, his hair was thicker, and he didn't have the sprinkles of gray in it yet. He had sideburns and walked with a bouncier step. His expression was different too; his face bore a look of contentment I'd never seen him wear. Usually his features were hard and set like marble.

I realized this was his school, where he'd worked as a principal before he'd founded Digital School, Inc.

He acknowledged students as they passed with nods and smiles and he fell into step with a teacher who approached him. I watched him walk down the hall and then turn the corner, out of sight. I watched, fascinated by the crowd of kids wearing a colorful mixture of expressions, all individual and interesting. It was like being inside a moving piece of artwork. Another bell rang and the students started to disperse.

The door of the admissions office opened in front of me and a boy walked out. He wore a heavy red winter coat that looked two sizes too big; it fell below his hips. A hat was pulled low over his head, the brim shading his eyes. His black jeans dragged along the ground. He strutted down the hallway like he owned the building. He headed straight for me, and I moved aside at the last second to avoid a collision. He didn't even say *Excuse me*.

"Punk," I mumbled when he was out of earshot.

"Hey, Thiel," somebody yelled. I turned to see a group of kids coming down the hall in my direction. A clan of guys and a few girls clung so tightly together they moved like one creeping animal. A boy in the center of them, short, with black, spiky hair, seemed to speak out for the group. "Where have you been all week?" he asked the boy in the red coat.

They held each other's eyes in a stare-down. I looked from one to the other and backed away toward a closed door. I pressed down on the lever, but it was locked.

"I got expelled," the kid answered back.

"You still owe me money," the other boy announced. His friends snickered and nodded in agreement. They formed an eight-headed creature. Sixteen eyes glared at him. "Six grand," he said. The group inched closer until they were right in front of me.

The boy raised his arms in his heavy coat. "I'm all out. I told you I quit."

"You quit?" The animal sneered. "You're not out until you pay your debts. Then we decide if you're out." His friends nodded, and the girls in the group watched the interaction with cocky smiles.

I slowly pieced together what I was seeing. I started to put faces with names. I remembered photographs in the news of all the kids who'd died in a school shooting—the school shooting my father had to break up by killing the gunner himself, a kid named Aaron Thiel.

"Do I need to come over there and beat the money out of you?" the guy asked, and he broke off from the rest of the group.

I knew what was coming. I watched the boy lift up the waist of his red coat and reach his hand inside. I didn't wait to see him pull the gun out. I already knew the ending. I knew the story it would begin.

I turned and started to run.

"Dad!" I screamed out as gunshots roared through the air, shaking the ground under my feet. I tried to get past the mob of kids, but a body fell against me and knocked me to the ground. I wriggled myself free from the weight of a boy twitching on top of me. Screams ricocheted off the walls. The glass panes shattered and fell around my body. I wanted to shut my eyes, but they stared around me, wide open.

I tried to get up but my feet slipped on a smear of blood and I fell over into shards of glass. The ground was wet and slippery, shining in a crimson red. People shouted. Doors opened. More gunshots. Blood splattered the walls. There were bodies slumped over bodies, some still moving. I tried to get up but I couldn't use my hands. Footsteps crunched over glass. I could see the red coat out of the corner of my eye. I looked up, and the black barrel of a gun was a foot away from my head. It was aimed between my eyes, and it quivered just slightly. I felt the impact at the same time I heard the roar of the shot. It was like someone had smashed my head with a baseball bat. Then there was heat, and pressure, and then it lifted and I was slipping.

CHAPTER *twenty-six*

"Wake up, Madeline."

Gabe's voice was distant and it echoed like he was talking in a tunnel. I wanted to reach out for him but my arms were too heavy to move.

"Wake up."

I willed my eyes to open but they felt sewn shut. I moved them under the lids. I felt safe underneath their curtain. There's something comforting about being blind. You don't have to see your world falling apart.

"We need to go. It's almost midnight," he pressed.

He snapped on the bright overhead light and the curtain of my eyelids turned from black to yellowish red. A warm hand grabbed my arm and I yelped and cowered deeper in my bed. I pulled the sheets around me, the curtain tighter.

"What's the matter with you?" he asked. "Oh my God," I heard him mutter.

I knew what he saw. I had thrown up again. I could smell the acidic stench all over my sheets. My hair was matted to my face.

Sweat drenched my clothes; even my sheets were wet. I curled up in a tight ball, and the plastic mattress pad under my sheet crinkled from my shaking body. I managed to open my lids, just a slit. The room was fuzzy. He bent down to look at me.

"I thought the nightmares were over," he whispered. My lips were trembling so hard I couldn't answer him.

"I'm going to pick you up, all right?" he asked. "I'll take it slow, I promise."

He carefully slid his warm arms underneath me. He scooped me out of bed and I tucked my head under his chin and pressed my head against his chest because it was warm and moving with breath and blood and heartbeats. He carried me down the hall, into the bathroom, and helped me stand up next to the showerhead.

"Rinse off," he told me. "I'll grab you a change of clothes."

After he left I peeled off the wet, sticky scrubs and threw them against the wall. I turned the water on and the hot jets pierced my skin and forced my eyes completely open. I took deep gulps of air. My lungs started to expand. I reached my arms out in front of me and touched the warm spray with fingers so cold they were almost numb. The hot water burned each tip, and the pain slowly woke me up. My thoughts were starting to thaw.

❖

By the time we got downstairs, we were almost an hour late for the meeting. My hair was still wet and dripping onto my sweatshirt. Justin took one look at my weary face and bolted out of his seat.

"What happened?" he asked. Gabe held his hand up to warn Justin to stay back. He helped me into a chair in the corner of the generator room and I sat down and sipped at a bottle of water.

Gabe handed me a blanket and I spread it over my lap. My mind was still fragmented, still coming out of its hiding place. I couldn't look at anyone directly.

Everyone waited for me to say something.

"Abort mission," I said flatly.

"What?" Pat asked.

"System failure."

"What is she talking about?" Clare asked.

"I don't understand," Molly said. "You shouldn't be reacting. I thought the counter-drug was working."

"It's over," Gabe said. "They caught on. They know they can't break her with the Cure so they're giving her something else." He looked at me, his face severe. "You need to get out of here, Maddie. Tonight. It's suicide if you don't."

"What are you talking about?" Molly asked.

Gabe sighed impatiently. "Remember when I told you Maddie was one of the only students who've talked to me in the six years I've been here?" We all nodded. Gabe looked down at his hands. "The other two passed away. The second one happened last year. The DC claimed each time that it was some kind of a virus," he said quietly.

"Are you sure it was a virus?" Molly asked.

Gabe shook his head. "I got to know that second guy pretty well. He was a lot like Maddie. Determined. Stubborn. So confident it got him into trouble. They couldn't crack him. They pushed him through a second round of counseling sessions when he didn't break after six months. That's when he started to get sick. He couldn't keep any food down. He started having seizures. Then one day he wasn't in his room."

"How can they get away with this?" Clare asked.

"They hide everything," Gabe said. "They have food stations on every floor, and I have to empty them and restock them each month, even though no one uses them. I throw away all the food and replace it, just in case people ever get suspicious and come in here for an inspection. It's all a front so the DC looks humane."

We were all quiet for a few seconds. The even moan of the generator was the only noise.

"You're saying they tried to kill her today?" Justin asked.

Gabe swallowed. "They don't let people win in this place. They don't accept failure. One of these days she's not going to wake up."

Justin pulled on his hair and sat back down so his eyes were level with mine. He asked me to tell him everything I remembered.

I did my best to recap what happened the last few days. I told them everything from my father's visit to Richard's personal counseling session. I admitted to everyone I filled my father in on what we were trying to do.

"You told your father our plan?" Molly said with exasperation. "Why not just sky-cam it to the entire country while you're at it?"

I was too tired to argue. "I'm sorry. When I saw him, it all made sense," I said. "My dad can help us. If he's willing to back us up—"

"Why would he ever help us?" Molly asked. "We're trying to take down his system. We're the enemy." She laughed but there was no humor to it. It sounded like a cry of defeat.

I looked at Justin, and his face was unreadable, lost in thought. It would kill me to think I let him down.

"But we're not fighting my dad," I said. "And he knows that. It's this insane asylum Richard's created. My dad had no idea what was going on in here. Richard refuses to let him tour the DCs. But now he knows."

"So what?" Pat said. "Is he suddenly going to join your side now?"

"He won't quit until he knows what's going on. If there's one thing I know about my dad, he wants people to be safe."

We were quiet as we all thought about this. Clare tapped her feet; Gabe fidgeted; I chewed my nails. Molly and Pat paced across the room. Justin was the only one who sat motionless, absorbed in thought.

"What do we do now?" I asked. "Gabe's right, I'm worthless to you if they put me through a second round of sessions."

"You're coming with us," Justin said. I looked around at everyone's reaction. Molly looked anxious; Pat relieved. Clare was beaming.

I worried about Gabe. "Won't you get in trouble if they notice I'm gone?"

"I can buy you some time," he said. "Maybe a week, until your next counseling session comes up."

"One week?" Molly squeaked. "We need to try to free everyone in this place *in one week?*"

"The counter-drugs are working," Gabe said. "Students aren't scared anymore. Connie had to break up a floor of guys gaming yesterday. Practically every student has violated at least one of the rules in the last month. Vaughn has scheduled an all-staff meeting for next week—it's the first one the DC has ever had. They've had to put floor security in the dorms because the Eyes aren't working."

"They're down?" Justin asked.

Gabe shrugged. "One of the kids got out of his room at night and took a camera apart. It deactivated the whole system. All students have to be escorted when they leave their rooms now."

Justin laughed out loud at this. "That's just too easy. And the entire staff will be together? In one room?" he asked.

Gabe nodded. "A week from today."

"Well, now we have the date finalized," he said. "In one week, we shut this place down."

"We can't plan it that fast," Molly argued.

Justin raised his hands. "We don't have a choice."

"He's right," Pat said. It was the first time I'd heard him step up and agree in a long time. "This is like a winning lottery ticket. We can't pass it up."

"We'll conference-call in two days," Justin said. "Tonight, I just want to get Maddie out of here."

Everyone quickly got up but I dawdled. It was all happening too fast. I looked around the dingy basement and felt a sense of nostalgia. This room had become a sanctuary.

I stood up and Gabe offered an encouraging grin. I hated leaving here without him. I felt selfish, like I'd used him as a stepping-stone and now I was kicking him to the side.

"You don't have a choice this time," he said, reading my thoughts. "You're not coming back with me." He reached his hand out so we could shake on it, but I surprised both of us and leaned in and wrapped my arms around his shoulders.

"I promise we'll get you out of here," I said, and when I let him go, the blood rushed to his cheeks, staining them red. "Wherever we are, you're always welcome. You're our family now," I said.

Before I left he handed me something red and smooth. I took my journal and smiled.

"Good luck," he said.

I followed Justin to the exit. Adrenaline pumped through my body, enough to ward off the fatigue the new drug caused. Richard's warning echoed in my head: *Defiance has its limits.* He was right. There is only so much fight in a single human being. A single person can quickly get beaten down. But when we combine forces, we build a wall of hope. And you can't put a limit on hope.

◈

We headed down the dark tunnel and this time I didn't cower. I felt reborn. I led the group, with Justin's hand wrapped tightly around mine. When we reached the night air, a warm breeze whipped around us. Clare leaned forward to grab me in a hug but then caught herself and held back. She told me she'd see me soon.

"You're free," she reminded me with a smile.

I told her it was going to take a while to sink in. "I'm still just a fugitive."

"Justin will take care of you," she said. Then she stopped and considered her words. "Actually, I take that back. You can take care of yourself."

I smiled and turned to Pat. "It's good to have you back," he said. "Try to behave this time."

"Thanks for being here for me," I said. I knew Pat gave everyone a hard time only because he genuinely cared about me.

"I did it for you," he said before he turned away.

Molly nodded in our direction and wished us luck. They all headed down the street, and I watched their silhouettes fade into the darkness. Tonight, all I wanted was to forget. Just for one night.

I turned to find Justin watching me. He blew out a long, slow breath, like something heavy was being pushed out of his lungs.

"You okay?" I asked.

"I've just been waiting a long time for this moment. I want to enjoy it for a second."

He stared at me and I felt shy from the attention. I didn't know what the night had in store. Justin and I always knew our meetings were short. We always knew how the night was going to end. Now, possibility surrounded us and I'd forgotten what to do with that kind of freedom. I was so used to my story being dictated to me, it was overwhelming to write it for myself again.

"What do you want to do now?" he asked, and waited like he was expecting a long list. But I could think of only one thing.

"I just want to be with you," I said honestly. For a second I was afraid he'd tell me no, that he had too much planning to do in the next week. I didn't want to be a burden. I knew, now more than ever, that his time was valuable. But I selfishly wanted him all to myself. No phones. No wires. No distractions. Just us.

"I think I can handle that" was all he said.

I followed him down the block to a motorcycle parked on the side of the road and he held out a silver helmet.

"Are you up for this?" he dared me. I took the smooth helmet in my hands and studied the bike.

"Did your dad build this thing?" I nodded to the motorcycle.

"Unfortunately, no," he said. "This one doesn't fly."

"Or even hover?" I asked. He laughed and swung his leg over the leather seat.

"If I get enough air off a jump, I guess you could call it hovering," he said.

Before I could argue, he grabbed my hand and pulled me down on the seat and promised to drive slow.

"Isn't it every girl's fantasy to ride on a motorcycle?" he asked.

I slid the helmet over my head. "Yeah, especially while wearing green hospital scrubs and grandma sandals," I noted. "That defines sexy." Just like that, I was back. Without trying, I was me again. Justin always had that effect on me. He helped reveal parts of myself that most other people tried to bury. There's a security in people knowing you because sometimes you forget and you need to be reminded of who you are.

He started the engine with a kick of his foot.

I asked if we were going to Pat and Noah's apartment.

He shook his head and glanced at me over his shoulder. His lips turned up at the corners and his dimples were deep. My heart almost stopped. It was the first time I'd seen a genuine smile on his face in months. I realized he hadn't worn a true smile since I'd been in the DC. I'd forgotten how beautiful it looked on him. I'd forgotten I was one of the few people who brought it out, as if he saved his smiles for me. He slid his helmet over his head.

"Don't you want to see where I live?" he asked.

PART 3

Middle Ground

CHAPTER twenty—seven

We drove up a winding road that crawled above the city like a vine wrapping its way up a trellis. Homes were concealed down long driveways and hidden from the street behind plastic shrubs and trees. We came to a stop next to a two-story white house built on the edge of the hill. Wide windows stretched across the entire second floor, and the first floor was nearly camouflaged behind miniature palm trees and bushes. The air was warm and smelled like salt from the ocean mixed with the blacktop on the streets. I'd spent so many months at the DC, I forgot that winter was over and it was already spring.

"You're renting a whole house?" I asked Justin. I doubted he needed the space. I took my helmet off and handed it to him.

"Just the second floor," he said. I asked him if he had been renting it the whole time I was in the DC, and he nodded.

"Why?" I asked. He stared at me like it was a ridiculous question.

"So I could be closer to you." He shoved his helmet in the seat compartment and pulled my journal out and handed it to me.

We went through a metal gate that buzzed open when he touched the handle. We walked along a stone path to a side entrance and up a flight of stairs. Two lamps snapped on when he opened the door, illuminating a large open room with high ceilings. The hardwood floors shone, and the walls were painted a warm yellow. There wasn't a single wall screen, which didn't surprise me. There wasn't much of anything.

I followed him down the hall and he pointed out a small kitchen, barely large enough for both of us to fit in at the same time. So few people cooked these days, kitchens were designed smaller and smaller. Some homes didn't even have them—they used cooking closets, which were adequate. People saved the space in their houses for their living rooms, their family rooms, their entertainment centers.

We walked past the kitchen and he pointed out the bathroom. I looked inside and there were just basic essentials: a few towels stacked on the white counter, a single toothbrush, soap, a bottle of lotion. I was fascinated with what he owned, even though they were such basic things. I stared down at the blue toothbrush; I touched the white hand towels and the tube of toothpaste. I marveled at his things because they were tiny pieces of him, just the smallest hints of who he was. There was a chipped blue soap dish holding a white bar of soap. I wanted to know where he bought it, how the chip happened.

Looking around, I couldn't believe he'd been here almost six months. It looked like he'd just arrived.

We walked back to the living room. I noted the minimal furniture. All he had was a couch and a mattress in the corner with sheets and pillows thrown on top of it. He wasn't the neatest person in the world, but he wasn't a slob either. It looked more like he was always leaving.

The couch was against the wall of windows, and it was covered with duffle bags and jackets. He told me he would have cleaned up if he knew he was having company tonight, and he started to toss the bags onto the floor next to a black suitcase in the corner.

There wasn't a single picture or poster hung on the wall. Nothing to hint at who he was, other than mysterious, and I already knew that about him. All he had for entertainment was a stack of books lying next to the bed. I bent over to read a few of the spines. A collection of Rumi was there, one of my favorite poets. I recognized *Zen and the Art of Motorcycle Maintenance.*

"What would you call your decorating style?" I asked. "Boring-bachelor? Or messy-loner?"

He looked over at me. "More like distracted-about-my-detainee-girlfriend," he said. "I'm not here very often. It's not like I'm hosting dinner parties."

"You're definitely not a homebody," I agreed. Even though his clothes were here, there was a vacant energy to the place. But I remembered him telling me once he didn't own anything more than what he could carry on his back. I also noticed that the few things he did own were nice. The leather jacket he wore fit his arms and shoulders so well it looked tailored. It was probably custom-made. His jeans and shirts and shoes were expensive sports-company brands. I noticed his lotion in the bathroom had a French label. He had access to every gadget technology had invented, but he didn't care to use any of them.

"I crash here twice a week."

"After you meet with me," I figured.

He nodded and kicked off his tennis shoes. "That's right. Anyway, it's a start. It's the only place I've ever had to myself."

I sat down on the tattered gray couch. It was soft and broken-in. The apartment was a palace compared to the dungeon I'd just escaped from. I looked up at Justin. "It must be scary, the idea of settling in one place."

He took off his coat and tossed it on top of a pile of jeans. "Actually, it's kind of nice." He pulled back the curtains that blocked the wall of windows. "I rented it for this," he said. He turned off the lights and climbed onto the couch next to me. We looked out at a jagged skyline below us. In one direction we could see downtown, toward South Central, and all the skyscrapers looked tiny, like I could hold them in my hand and touch their yellow windows with my fingertips. We watched trains move like glowing snakes through the city streets, and ZipShuttles dart between them like fireflies. A million lights twinkled. It was a man-made constellation. We could see all the way to the ocean in the distance. We watched the water glimmer by the light of the wave generators.

"I could see you from here," he said. He pushed his finger against the pane and pointed in the distance, toward the ocean, and I followed his eyes. I couldn't make out the detention center. I didn't even want to imagine it. I wanted to block that life from my mind.

"I liked the idea I could always keep an eye out for you," he said. "It made me feel a little bit better." Our eyes met and his were lighter than I ever remembered seeing them. There was relief on his face, but also exhaustion, like the last six months had been a kind of torture for him too. I'd never thought about my situation from Justin's perspective. If I knew he was trapped, that I couldn't be there for him or understand what he was going through, I'd go insane. I'd riot and storm through the doors. I'd tear the place down. I'd only want to save him. Looking at Justin, I understood how much support he gave me. Even though it tortured him, he let me make my own decisions and was there to back me up.

He lifted his hand and ran his fingers through my hair. My heartbeat immediately picked up. His hand was slow and his body was close, but not too close. He was tentative with each movement, like I was a wild animal whose trust he was trying to gain.

Everything moved in slow motion. He leaned his forehead against mine and we sat like that, just leaning in and breathing. My fingers traced the part of his chest where the scars were. I was trying to get to know him again. I was trying to know myself. I still felt disgusted with my scrawny arms and waist and ribs that stuck out nearly as far as my chest. I hated being skin and bones. I felt like I was too pointy to touch, all angles and edges.

But Justin's hands never left my skin. They traced my nose and my lips and eyebrows until my lids felt heavy and closed. He pulled me on his lap and I fell asleep that way, curled up in his arms.

❋

The next morning, I woke up new. I woke up in white cotton sheets that smelled like Justin, warm and soapy and clean. I woke up to the sun filtering through the window. I hadn't let him close the curtains last night; I wanted to see the rays paint the walls gold. I stared at the brightness all around me and felt it inside of me, warm and tapping my bones.

I rolled over and stretched my arms and legs, and the warm sheets felt like silk. I reached my hand out and touched the sunlight and it made the tips of my fingers glow. I eyed Justin's phone lying on the floor next to the mattress and picked it up with curiosity. I hadn't used a phone in six months.

Justin stirred next to me; he was lying on his stomach, and his dark hair spread over the pillow.

I turned his phone on and informed him he had fifty-seven

messages and twenty-eight missed calls. His hair fell over his eyes, and he had to brush it away to look at me.

"Have you ever considered getting a secretary?" I asked.

"You know I'm terrible at checking in," he said, his voice slow and lazy. It was a side of him I'd never seen before.

"True," I said. "She'd fire you."

He grabbed the phone out of my hand and threw it on the couch. "You need to let me savor this," he said.

He rolled toward me and leaned up on one elbow and tucked a strand of hair behind my ear and stared at me. I knew how battered I looked after six months at the DC. I could probably model for a brochure on malnutrition, bad hair, sleep deprivation, or all of the above. But Justin looked at me like he was enamored, which made no sense at all. Meanwhile, I felt like I'd woken up next to some Hollywood supermodel.

He kept watching me and his brown eyes were golden in the sun. I finally nudged him out of his daze. He was freaking me out.

"You should return those calls," I said, trying to take the focus off me.

"I'll get to it," he said. His eyes didn't budge.

I covered my face with the sheet and mumbled he couldn't look at me until after I showered.

Justin rolled out of bed, wearing nothing but a pair of black boxers. I couldn't help but stare at him as he walked over to the corner of the room and dug through a pile of clothes until he came up with a pair of jeans. He told me where the towels were and said we could get coffee down the street and rattled on about the breakfast specials, like talking in our underwear was our typical morning routine. I stood up and the floor was warm on my bare toes and I stretched my feet to soak up the heat. I was used to the ice-cold floors in the center. I was used to curling in on myself. Anything that touched my skin was a threat.

He pointed out a duffle bag on the floor with a few changes of clothes inside.

"Not that you don't look hot in my T-shirt," he remarked of my nightgown. I looked down at my skinny bare legs and felt myself blush. I picked at the hem of the shirt and nodded at his mound of clothes on the floor.

"So this is your idea of moving in?" I asked, to change the subject. "It looks more like you're leaving."

He nodded and pulled a gray hoodie over his head. "My life's one long trip."

I looked around the room at the simplicity. I had a feeling my own life would mirror this existence for a while.

"What's your advice?" I asked. "How do you live your life without settling?"

"Own as little as you can. Travel light." He smiled at me. "I'm not going to completely drop anchor anytime soon," he said. "You've got to know that by now."

I felt a twinge of disappointment at his words. He would never give up. He would never back down. He was right; his life was always on the road. And he didn't say anything about a traveling companion.

"We need to get out of here," Justin announced, and turned my shoulders toward the bathroom. "And you need to eat something."

"Where are we going?" I asked.

"Eden," he said. "I think you could use a little one-on-one time with reality."

❀

I showered and took my time shaving and washing every crevice of my body, as if the last six months of memories could be rinsed off if I scrubbed hard enough. The steaming mist of water was a luxury; so was a washcloth, and so were shampoo and conditioner that didn't smell like kitchen-cleaning products. They gave us dull plastic razors at the DC so we wouldn't hurt ourselves, so my legs were red and always prickly with short stubble. My skin was dry, chapped, and flaking from the hard water. I helped myself to Justin's lotion and it smelled like aloe and rosemary.

It was my first time back in jeans in six months, and I slipped them on slowly. I finally wore a T-shirt that was soft and fitting, not a scrub top that hung on me like a bed sheet. I looked at my reflection in the bathroom mirror, at my long hair that needed a cut, at my wispy frame, and at my face that was still too thin. But my cheeks had a hint of pinkness from the heat of the shower, and my eyes were glowing. For the first morning I could remember I was excited to start the day. Usually I dreaded time; now I craved it and clung to it and wanted it to slow down. The day was something to celebrate, not just something to get through. So much of my life up to then had been something to endure, not experience.

I met Justin in the living room and we walked outside into crisp morning air. The sky was light blue, still sleepy, with the sun low in the sky. We walked down the street to a café called Firefly, a few blocks from his apartment.

I noticed people were out. I noticed because I jumped whenever someone passed us. Two women jogged by with their dogs, and when they said hello I was so startled I tripped over the curb. Justin grabbed my hand and held it to keep me steady. A young mother passed us with a stroller. A pack of guys rode by on skateboards, and the whirring sound of their wheels made me panic and I let go of Justin's hand so I could latch on to his entire arm.

"Do you want to turn around?" he asked me, his face worried. "Maybe you're not ready for this."

"No," I said. "I'm not scared, just jumpy. I'm not used to so much—life."

"Sensory overload?"

"Yeah, but in a good way," I assured him.

Justin talked to keep me distracted. He told me this was the only neighborhood in L.A. that was unplugged. People referred to it as Freak Street. The road was lined with boutiques and cafés and tattoo parlors, art galleries and old cinemas. He told me they even had an antique bookstore.

"People actually walk around here," he said. "They come outside during the day."

"That debunks my theory," I told him.

"What's that?"

"That people have all mutated into vampires and that's why we stay inside all day. It's a lot more glamorous than the idea that we're all sitting around staring at screens."

He smiled at me. We passed restaurants with outdoor seating and old-fashioned handwritten menus hung in their windows.

"At least these neighborhoods still exist," I said.

"Barely," Justin said. "Most of these places are going out of business. Even Eden is struggling. Its population is shrinking every year."

He stepped under a yellow awning and opened the entrance for me and a bell chimed when it banged against the door. It made me jump, of course. I sucked in a breath and reminded myself to relax. I had to clasp my hands together to keep myself from grabbing Justin's arm again. *Contain your inner freak show, Maddie,* I told myself.

The floor inside was covered in black and white checkered tiles. A few people sat at tables, mostly staring into their flip-screens. We walked up to the counter and Justin ordered us coffee and sandwiches to go. The barista, a young girl with auburn hair tied back in a low ponytail, turned his money card away when he took it out.

"You know your money is no good here." She flashed him a smile and I raised my eyebrows. "Think of it as a donation to fighting DS." He thanked her and offered her a smile, which made her gush over the counter like he'd handed her a bouquet of flowers.

She looked over at me. "Looks like you had a rough night," she said, and glanced at Justin. "Is this your latest interception?"

"Actually, this is my girlfriend. Maddie Freeman. You might have heard of her."

The barista's mouth dropped open. "As in Kevin Freeman's daughter?" she asked.

I smiled. "That's right." I couldn't tell what surprised her the most: my scruffy appearance, my bloodline, or Justin's she's-my-girlfriend announcement, which had shocked me as well.

"Are you two insane?" she asked. "Warring families? Haven't you ever heard of Romeo and Juliet?" Another worker handed us our coffee and sandwiches.

"Yeah, but there's one big difference," Justin said.

"What's that?" she asked.

"Romeo was a pussy. Thanks for the coffee," he said, and we turned to leave. I followed Justin out the front door and we sat down on a bench tucked between pots blooming with yellow tulips. He handed me my coffee.

"Sorry," he said. "I should have warned you Chrissy's a little outspoken."

"I can't believe you disrespected the Bard," I told him. "Did you see her face when you told her I was your girlfriend? I think you filled her gossip quota for the next century."

He smiled and leaned in and kissed me. I leaned in and kissed him back, and then we forgot about our coffee for about ten minutes.

❋

We took our time heading back up the hill, sipping our drinks. I pointed out everything we passed, like we were walking through an art museum. It was the intimate details of life I'd missed the last six months. I savored the sun warming the back of my neck, this rare morning alone with Justin, the good coffee, the worn-in jeans and flip-flops, and a world around me with no walls, spread out like life was intended to be. I absorbed the sounds of the city—the sighs and breaths of trains. I noticed the leaves hanging from trees like mobiles, the smell of dust and concrete in the air, the way grass grew up through sidewalk cracks like it was trying to win back its territory. I watched an older couple walking in front of us. The man rested his hand on the woman's shoulder and then leaned down close to listen to what she was saying. That small gesture said so much.

I pointed out another man, walking slow with his shoulders hunched, as if his thoughts were heavy. He took his phone out of his pocket, hesitated, and put it back. Then he took it out again. He dragged his feet. I wondered why he was hesitating and who he wanted to call. I wanted to tell him to make the call. Life's short, don't hesitate. Just make the call.

We stopped at Justin's apartment to grab our bags and then walked around the side of the house to the garage. He opened the door and a red sports car was waiting inside.

"Of course you don't want to use the train," I noted.

"Of course you are currently a fugitive, so that's not possible," he said.

I groaned at the reminder. It seemed my destiny. "Do you think I'll ever have a normal life?" I wondered out loud.

"No," he answered easily and opened the passenger door for

me. "That would mean you'd suddenly become obedient. Again, not possible. And boring."

He got in the car next to me, and he smiled and I smiled and our eyes caught and he was kissing me again. He broke away after a couple minutes.

"Guess when the first time I almost kissed you was," he said.

I thought about it. "During my dance of seduction?" I asked.

"No—well, yeah, but it was before that."

"Before that?"

"It was the night we drove out to the coast, when I showed you an interception."

"That was a good night," I said.

He nodded. "I almost kissed you that night, on the bed in that house, in the car when I dropped you off . . ."

"So that's when you started liking me?" I asked.

"More like loathing you," he corrected.

We backed down a steep driveway onto the winding road and he flipped on a dashboard screen to see a list of calls waiting for him. I was a little resentful. So many people needed pieces of him, all the time; I wondered how he could handle always stretching himself so thin. I pulled the seat belt across my chest and looked at the screen.

"Shouldn't we stay here while we figure out plans for next week?" I asked.

"I need to talk to my dad," he said, "and I'd feel better putting some distance between you and the DC right now." He looked at me. "Do you really want to stay here?"

"No. I just don't want to be a burden anymore," I said, and rested my head back against the seat.

"I need you to understand something, Maddie," he said as we got on a freeway ramp. "You will never, ever be a burden to me. You're the most important thing in my life. That's why I'm here.

It's an honor to be with you, not a burden. Never think that again. Got it?"

My mind lingered on the word *honor* and I sipped my coffee and nodded casually to try to downplay the best compliment he'd ever given me.

❀

We followed the coastline back to Eden, the same highway I drove six months ago in the opposite direction. Sometimes your life comes full circle. Sometimes you set off only to end up where you started because the places you belong always pull you back. That's when you know you're home.

We pulled into Elaine and Thomas's driveway just before dusk. Justin's parents dedicated their careers to fighting for human rights, and after their last protest nearly cost them their lives, they'd retired on the coast with a community that preferred to live unplugged.

People were sitting outside on the porch. A group of kids played in the front yard. Bikes and soccer balls and Frisbees littered the lawn. It looked like a family reunion but it was just the normal chaos of their house. I realized why Justin wanted me here. He wanted to pump life back into me, to remind me of the life I was fighting for before we tried to take on the world.

For months I've been slowly dying. So today I made it my mission to walk around and focus on things that are living. I want to learn their secrets, not think about how to change them or multiply them or use them for myself, just study them as they are and appreciate the fact that they exist. Maybe that's how I want people to see me.

Thomas and Elaine have a chicken coop in their backyard. I've seen the coop before, but I never stopped to study it until now. I've never been so enamored with life. I took it for granted before.

I watched a dozen chickens, white and tan and chocolate brown, plump and feathery. Their curious beady eyes stared up at me. They walked with brash steps, jabbing their heads and clucking to no one in particular. Their life is simple—the way they build small coves inside the hay, the way they huddle close together, chatting in the shade or pecking in the sun. They don't look stressed or anxious or displeased with anything. They look more content than almost any human I have ever seen.

It made me want more of nothing. Less of things, more of air and freedom and space and quiet and sunshine.

But how do you ask for nothing? How do you empty yourself so you can make room for what's most important? People aren't trained to want less. We own until we overflow. We're the only animals that willingly drown ourselves with things.

I stared into the coop and couldn't believe I was jealous of a dozen chickens. Their tiny brains understood how to live life better than our complex ones.

I walked around the side of the house and studied the wraparound porch where hanging baskets overflowed with tendrils of vines and flowers. The colors that burst around me inspired me to open myself up to the elements. My whole life I've been taught to curl in on myself, to close myself off, because if you expose too much, you're vulnerable. But these flowers expose everything. It's remarkable how much beauty is wrapped inside a single bud. What if plants were like people? What if they were too afraid to open themselves up to the elements? Imagine all the colors we would lose.

Maybe people can learn more from nature than they realize.

I continued to walk around the yard and through Elaine's flower garden. The rosebushes were beginning to bud with delicate green and red leaves. Pink blossoms on rhododendron bushes peeked through green cocoons. Everything is reborn. It reminds me pieces of myself have to wither once in a while. Some parts need to die in order for new sprouts to open up. You need to trim off dead branches so new ones can grow.

The house is bordered with sharp leaves of tulips reaching for the sun and daffodils bowing their yellow heads. So much life surrounds me here.

I strolled inside and stared at the display of guitars in the living room and mandolins and banjos and an old wooden piano with the cabinet missing, exposing its keys and strings like ribs. The keys are chipped from so much use.

Baskets hang in the kitchen stuffed with papayas, mangoes, and bananas. Others are stocked with potatoes, onions, garlic, and avocados. Food that grows. Food that's alive. I noticed a picture frame made out of tree branches. A photograph mobile made out of twigs and sticks hangs in the hallway.

I walked out to the back porch, where I saw the ocean flip and roll in the distance. I realized my dream had come true. A wave did come and sweep my old life away. And it was cleansing. But it took more than water. It took a mixture of people and love and friends, and those elements, when combined, are the strongest force of all.

At night we play games. Elaine's house is full of them. Word games, board games, card games. Thomas taught me how to play cribbage, and Elaine taught me how to play chess. We read stories out loud by candlelight. Some people make up their own stories. There's no television to turn on. We get more out of the night because we make our own authentic performances.

Tonight we sat out on the front porch and stared at the sky. Science can answer most of my questions — which stars are in which constellation and how far away they are, why they light up, why some shine brighter, why they fade. But I prefer not to know all the specifics. I like to make up my own theories.

I see light everywhere around me tonight. It starts in the sky and ends in the town lights at the bottom of the hill. It's all starting to connect.

CHAPTER twenty-eight

Without telling me I needed this time to unwind, Justin showed me. The next few days I learned how to clear my head. I learned how to enjoy time again. I didn't need medication to do it; I didn't need a counter-drug to keep me going. I just needed the right perspective.

Justin and his dad worked on plans for the detention center, and Justin worked with Gabe by video calls to design a virtual display of every floor in the dormitory. They reconstructed the layout of the grounds, the courtyard, and the electric fence. They labored over the subway lines, like doctors looking over a patient, trying to analyze which arteries led to which organs.

He wouldn't let me work more than a few hours a day, maybe because re-creating the detention center forced me back there, and he wanted me to heal. I had only physically escaped; he helped me to mentally leave.

After three days, I'd nearly forgotten my six-month sentence. It felt like a life removed. It's easy to forget your problems when you can run away from them. It's easy to forget other people are suffering when your own life is secure and comfortable and perfect. It's tempting to stay contained in that safe bubble forever.

❋

It was a sunny afternoon and I grabbed a box of chalk and a few poetry books from Elaine's bookshelf in the living room. Elaine was planting tulips along the sidewalk at the edge of the yard. I joined her and set the books on the grass. I crossed my legs and skimmed through passages and dog-eared my favorite pages.

I looked up and noticed Elaine studying me from under the brim of her straw hat.

"You're getting color back in your face," she told me.

I nodded. "I'm feeling better," I said. "I'm still trying to get the crazy out of my system."

"Oh, don't do that," she said, and patted soil around a green stem. "Crazy isn't your problem. One in three people is crazy. And the other two are liars."

I laughed and told her it was probably true. "You seem pretty grounded," I said.

She shook her head. "Your only normal friends are the ones you don't know very well," she said. "But I always tell Justin, I'd rather be off my rocker than in one." She smiled, Justin's smile, wide with dimples. "You just need to unwind, that's all," she said.

I lay on my stomach in the grass and started to write poetry on the sidewalk, just like I imagined doing when I was in the DC. Elaine helped me. We dug through poems by Frost, Wordsworth, Rumi, and Shakespeare. We pointed out our favorite passages. We wrote words on the sidewalk with red, yellow, and green chalk until our fingers were as stained as paintbrushes. I didn't notice Justin walk up to us until he cleared his throat. I blinked up at him and squinted through the sunlight.

"Here's your birthday present," he informed me. "Sorry it's a little late, but I couldn't really bring it to the DC." His hand was wrapped around a plant standing next to him. It was almost as tall as him, and its roots were wrapped tightly in a burlap bag.

I picked myself up and examined my gift. The trunk was thin enough for me to curl my fingers around. It looked scraggly and weak. It was real, that much I could tell from the thin texture of the tiny leaves and the earthy scent of the roots.

I looked from him to the plant and back. "This is for me?" I asked.

He watched me with amusement and nodded.

"Um, thanks," I said, and tried to take it from him, but its shape made it too awkward to lift. I scratched my head. "Should we put it inside?" I asked.

Elaine snorted.

"It's a tree," Justin informed me. "I thought you could plant it," he said. "Leave your mark."

I nodded slowly and walked around it. "What's wrong with it?" I asked. "It looks like it's dying."

"Dying?" he asked.

"It's so small and skinny. Is it sick?"

Justin tried to fight a smile.

"Hey, I didn't take botany in high school," I reminded him. "Not much use for it these days."

"It's a sapling," he said. "This is what they look like."

"Wow." I tugged on one of the branches. "No wonder people run out of patience planting them. They must take a lifetime to grow."

He ran his hand through his hair and Elaine snorted again.

"Believe it or not, they begin as seeds," Elaine said.

Justin grabbed the gangly trunk. "This is how they're supposed to look—not like the full-grown God-awful plastic monstrosities people get shipped to their homes and then tack into the ground like chintzy lawn ornaments," he said.

"Well, it's a good thing you're not bitter about it," I said.

I studied the tan, smooth trunk and the thin branches spilling over the top speckled with small mauve-colored leaves. The longer I observed it, the more I felt a connection to this tree, like we were both waiting to be planted, to land somewhere solid and let our roots unwind.

"Can we plant it right now?" I asked. Justin nodded and picked the tree up by the base.

"Pick a spot," he told me. He followed me back to the house and I examined the lawn like a critic evaluating a painting, looking for textures and depths and shades. I walked around the entire yard before I made a decision. I tried to imagine the best place for it to grow, an area where it would thrive. I chose a spot east of the house, a sunny space where the ground rose slightly and the ocean was visible down the slope of the hill. You could still see the road and observe who was coming and going from downtown. You could people-watch or stare at the stars. If I had to plant roots anywhere in the world, this is where I would choose to be.

"Here," I said, and pointed with my foot.

Justin set the tree down and jogged to the garage, coming back with a shovel and some work gloves. He stood next to me and talked me through it, but he made me do all the work. I pierced the ground with the shovel, and the grass gave way to thick brown soil, the texture of clay. I had to stand on the shovel in order to dig through the stubborn ground. Justin was patient (since my muscle strength was lacking these days) and explained how deep to make it. Once I was done digging, he showed me how to score the sides of the hole by making grooves in the dirt with the edge of the shovel. He told me it would give the roots a place to expand.

My muscles ached in my shoulders and all the way down my back. For the first time in months I was growing instead of deteriorating. Sweat dripped down my forehead and nose and I licked it up with my tongue. I could feel toxins seeping out, and sunshine flowing in. It was the best medicine I'd ever been prescribed. It was a relief to use my hands and legs and muscles for a purpose. I loved the ache and the burn in my arms. Why have a body, why have this collection of muscles and tissue, if you don't put it to use?

I wiped the sweat from my forehead with dirty gloves and we took a break to drink lemonade before we planted the tree.

He handed me a pair of shears and showed me how to cut the rope and remove the burlap bag. I tugged the bag free and there was a tight mound of roots held firmly together. I handled it delicately, like a surgeon transplanting an organ from one body into another. I lowered the roots into the ground and Justin helped me mix fresh soil and fertilizer with the rest of the dirt we dug up. I filled the hole slowly and carefully like I was wrapping the roots in blankets and pressed my feet around the base to pack it down. I couldn't escape the idea that I was planting a piece of myself that day.

We stuck two stakes into the ground and attached them to the trunk using rubber chains, to keep the tree steady in wind gusts. I stood back and studied my first planting project.

"You left your mark," he told me.

I leaned my arm on the shovel.

"We just have to water the soil so the roots can settle in and we're done," he said. I arched my eyebrows in surprise. This wasn't so hard. A little time-consuming, but not in a bad way. My fingers were gritty with dirt and my arms and face were flushed from the sun and I felt more of a sense of accomplishment in that afternoon than I'd felt in all my years in digital school.

"That's it?" I said. "Why don't people plant trees more often?" I wondered.

Justin shrugged and reminded me it took time. "It takes ten or fifteen years for them to grow up," he told me. "That's like five thousand years in digital time. There's no instant gratification." He pointed to the trunk. "There's nowhere to hang a wall screen or plug in a cord. Makes it pretty useless to most people these days."

We pulled off our shoes and Justin stretched a hose from the side of the house and we sprayed the ground until the soil was dark and saturated. I stood back and admired it. I liked the idea it would get stronger every day.

I lay down on the warm grass and I stared up at the tiny dark leaves, like little hands waving to the sky. Justin flopped down next to me and held my hand against his chest.

"Thanks for the present," I said.

"You like it?" he asked.

I nodded. It was the best gift anyone had ever given me. "I love that you show these things to me."

"I love showing you."

I asked him why.

"Because you absorb it. Most people let experiences bounce right off them. But you soak it all in. And that's the only way it stays."

❧

We sat in Thomas's basement for our last conference call. The wall screen projected several scenes: one was of Gabe and Clare talking to us from a flipscreen in the basement of the detention center. She'd stayed in Los Angeles to help Gabe, since he didn't know how to use the computers to contact us.

Another screen showed Molly and Scott sitting around an apartment with a roomful of recruits, all young kids in jeans and T-shirts. Pat was on another screen, in his apartment in Hollywood, with a few more volunteers.

Riley and Jake sat in the basement with us. Riley and Justin would fly a plane down to L.A. tomorrow afternoon to transfer half the students. I'd drive down separately with Jake.

Clare had organized the hideouts in three different sites: one outside Santa Barbara, one at a retired airport on the coast, and one in a valley south of Sacramento. We separated ourselves into teams responsible for transporting groups of students.

"You think they're ready for this?" Molly asked Gabe.

"You kidding?" he said. "It's a zoo in here. Eight staff members can't handle eight hundred squirrelly teenagers. One kid already figured out a way to hack through elevator security. He got about thirty guys onto one of the girls' floors before they broke it up."

"And the staff meeting is still scheduled?" Justin asked.

Gabe nodded. "Vaughn flies in tomorrow morning. I heard some doctors talking. Rumor is he's introducing a different drug in this place. He's caught on that the current one isn't working anymore. They've suspended all the counseling sessions."

Gabe and I discussed the details of how to move around in the DC, since we knew the layout. I dictated who I wanted, where, and when. I showed them how to make our move inside and how I wanted people situated. I told Gabe how I needed him involved. No one questioned me; everyone was busy taking notes and listening. It wasn't until a half an hour into my speech I realized I was calling all the shots.

Justin did a final recap to make sure the counter-drugs were ready and the transportation was set.

"I think we've covered everything," Scott said to wrap up the call. "If there are any more questions, Maddie will be the one to touch base with." He caught himself and looked at Justin. "I mean—"

"No," Justin said. "She can handle this. She knows this place better than any of us, and Gabe will be in the staff meeting."

There wasn't a single objection to this.

"See you all tomorrow," Justin said. "Los Angeles."

Everyone nodded. "Los Angeles," we echoed together.

CHAPTER twenty-nine

"Come on," Justin said when he walked into the kitchen. "Field trip."

It was early in the morning; the sun had barely risen but I was already downstairs making coffee, too anxious to sleep. I was starting to get sick thinking about the risks involved with freeing the students in the detention center, but more than anything I was sick with the idea of going back. I was afraid I'd have a relapse, that I'd panic once I was inside and be worthless. I chewed every one of my nails to a stub.

Justin could tell I needed a distraction. He pulled a jacket on and moved past me and out the screen door to the back porch. I slipped my sneakers on in the hallway and caught up to him. We walked through the backyard, past the tree I planted. We headed down to the beach and turned south. The morning wind whipped at us and I fastened my hair to keep it out of my face. We walked for about ten minutes until we found an open path and I followed Justin up a dirt trail cut through the low shrubs. The ground steepened to a climb and we hiked up a winding trail. By the time we reached the top I was panting for breath but I was distracted as soon as I was met with the view.

Houses up and down the cliff were burned, all of them black and crumbling. A few were nothing more than piles of debris with some blackened support beams hanging on to scraps of roof that hadn't caved in yet. One of the houses had only had its windows blown out, and the hollow spaces were boarded up, but the smoke and heat had warped the paint to a charcoal gray. The house that stood directly in front of us was gutted, like a decaying corpse. The rotting walls that were still standing were black from the soot and ash, but a few beams from the white porch were still intact. The contrast between the white porch beams and the black background was startling. I imagined the homes when they were living and breathing.

"How did it happen?" I asked.

Justin walked up closer to the white beams. "It was a group of arsonists," he said. "They doused every porch on this block with gasoline and set fire to them all at the same time. They called the fire department and reported a fire in another town, twenty miles away, to create a diversion. By the time the trucks made it back, they were too late."

"Clever," I said, and picked up a pile of what could have been blue jeans that had been welded together in the heat. I tossed them back on the ground. "Were they caught?"

He nodded. He said they were convicted of twenty counts of attempted murder.

"Why did they do it?" I wondered.

"They don't like the way we live. They don't like that we build wood homes and that we burn fires at night and we hang out outside. They said we were a bunch of savages."

I sat down on a flat rock and looked at the house. I focused my

eyes on the white pillars of wood that survived. There was something beautiful about them. They stood out more than anything
else. Then my eyes found more evidence of survival. A window
intact. The trees around the house were still green and growing.
Grass was growing around piles of debris. The graveyard of houses
had turned into something living. I just had to adjust my eyes to
see it.

The DC was doing the same thing as the arsonists, trying to
scare me out of my mind, make me hollow and useless. But it
didn't mean I couldn't go on. I just had to start over. I had to
focus on the pieces that were still standing and attempt to re-
build.

"I know why you brought me here," I said quietly.

"Yeah" was all he said. He sat down next to me on the rock. He
told me they were tearing this all down soon. Time to start new.

"It's not so much about moving on, is it?" he said. "It's more
about letting go. There lies the challenge."

I put my face in my hands and took a long breath and then I
was crying and I wasn't embarrassed because I knew it was what
my body needed to do. I still had a layer of soot on my heart. It
was still hard and callused and charred, and I needed to push that
heaviness out or it would always weigh me down.

I dried my eyes on my sleeves. "This probably wasn't what you
expected," I said, and sniffed the tears away.

"Things never go the way I expect with you," he said. "I learned
that on day one."

I already felt better. I could dwell on what life takes or focus on
what it gives me. Now, looking out at these homes, I saw something beautiful in the destruction. I saw the potential for what
could grow. It could be the same with me.

"They're building a school here," Justin said. "The families all got together and agreed to donate their land to the city. They're calling it Bayview Alternative School. Their mascot's a phoenix."

"Isn't it illegal to build a school?" I asked.

He shook his head. "Not for long. The national vote's coming up, to decide whether or not digital school remains a law. Things could change."

"What if we lose the vote?" I asked.

"That's not an option," he said. "You only lose when you give up. That will never happen."

I was quiet and I watched the ocean and I started biting my nails. Justin looked at me.

"Worrying about it isn't going to make today any easier. Try to keep your head clear."

"Fine," I said. "Tell me something about yourself. Something personal. Five things you like, other than fighting DS."

"Okay," Justin said.

"What if I screw up today?" I asked.

"That's not changing the subject."

"Does it bother you that I'm leading this?"

"No, it impresses the hell out of me," he said, and smiled. "Taking on the world is extremely hot."

"Great," I said. It only made me feel worse. "I didn't ask to *lead* this."

He shrugged his shoulders. "That's how it works. You fall into the role because people look up to you. It just happens. You earn it. People are always going to look up to you, Maddie. You're confident. You carry an energy people gravitate toward."

It was strange to hear him describe me like that, since confidence was always what attracted me to him. It's what I fed off of when I was in the detention center to keep me strong.

"What if I don't want the responsibility?"

"People are counting on you. I know you won't let them down, you're too loyal for that."

I nodded but that was only part of my restlessness. I wasn't just afraid of failing. I was afraid of winning. That would open up another world of responsibilities. Sometimes it's scary to know exactly what you want. It can be easier not knowing; if you don't know what you want, at least you'll never worry about failing to get it.

Justin was reading my thoughts. "You're not going to screw up," he said. "Don't even think about it. If you don't consider failing, you won't."

"What if something happens I didn't expect?"

"Things never happen the way you plan. Take it a second at a time. Stay in the moment. It's the only way to control it. Your thoughts can paralyze you. They make you second-guess and that's when you lose. You mentally beat yourself. Believe you can handle anything. Look at something that's bigger than you and take it all in, the enormousness of it. Drown in it. Then take a step back. Compartmentalize it. Remember, anything's attainable. And take every risk you can, as long as you trust yourself."

I felt a groan grumble in my throat and I buried my head in his shoulder.

"Basketball," he said.

I blinked at him. "What?"

He grinned. "Five things I like," he continued. "Basketball. Books. Chocolate. I like driving at night with the music loud and the windows rolled down. Music always sounds better at night."

I nodded because I'd been there to observe it. He was always at his best when he was moving. "I like your skin," he said, and slowly ran his fingers over the ridges of my knuckles.

"My skin?" I asked.

"It's warm," he said. "And I like the way it tastes. It's sweet."

He pressed his lips against my neck and pulled me closer. "I like all of you," he said. I rolled my eyes because I had never felt more unattractive.

"I look like I just got released from a concentration camp," I said.

Justin shook his head. "You'll bounce back," he said, and leaned over until his lips were almost touching mine. "You're the most beautiful thing I've ever seen."

"Even now?" I asked.

"More than ever." He pulled a strand of hair away from my face and tucked it behind my ear. "You told me once you didn't think you were brave," he said quietly.

I nodded. "I didn't think I was."

He moved in until his lips were just brushing mine. "You're the bravest person I've ever met," he said against my mouth.

"You're rubbing off on me," I whispered back.

"No," he said. "I'm just showing you."

CHAPTER *thirty*

Later that afternoon, Jake and I pulled up to an abandoned loading dock about a mile away from the LADC. We met the rest of the group inside an empty warehouse. Scott was doing sound checks and Molly sorted equipment and stuffed syringes into a backpack. We dressed like a street gang getting ready to rob a gas station. We were a ragged assortment of kids, mostly teenagers and a few that looked older, just out of DS. Our version of uniforms was hooded sweatshirts, jeans, baseball caps, and tennis shoes. We were just a group of outsiders, a dissident society, and that connected us. We had one bond that brought us together: we believed in the same kind of life. We wanted to burn the rules, sweep them out, and start again.

Scott handed out equipment: scanners, tranq guns, and radio headsets that would keep us all connected but were encrypted so no one could pick up our signals.

"Ready to be the ringleader?" Scott asked as he handed me an earpod. I stuffed it in my ear and nodded. I looked out at a roomful of people who trusted me and I was still afraid, but not the kind of fear that's limiting—the kind that's empowering.

Justin seemed to be reading my mind. "We're all going to be with you," he reminded me. "This is going to be fun. Think of it as crashing a party."

The staff meeting was scheduled for five p.m. At four o'clock, we headed for the tunnels. We moved underground, using old subway lines that had been closed and forgotten after the Big Quake. Justin had had recruits scout out the area and find a path that would take us to the DC artery. Half of the tunnels were eroding; most of them had cracks and damage from the quake. A few had caved in and had so many rocks blocking the path that we were boulder-hopping to get through.

We threw down flare lights to guide our way so we wouldn't have to bother with flashlights. We all stayed quiet; the only sounds were twenty pairs of feet brushing against concrete and twenty people breathing steadily. It took us almost an hour in the tunnels to find the detention-center entrance. As he'd promised, Gabe had left security keycards and a list of codes outside the door. We all huddled near the entrance. It was just after five o'clock. Gabe had also left us a note, scribbled in frantic writing.

The Eyes are back on. I will reboot them right before the meeting, at 5:00, to give you some time. It takes eighteen minutes for them to reprogram, and after that, any un-authorized movement in the DC will set off the alarms. You have until 5:18 to get out of there. Guards are doing rounds on all the floors.

I looked down at my watch. It was 5:07 and we couldn't even make a move until we got the signal from Gabe. I frowned up at Justin but his face was calm. The time crunch didn't seem to worry him.

"We'll be fine," he said, below a whisper. "They're worried about protecting the ideas in this place, not the building itself. They aren't expecting this."

We waited in silence for Gabe's signal that the meeting had started. I was backed against the door, between Justin and Pat. The only sound was a chorus of breaths. The only communication was passing nods of encouragement. The flare light was fading, and the faces around me dimmed until eyes became dark shadows. Time slowed down to a suffocating crawl.

At 5:11, the sensor on my wrist vibrated. The meeting had started.

Scott did a quick sound check to make sure all the lines were live. Justin did a final check with all the transportation drivers who were waiting at three different exit spots in the tunnels and nodded to me. Everyone was ready to go.

We opened the metal door and we trickled, one by one, into the basement, then we hurried past the generator and around the corner into the hallway. I opened the stairwell entrance using one of Gabe's keycards and put in the access code.

My heart was pounding and my hands shook as I tried to type in the code. I imagined Richard Vaughn, Dr. Stevenson, and the other staff members sitting around and willingly plotting how to destroy people—how to treat kids like psychological experiments. I held on to that image with my mind and let it carry me forward.

I opened the door, and ten of the recruits swept by, their steps light. I looked down at my watch: 5:13. We had five minutes left. We quickly climbed four flights of stairs to the ground floor and waited. I stood between Justin and Clare. Molly and Pat were a few steps below.

"Something's going to get mucked up," I whispered.

"They know what they're doing," Justin told me. I looked at

my watch again. Four minutes. Justin never once checked the time. He was taking long, calm breaths. I wondered if he was counting.

The tranq guns we used were silenced, so we had no way of hearing the shots. Voices came over our radios and told us two of the guards were down. One of our recruits was down as well, they told us. I pressed my back against the wall. Trying to stand completely still takes more effort than running. My muscles ached and time slowed to a stop.

Nothing happened. I looked at my watch. Three minutes. Sweat rolled down my neck. We should have planned better. We should have come up with other options. Just when I convinced myself we were caught, Jake's voice came over the radio. He told us we were clear.

Justin already had the door open and we followed him out to the lobby. We turned the corner, and a security guard was sprawled on the floor, next to a desk chair. Justin didn't hesitate; he moved like he knew this place as well as me. He took the guard's hand and swiped his fingerprint and then used codes Gabe gave us to unlock the students' doors and disengage the alarms. Two more recruits were coming through the entrance doors, dragging security guards that had been stationed at the kiosk and the office building. If all went according to plan, they would join the rest of the staff in a few minutes. I looked down at my watch just as it turned 5:18. I inhaled the first deep breath I had taken in hours.

Justin mumbled something into his headset and we followed him outside, across the courtyard to the office building. The door was unlocked and the rest of our group hurried in. All I could hear was my heart beating. It pounded in my ears and shook against my ribs. I had to remind myself to breathe. We gathered together in the lobby.

This was it. I'd fought an uphill battle to reach this summit. I had finally made my way to the top and was ready to take in the view.

I looked down the hall and knew the conference center was at the far end, around the corner. We could hear voices trickling through the empty space. I stared down the gray hallway, lit up with advertisements, and stalled, but I felt Justin's hand on my arm. He was grinning. Beaming. I forgot how much he loved this.

"No hesitating with me, remember?" he whispered. "This is the fun part."

"Fun," I whispered back. I glanced around at my friends and they each gave me one last nod of encouragement. I turned and walked forward. My spine naturally straightened. My chin rose up. With each step I felt a wave of determination. We pushed ahead and I stopped trying to muffle my footsteps. Justin walked next to me. There was no point in hiding now; we were in. It was time to make our presence known. I could feel my walk turn into more of a strut.

"I get Vaughn," Justin mumbled. When we were at the door, he kicked it open, and we were met by a series of gasps and shrieks. Two staff workers jumped up from the table, but they weren't quick enough. Justin had already fired a shot, and Molly took out the other. The workers fell forward on the table and smashed their faces into their flipscreens, then rolled to the floor, toppling chairs over with a crash. I raised my gun and pointed it straight at Dr. Stevenson, who sat at the end of the table. The rest of our group streamed in and each one of us raised a gun at a target, daring people to move.

"Stay in your seats and put your hands where we can see them," Justin said calmly. A few people did exactly as he said but others froze.

"Now!" he demanded, and a wave of shaking hands fluttered up in the air above shocked faces. "You don't move without permission. You don't speak unless I address you," Justin ordered. Molly swung a backpack off her shoulder and unzipped it. Inside were eighteen plastic syringes that glowed with bright orange liquid. Just looking at the drug made my stomach churn.

Richard sat at the head of the table, his mouth clenched shut like a fist. Justin pointed the gun at him and took a few steps closer.

"You didn't invite us to your meeting," Justin said. "But we have a few concerns of our own to discuss."

Richard's face fell into a sneer. "Justin Solvi," he said with a knowing glare. "We finally meet. I was starting to think you were a hoax. Hiding behind secret identities. Hiring other people to do the dirty work for you. It's pathetic that so many people worship a man who's too much of a coward to ever show his face."

I glared at Richard. He knew how to mess with people's emotions. It was his weapon. But his words bounced right off Justin.

"I show my face everywhere but on a screen," Justin informed him.

Richard's eyes searched the room and then settled on mine.

"I warned you," I said to him. "Next time, you should take a rebellious teenage girl a little more seriously," I added.

Molly walked around the table and told all the staff members to pull up their sleeves. I looked around the room at the stunned faces of Connie and a few other workers I recognized. I met Gabe's eye for a split second and he slowly got up from his seat and joined us, standing against the wall, next to Clare. Richard watched him and shock passed over his face as he registered the traitor among his staff.

"All it takes is one person," Justin said to Richard. "We're freeing the entire center. Your methods haven't been working because people are stronger than you. Now we have eight hundred witnesses to attest to what's been going on in here."

Richard was calm. "You won't be able to prove anything," he said. "You've wasted your time and endangered all of these kids. All that's been going on here is safe and necessary rehabilitation."

"Is that what you call the deaths of students?"

"This is a clinic," Richard said tightly. "Kids in here are sick. People die in clinics all the time." The rest of the staff was silent, all looking at Richard.

Molly began the injections, one by one.

"What the hell is going on?" Richard demanded as Molly stuck Connie's arm with a needle.

"Just giving you all a taste of your own medicine," Molly said.

"It's just the Cure," I said flatly. "There's no physical effects. We want to help you open your mind."

I kept the barrel of my gun aimed at Dr. Stevenson. One of the staff members made a lunge for Molly, but before he could touch her, he slumped down and hit his forehead on the table and then rolled out of his seat. His body fell limp on the floor, stunned from the tranquilizer gun.

Justin turned his gun back to Richard. "Anybody else want to object?" he asked. The room was sullen and silent in response. The DC staff sat like stiff columns, too scared to move.

"Be careful," Richard said, looking at me. "This all goes back to your father. He signed all the legal documents when I designed this facility. It's all under his name." Richard smiled.

"You're bluffing," I said.

He smiled wider. "It won't even come back to me. According to the legal terms, I'm simply a sponsor. Besides, do you really think the public can afford to question me?"

I stared back at him. My hands started to shake.

"This is your father's head, not mine," Richard informed me. "Are you ready to turn him in? He'll be executed for this."

I swallowed and looked at Justin but he just shook his head.

"Wait," I said when Molly approached Richard. "I want the honor." I grabbed the syringe from her hand and headed to Richard and told him to roll up his sleeve. He glared at me, and his mouth pinched into a frown.

"You won't get away with this," he hissed.

Justin raised his gun and pointed it at Richard. "Neither will you," he said. "Now pull up your sleeve or I'll do it for you."

Richard shoved his sleeve up his arm. I pierced the needle through the soft skin below his shoulder and pressed down on the syringe with satisfaction as I watched the orange liquid flow inside. His arm flinched from the needle.

Once the drugs were administered, we ordered everyone to stand up and head down the hall to the dormitory. The staff met each other's eyes with concern.

"To the imagery rooms," I informed them. We escorted them down the hallway in a single-file line, and they moved slowly, their hands clasped behind their heads. Justin called for a couple of the recruits to go back for the guards who were knocked out. As we approached the door, we could hear a storm building strength outside. It sounded like thunder approaching. I was the first person to reach the metal doors and when I pushed them open the roar from outside was deafening.

CHAPTER thirty-one

All the inmates were standing in the courtyard; eight hundred bodies were huddled around the office building. They separated on each side of the doors to form a narrow path between the office and the dorms.

All of them looked skinny, their physical bodies still bouncing back from the treatment. The guys had long, scraggly hair and the start of scruffy beards. The girls were haggard and pale. But all the students' eyes were alive and untamed. Their faces were determined. And their voices were pissed off.

Cries of outrage thundered through the air around us. The staff members bent their heads as if they were trying to dodge hail, and some of them covered their ears to protect them from the flood of screams.

We slowly pushed our way through. Students berated the staff. They pumped their fists and a few of them lunged out and had to be restrained by recruits who were working like security guards holding off the angry mob.

Justin didn't force the staff forward quickly. He allowed this to be a slow progression. He made them listen and look and absorb all the hate pouring out from kids they had been abusing. I felt chills rush over my body. It was like a public stoning. I watched the staff wither and cower.

We made our way to the dormitory and onto the counseling floor. We divided them up; each staff member was assigned to an imagery room. Justin and I escorted Richard, one on each side of him. We opened the door and Justin waved him in. Before the door shut he turned and glared at us, sweat rolling down his fore-head, his eyes narrow.

"This isn't over," he told us.

"You're right," Justin said. "We're just getting started." With that, Justin shoved him in the room and slammed the door. Once everyone was inside we looked around for Gabe. He was standing at the end of the hall, a little flustered from all the chaos. Mind-Readers were draped over his arm.

"The screens are ready," he said. "The MindReaders are pro-grammed. They'll be reliving M-Twenty-Eight for the next eight hours."

Justin shook his head. "I don't want you to download it," he said. "I don't want to stoop to their level. The imagery screens will play whatever messed-up thoughts are in their minds right now. That should be terrifying enough."

Gabe nodded and looked relieved to hear this. We all turned down the hallway, heading for the stairs. When we got outside, the DC students were being separated into groups. It wasn't time to celebrate yet. Something in my gut told me this had been the easy part.

Justin grabbed my arm. "You're getting a ride up the coast with Pat. You guys can take off," he told me. "I'll handle it from here."

I narrowed my eyes because I knew what he was trying to do. Now that our plan had worked, his only concern was to keep me safe. I didn't want to take the easy way out. I wasn't scared.

"I'm not leaving here until I know that every student is out."

Justin motioned for Clare to go ahead and she ushered a line of students through the dormitory to the basement.

"You've done enough, Maddie," he said. "You risked your life for six months. I just want you out of here. Okay? Do this for me." People swarmed around us.

"Let me finish this," I said. "I'm not trying to be a hero; it's just something I need to do so I can let this go. I want to be the last one out of here. It's personal for me." We were getting pushed along with kids now.

He couldn't argue with me on this point. He sighed. "Fine, then I'll stay back here with you," he said. "We'll switch some people around."

"There isn't time. Just get out of here. You're in charge of the most kids."

"Justin," Clare shouted. "Your group's ready to move." Justin looked over at me. His expression was skeptical.

"I'll be fine. I'll see you on the coast," I said.

Justin fixed his jaw and nodded, knowing it was a waste of time to argue. He leaned down to kiss me.

"If anything happens, I want you to run, okay? Keep running. I'll come back for you." I nodded. "And trust yourself," he told me. "If it feels crazy, it's probably right." He took off after Riley and the rest of his group.

Pat and I waited in the courtyard while students trickled out, gliding like a long, green caterpillar through the dormitory entrance and downstairs to the subway tunnels. We worked as ushers to keep the lines moving. Pat told me we had a van waiting for us and any stragglers left behind.

Scott kept us updated on everyone's status, notifying us when each group of students had safely left. The courtyard was emptying now. Clare and Gabe had left with their group on a shuttle bus. He notified us when Molly had gotten out safely and, finally, when Justin and Riley's plane was loaded and ready to take off.

"Should we start moving?" Pat asked.

"When this is finished," I said, standing my ground. I looked around at the buzzing fences and still had the eerie feeling I was being watched. When the courtyard was silent, the ground dusted with footprints, Pat and I moved to the dorm entrance.

"Okay, you're clear," Scott said. "We did a head count and everyone's accounted for except you two," Scott told us. "Get out of there."

We hurried down the stairwell, through the basement corridor, and out into the subway tunnel, following flares that were still glowing dimly from the other groups that moved out ahead of us. I asked Pat where the van was parked.

"It's two stops from here," he said. "About a mile east."

I checked my watch impatiently. A mile hike through the subway lines wasn't my idea of a fast getaway. I felt my intuition kick in, and I picked up and started to run. Pat kept up with me.

We swerved through a labyrinth of tunnels, passing cracks and eroded holes of rocks and cement where beams of light poured in from outside.

We turned another corner and Pat said we were getting close. He pointed to a bright beam of light in the distance and my feet picked up speed.

"We did it," I said, and the words tasted victorious on my tongue. "We actually did it." Maybe I *was* a natural at this. I let my imagination fly—to news stations finally broadcasting the truth about digital school, to all the detention centers being closed, to digital school finally becoming a choice, not a requirement.

"You guys, stop." Scott's voice snapped me out of my daydream like a foot tripping me. My feet stuttered to a stop. "The cops picked up on this. It just came up on the dispatch."

I stared out at the sunlight ahead of us, so close I could see dust circling inside of it.

"Is this a joke?" I panted.

"Somebody tipped off the van's location," Scott said. "They're headed there now, you need to turn around."

I tried not to panic and told Scott we could hide out in the tunnels. We'd be fine. We'd wait for Justin to bring the plane back for us.

"You need to get out of the tunnels," Scott insisted. "They're sending a search squad down there. Someone ratted us out."

"You got any bright ideas of where to go?" Pat asked as we turned back the way we had come.

"Shit," Scott replied.

"Anything else?" I muttered. Scott tracked our location using our earpods and looked for possible exits. There was enough daylight seeping in from ground cracks to light our way now, and our eyes adjusted to the dimness. We sprinted through the tunnels, our tennis shoes padding heavily on the concrete. Fear trickled its sharp fingers down my back. Pat asked Scott if he found anything.

"At the next fork, go right," he told us. "The only place you might have a shot of hiding is the Hollywood River exit."

We followed his advice and turned down the tunnel. I asked Scott what we'd find at the exit. He said it was barren. There was an old research lab down there, but it closed down years ago. He said we shouldn't find anybody. Pat suddenly grabbed my arm and twisted me around to face him. He turned off his earpod and motioned for me to do the same. I took it out of my ear, still panting.

"What's wrong?" I asked.

"This is crazy," Pat hissed. "Why would Scott send us to a dead end?"

I glared at him. There wasn't time to think. I told him maybe Scott was right, that the police wouldn't expect us there.

"We need to trust him," I said. "He's the one with eyes right now. We're the ones in a rat race." I started moving again.

"I think he's setting us up," Pat said, keeping pace with me. "I've never trusted Scott. Maybe he's the one that turned us in."

I shook my head. I couldn't believe it. "He wouldn't," I said. I prayed.

"I say we go back to the van," Pat pressed. "If there actually are cops, I can hold them off," he said, and pointed to his guns, one strapped at either side of his waist.

"If Scott's right, we can't get past an entire squad of police," I argued. In my heart I knew we could trust Scott. I pulled Pat along. "There's got to be a place we can hide out there," I insisted. "We can hold out until Justin brings the plane back for us."

We ran out the mouth of the tunnel and were met by a steep walkway crudely carved out for the research lab to use. It was more of a gravel trail than a sidewalk and it snaked down to a lopsided pier bouncing in the river current. Steep cliffs shouldered both sides of the canyon and blocked out the setting sun. All that was left was a ribbon of pinkish blue sky. I looked down in each direction and Pat was right. We were trapped. There wasn't even a crevice to conceal us.

I pointed down to the pier, the remnants of the research station, and told Pat to follow me. We hugged the side of the canyon wall and I had my eyes set on one thing: a garage made out of corrugated metal, docked at the bottom of the cliff over the water. I ran down a narrow row of steps, past the abandoned research shack, and down to the garage, Pat following close behind.

The side door was locked and there weren't any windows to try to break through.

"Can you dive down underneath?" I asked. "Maybe we can get in through the water?"

He frowned at the green sludge cemented to the sides of the dock. "Underwater break-ins weren't in my training," he informed me.

"Fine, help me to the roof," I said, and he lifted one of my feet up and I pulled my weight the rest of the way. The metal was warm and sturdy and there was a square air vent in the corner of the roof. Pat handed me a pocketknife and I used its screwdriver to twist off one screw in each corner of the vent. I pried the metal grate up and stuck my head down in the musty, stagnant air. I heard splashing below, and my eyes adjusted well enough to see a boat looming next to the dock.

I lowered myself down the hole and dropped two feet until I landed inside the garage.

"There's a boat," I yelled. I opened the garage door and unlocked the side entrance to let Pat in. Pat looked at the speedboat, which had a small life raft fastened to its stern. I found the key hanging on a thin silver chain next to the door.

Pat looked out at the river while I jumped into the boat and started to unfasten the rope from the cleats. "This is insane," he said.

I nodded. "The best ideas always are." It was crazy. That's why I was confident it would work. Pat was standing on the pier, hesitating.

"What are you doing?" I said. "Help me."

"No." He shook his head stubbornly. I glared at Pat. I knew he had been a gopher, someone who intercepted people, for years. He knew how to drive a boat.

"What's your problem?"

"We're trapped, Maddie." He looked up and down the bank. "There's nowhere for us to hide out there. I say we stay in the tunnels."

"And turn ourselves in?"

"The wave-generator plant is down there." He pointed down the river. "It's suicide."

"There's got to be a way around it," I argued. "Scott will help us."

"You're not thinking straight, Maddie. You're still messed up. This won't work."

He grabbed my arm and tried to pull me out of the boat but I wouldn't budge. "What's the matter with you?" he shouted.

"I have a no-surrender-to-the-cops policy," I said through my teeth.

"No, that's Justin's policy and he's insane," Pat said, his face furious. "You don't have to agree with him on everything. If you keep listening to Justin you're going to get yourself killed," he shouted at me. "He's dangerous, Maddie. Look what happened to Kristin. Look what's happening to you."

I pressed my lips together. "You want to go to jail?" I asked. "You know the cops are back there looking for us." Pat shook his head and then he smiled, manipulatively.

"They'll bargain with us," he said. "They let us go if we give them someone they want."

"Who's that?"

"Who do you think?"

"You would turn Justin over to the cops?"

"He's no different from those wave generators. He'll use you and chew you up and spit you out. I've seen him do it. He doesn't care about you, Maddie. Has he ever *told* you he has?"

I couldn't do this. I couldn't let in any doubt right now.

"He saved me, Pat. You don't understand."

"I care about you. I can't watch you throw everything away because he's brainwashed you. What he's fighting for is pointless."

He tried again to pull me out of the boat, back onto the creaky ledge. "Trust me," he said. But that was the problem. I didn't.

I let him help me onto the dock.

"Okay," I said. "We'll go back." His chest rose with a deep breath. Just as he turned to the door, I slid my gun out of the holster at my waist.

"This is the best way," he assured me, his back turned.

"You're right," I said. I knew there was only one thing I could do and I felt terrible but I couldn't let Pat interfere. Maybe I had lost my mind or maybe I was the only one thinking clearly.

I unlocked the safety and Pat met my eyes for an unbelieving second before I pulled the trigger and the tranquilizer shot pierced his neck. His body immediately slumped to the side and I caught him before he fell off the dock.

CHAPTER *thirty-two*

I put the earpod back in my ear with shaking fingers. I stared down at Pat's frozen body. Panic prickled down my back, but I kicked the feeling aside. I remembered Justin's words that doubt would back me into a corner. And now I was responsible for two lives.

"Scott?" I asked.

"Where the hell have you been?" he shouted, and the noise made me wince.

"There's a boat down here," I told him.

"What? Are you guys onboard?" he asked. I groaned at Pat's weight as I reached my arms around his chest and dragged him over the gunwale.

"You could say that," I said. Pat's long legs flopped lifelessly over the side and I laid him down on the ground as gently as I could. I grabbed an orange life jacket from a cubby under the steering wheel, put it on, and fastened the belt around my waist.

"Where's Pat?" he asked.

"He's fine," I said. "There isn't time to explain. Just get me out of here." I turned the key and the engine coughed to life and the propellers cut gentle divots into the water. I finished untying the boat and pushed us away from the pier. Once the boat inched its way out of the garage, I slammed the throttle forward and sent waves spraying up on both sides.

"Head west, for the ocean," Scott said. "Once you hit the open water look for red flare lights on the coast," he said. "It's about a two-hour ride. I'll set them up."

I brushed away the hair blowing in my face. "What about the generators?" I asked. "What if we can't drive around them?"

"Then I'll turn them off," he promised. "I'll get you out of there."

I curved around the twisting river. My hands were shaking so bad I could hardly hold the steering wheel. I wasn't thinking. I was only capable of moving now. I had to trust my instincts. I pushed the throttle forward as high as it would go. "Come on," I yelled at the engine as if shouting would speed it up. I looked up at the jagged cliffs. Rocks balanced precariously at impossible angles, ready to slip at any moment. I wondered what held them together. Will? Force? Strength? They were both daunting and beautiful, not moving but not completely resting either. Just waiting, waiting for the right time to slip.

The water was a cloudy gray and I couldn't see anything through the surface. I lifted my head and let the wind whip through my hair. I was starting to realize I liked this sensation, this idea that anything could happen, that life was as unpredictable as those stones, holding on precariously, waiting to slip. I realized I liked the sensation of fear.

Scott's voice came over the radio but it was crackling. "Maddie," he said. "I'm going to lose you soon. The generator plant is breaking up the signal."

"Just tell me how to get around them," I shouted through the wind.

"I'm working on it," he promised.

I turned another corner of the river and in the distance the wave farm stretched across the entire horizon, like a white field.

I watched the sharp propellers of the generators slice through the water. The closer they came into view, the more impressive they were. They stretched hundreds of feet into the sky and then plummeted down with an immense force.

"Scott?" My voice came out in a whisper. "Why haven't you turned them off?"

"Slow down, Maddie," he said. "I'm losing you. I need more time."

I could barely hear him now. My eyes were mesmerized by the blades.

Scott's voice came again, muffled through static. He told me to wait.

The blades reminded me of a giant shark's mouth stretching for a mile and slashing everything in its path. The mouth waited. Its teeth were white and one hundred feet long and a menacing growl rumbled out of its throat. It clamped and bit and gnawed through the water, daring me to approach it.

"Maddie, did you stop the boat?" he asked, and his voice kicked me out of my daze.

I lowered the throttle but the boat still sailed forward, which was odd since the current should have been pushing against it.

"Weird," I said.

"What is it?" Scott asked.

"It's like I'm stuck in some kind of suction. I'm being pulled forward, even though I'm not accelerating."

There was a quick pause before Scott swore into my earpod. Then I knew what was pulling at me. I twisted the boat around but it didn't get us out of the vacuum. My grip was so tight on the steering wheel, my fingertips turned white. I shoved the throttle forward and all it did was slow our progress, like a brake that had gone soft.

Scott's voice was crackling in and out.

"Scott?" I yelled. "Do something."

"I'm trying!" he shouted back. "I'm in the company's operation page, but all the controls are encrypted. If I had more time, maybe . . ." he said.

I looked out at the blades. I was being pulled toward them faster now and the sound of the churning propellers roared at me. The boat started to rock.

I looked down at Pat for a second and my confidence disappeared and doubt flooded in. I saw extra life jackets and contemplated strapping one on Pat and jumping out. But I knew I couldn't swim fast enough to get us out of the suction. We'd probably die of hypothermia, if the blades didn't kill us first. And that gave me an idea.

I asked Scott if there was a temperature reading anywhere on the control page. He said yes, the water was fifty-two degrees. He told me not to jump in; I couldn't outswim the current if the boat wasn't strong enough to escape. But that wasn't my plan.

"Do you think the generators are temperature sensitive?" I asked him. He knew immediately what I meant. There's a reason wave farms aren't built on glaciers. There are no waves if the water's frozen.

I waited while Scott tried to freeze the Pacific Ocean in two minutes. Technology does have its perks. If Scott could tell the wave generators that the water was frozen, maybe the propellers would shut down.

"I'm trying, Maddie . . ." Scott said through crackling static. Then his voice snapped off and I lost him completely. I swore and yanked the earpod out of my ear and threw it on the dashboard. The boat lurched and rocked in the current. Giant blades, as tall as buildings, sliced the horizon.

The boat wobbled in white foaming waves as the water was pushed and squeezed around us. I held on to the steering wheel to keep my balance and, for the first time, I felt helpless. I wanted to cry. I wanted to scream. More than anything, I wanted to see Justin. Why wasn't he with me right now? At that moment, I hated him for having so much confidence in me. He'd built me up to think I was a leader and I'd believed it. Pat tried to bring me back to reality, but I wouldn't listen. And now I was going to get us both killed.

I unclipped the gun on my hip and considered it. I wanted to give up. The blades were so loud they rattled the boat. My teeth chattered.

I closed my eyes and thought about Justin. I visualized him. I imagined he was here with me. I squeezed my fingers tight, like his hand was inside mine. I thought about my family. I pictured my mom, Joe, and Baley. I pictured my father. An image came to me from when I was young. I remembered my dad carrying me on top of his shoulders. We were walking Baley at a park in Hood River, looking down at the Columbia River gorge and watching the wind sweep the water into whitecaps. Before M28. Before the chaos. Before he changed.

I looked once more at the chopping knives, so close now water was spraying up over the sides of the boat and in my face. I lifted the gun barrel and pressed the cold metal to my neck. I curled my finger around the trigger and started to press.

CHAPTER thirty-three

I heard a clap of thunder and I looked up at the sky for a storm. I waited for lightning. But there were no clouds, just pinkish-blue sky. Then I looked straight ahead. The giant propellers were slowing down.

My finger froze on the trigger. I blinked to make sure I wasn't imagining the blades were slowing down. I reached for the earpod to tell Scott, but the current suddenly slowed down and the boat lurched like someone had slammed on the brakes. I was shoved against the windshield and smashed my head on the glass. My earpod slid off the dashboard and into the river. The propellers slowed to a lazy crawl. The angry metal fangs turned into a garden of white petals, stretching for miles in each direction. The shark turned into a flock of birds and their white wings slowly flapped to a stop.

I was too relieved to care that blood was running down my forehead and trickling into my eye. I wiped the blood away with my sleeve. The propellers gracefully came to a stop. The side of the boat connected with a shining blade glistening with water, but it hit with a clang and then rebounded off.

I eased the boat slowly through the range of propellers while I had the chance. The engine coughed in response and we picked up speed. The generators were set up in rows. We entered a white tunnel, frozen still. I held my breath as the boat passed a field of blades on either side. I was listening for any sign the machines would turn back on. All I heard was the gentle purr of the boat and the sound of water bubbling around the motor. I was afraid to speak, as if it would wake the sleeping monster. I could hear my heart pounding in my ears, louder than the boat's engine.

I took a deep breath and held it when the end came into view. We passed the last row of propellers, and the ocean, like arms open wide, greeted us. I finally let my breath out, but we were still close enough to be pulled back. A line of orange buoys floated in the distance, which I assumed marked safe waters. As I sped away from the plant, the boat engine started to sputter. I kept my hand pushed stubbornly on the throttle.

"Come on," I said, and rubbed my hand on the smooth leather dashboard. "Don't give up on me now." The motor coughed, sounding like it had a throat full of phlegm, and then, with a labored sigh, it blew out and stopped. I looked over my shoulder at the wave farm. Everything was eerily quiet, like the sky just before a tornado strikes when nature is gathering up forces. The blades were sharks again. Sleeping. There were no sounds, just my heart jabbing against my ribs.

I ran to the back of the boat and tore the cover off the motor to find water bubbling over the sides, flooding it. I tried starting the engine again and the motor coughed weakly in response. I cursed and smacked the steering wheel, as if screaming at it would scare it into working. A siren wailed, like a foghorn, and it made me jump. A sweeping sigh filled the air, as if the sky were yawning. I looked over my shoulder. The propellers started to turn.

The buoys teased me in the distance. I was still a hundred yards away from safe waters.

I swore again and tried to start the engine, with no luck. I ran over to Pat and shook him, but he was still motionless. I looked out at the ocean and wondered how long I would last in the water if I could make it to a buoy. And then I remembered the life raft.

I hurdled over the driver's seat and jumped down to the stern of the boat. The extra craft was still there, attached to the hull. The propellers were gaining speed now, starting to churn the water. The boat began to inch back, jostled by the waves. There wasn't time to think. Only to move.

I ran over and pulled on Pat's sweatshirt to try to lift him. He didn't budge, so I grabbed him underneath his arms and dragged him across the deck. I struggled with his weight, and when we got to the back, I jumped down into the raft and pulled Pat over the edge until his legs swung down. I pulled Pat down and unclipped the harness that attached the raft to the speedboat. The raft had a small motor at the rear, and when I yanked its black nylon cord, the engine sputtered. I swore and gave the cord another pull and the engine kicked in, muttering a reply. I turned the boat out to sea and prayed we weren't too late. The boat crawled forward, already fighting against the propellers pulling us back.

"Come on," I said. "Come on." I kept my eyes on the target of the buoys bobbing calmly in the distance. I willed them closer, as if my mind could help power the boat. When I was certain the orange markers were approaching, I allowed myself a peek behind. I looked back to see the other boat caught in the suction, slowly being pulled to the blades.

I looked ahead again, and once we were safely past the orange buoys I turned in my seat to watch the fate of the blue speedboat. The propellers continued to lure it closer until the boat was caught in the blades and let out a squeal as the metal frame twisted apart. The boat exploded in a loud gust and splinters of wood and metal flew into the air. The blades chipped and pulled the boat apart in thin slices. It hacked the pieces of splintering wood into tiny fragments. The propellers cut and chewed until all that was left was floating debris of wood being tossed and spit out in the churning waves. I watched the pieces floating in the water, knowing it could have been my bones crunching under the blades, and my blood churning in the white teeth.

I steered the lifeboat north and prayed Scott would still have the flares waiting for us. The ocean was calm, the wind cool, blowing in from the south. I was careful to stay far enough away from shore that we wouldn't be spotted. I looked west in time to see the orange sun dip below the horizon. The sky seemed to be celebrating with me, dripping in pink and orange light. The roar of the wave generator cried in the distance, like a wild animal that had lost its prey just before the kill.

CHAPTER thirty-four

We glided through the water in darkness. The raft didn't have any lights or emergency kits onboard. All I had to navigate by was a thread of lights from the coast. Lighthouses dotted the shore and were spread out every few miles. As we passed them, I counted the rhythm of their patterns. The bulbs rotated every twelve seconds, sometimes eighteen, sometimes ten. There was a language in those lights, a romantic story they shared with the sea. There was no sound, other than the occasional planes flying over head, lost in the sky, their lights blending in with the stars. I didn't have a single digital tie to the world and for the moment I relaxed in the quiet calm. It gave me time to reflect.

I watched the shoreline for the red flares. I had no way of contacting anyone now. My earpod was lost in the river, and I checked Pat for his, but it must have fallen out when I dragged him into the lifeboat.

Even though all I could see was blackness, visions ran through my head like a montage sequence—images of what might have happened to Justin, Clare, Gabe, and Scott. I couldn't shake the

287

memory of the cops trying to break into the LADC. Someone had tipped them off. But I knew it wasn't Scott. In my heart, I was positive it could be only one person, and it made me sick to think he could turn on me. My father knew I was planning on freeing the kids in the detention center. He knew it was going to happen. But I never told him when. I didn't understand how the information leaked out. How could he infiltrate something that had no trace? There were no files. It was as if my dad could see inside my mind.

Pat stirred next to me. He moaned as he tried to sit up. He blinked around us, at the coast in the distance and our tiny craft. He looked at me then, his face puzzled. I didn't know what to say. It's not every day you shoot your friend in the neck. But maybe we'd both been going insane at that minute. Maybe we were both desperate.

"The speedboat wasn't small enough for you?" he asked, looking around at the dinghy.

It felt good to hear him joke. It settled my heart to think we could get past what happened.

"I wanted to downsize," I said. "I thought we could use one more challenge." He smirked and I told him I sacrificed the boat to the wave generators. "Call it an entrance fee," I said.

He pressed his hand against the side of his neck where I had shot him a few hours ago. He winced. "Why do I have whiplash?" he asked. "We used to shoot each other with tranq guns all the time, but they never gave me whiplash before."

I explained what happened to him, filling him in on the last two hours. I apologized for almost breaking his neck when I pulled him onto the raft.

"I was trying to save your neck," I said. He was quiet for a few minutes as he digested this. I expected him to yell at me, to be irate. But he looked relieved more than anything. He gazed out at the coast a hundred yards away, sprinkled in a dusting of lights.

"Wow," he said. "You pulled it off. I guess I shouldn't have doubted you."

I leaned over and rested my hand on his arm and he didn't jerk it away. "I'm so sorry, Pat," I said. "I just couldn't give up."

"I see that," he said but his eyes avoided mine. "You take stubborn to a whole new level."

"Are you mad at me?" I asked.

"Mad? For what? Shooting me in the neck?" He grinned. "That's what friends do."

"Thanks for being able to joke about it," I said. We both fell silent. I was afraid to bring up what he said back at the dock. I didn't want to start another argument. But I had to know if he meant it.

"You bailed on me, Pat. You were going to give up."

He didn't say anything. He kept his eyes on the water.

"Were you serious about turning Justin in?" I asked.

Pat sighed and finally looked at me. "No, I didn't mean it. You made the right decision, Maddie," he said. "I didn't. I was stupid. I panicked. That's why I don't lead these things. I'm not cut out for this, not that I want to be. When I was younger I helped Justin out, but I always did it for the kicks, not for the cause."

He looked out at the water. The ocean rolled the boat lightly back and forth.

"God, this is peaceful, isn't it?" he said. "This is exactly what I want."

I grinned at him. "What? To be stranded in the middle of the Pacific Ocean forever?"

He smiled. "To go with the flow. Life's all about the pursuit of happiness, you know? I'm sick of trying to make the world a better place. So I'm quitting before I mess it up for everyone."

I nodded because I knew this was coming.

"I'm starting to believe that all you can do in life is make yourself happy. And if you can make a couple of other people happy along the way, maybe that's the best you can do. And I'm okay with that. I'm not some rebel leader. I don't want to be."

He put his feet up on the side of the boat and I studied his profile. His face was content. "This is a good way to end my last mission," he announced. "You have to be crazy to keep this lifestyle going."

"You mean, crazy to give in to the lifestyle that exists?" I tested him.

He cracked a smile.

"Don't say that Justin corrupted me, Pat. This is how I feel, not because I'm pressured into thinking this way. He didn't brainwash me."

"I don't think the world is so bad, Maddie," he said. "People leave each other alone. There's hardly any crime these days. It's safe. Everyone is doing their own thing. Maybe this is the best it gets. Maybe you guys all expect too much."

I stared at Pat. How could he say this to me, especially after what I experienced the last six months? He saw it with his own eyes today—hundreds of people that had been mentally beaten and were enduring torturing sentences, just for wanting a choice. People were dying, just for wanting a life outside of their screens. I looked at Pat like I didn't know him anymore. Maybe I didn't.

"I want to be more than just okay with my life," I said.

"Life is what it is," he said.

"Life is what you make it," I argued.

"Is this how you want it? Running from the cops, almost getting arrested, almost getting killed. I know Justin gets some sick high off of it. He's an adrenaline junkie. But I think it's a waste of time." He looked at me. "You don't have to do it either, you know."

I nodded. "I know that," I said. "I'll never do anything I don't want to do. Trust me, it's not in my personality. And I appreciate everything you've done for me. But you lost faith in all of us. You turned on Justin. You don't turn on people, even when you panic, because trust is impossible to win back. Believe me, I learned that the hard way. Justin would take a bullet for you, and you were ready to hand him over to the police. And you called *him* selfish. I'm going to forget about what happened back there, because I know you're quitting and I believe you were scared. I'll never mention it to Justin because I believe you're sorry. But"—I eyed him coolly—"if he ever gets handed over to the cops, if anything ever happens to him, you're the first person I'm coming after."

He nodded. "I'm done, Maddie. I promise." He dipped his hands in the ocean and wiped them together with a symbolic gesture. "I'm washing my hands of this. It's all yours."

I leaned back in my seat, satisfied. "And what you said about Justin being dangerous. I know he's dangerous. You don't have to warn me. It's one of his best traits."

He nodded. "Yeah, after today I'm pretty sure you two are perfect for each other."

I sighed and looked out at the coastline and that's when I caught the faint red glow in the distance. I pointed out the flares to Pat and turned the boat in their direction. As we approached the lights, we saw a fire lit on the shore, and dark silhouettes moving, mixing light with shadows. The moonlight coated the wet beach in silver. The light of the flares caught our boat and a few people turned to look at us. People ran closer to the shore, and a girl screamed my name. I waved back and called out it was us. Her scream was contagious and soon everybody on the beach was there, circling our boat by the time we met the sand.

"Maddie?" I heard Scott's yell and the next thing I knew people were dragging me out of the boat by my arms. Scott wrapped his arms around me and pulled me against him. I stood there, stunned that Scott was actually hugging me.

I patted his back. "Um, I missed you, too," I said.

He let go of me and grabbed Pat next, practically lifting him off the ground.

"What's with all the brotherly love?" Pat asked him.

"How did you guys get out of there?" Scott asked us, shouting over the crowd that was piling in around us. I was afraid they were going to crush us and Scott yelled for people to back up and give us room.

"You turned the propellers off," I reminded him, like it wasn't a big deal.

"I didn't think it worked in time. Justin took the plane back for you guys and saw the debris from your boat floating around the wave farm," Scott said. "How did you survive that?"

I tried to explain what happened, filling him in on the lifeboat and how I pulled Pat and myself onboard, but I kept getting interrupted by screams and strangers throwing their arms around me.

I was pulled deeper into the crowd, through a mob of fans screaming my name. Everyone wanted to congratulate me. Some guy with long, shaggy hair wrapped his arms around me and announced he loved me. It was starting to freak me out.

I searched through the crowd for Justin or Clare, but Gabe found me first. He picked me up in his arms and lifted my feet off the ground. He hugged me so tight my ribs squeezed together.

"Ow," I said into his shoulder, and he set me down.

"We thought we lost you," he said. Clare found me seconds

later and tugged me away from Gabe. She threw her arms around me with so much force, I stumbled backwards. She said something to me, but I couldn't hear her because her face was smothered in my shoulder.

"I'm fine," I assured her, and hugged her back. Her swollen eyes looked into mine with relief.

"Maddie," she said, and then she started crying and couldn't find her voice. I wasn't prepared for this much drama. I just wanted to find Justin and the nearest place to crash.

"You guys are acting like I died," I said.

She leaned back and nodded. "We did think you were dead," she mumbled. "These past three hours, we thought your boat was torn up. We were just about to call your parents and tell them—"

"Whoa, I'm fine," I interrupted her. "Stop talking like that. I'm right here." I looked at her and tried to smile. "It was a close call, but we did it."

I scanned the beach, on the prowl for one person, craving one person. Where was Justin? I looked for the tallest guys in the crowd, trying to locate him. People were already beginning to disperse. I grabbed Clare's arm.

"Is Justin here?" I asked, and she hesitated. "Where is he?"

Clare and Gabe exchanged looks.

I felt a chill run over my skin. Why were they stalling? "What happened?" I demanded. "Is he all right?"

"He's . . . okay." Clare seemed at a loss for words.

"Just okay?" Was he shot? Hurt?

Gabe finished for her. "You don't understand, Maddie. It's been like a funeral here the past couple hours."

Clare nodded. "He went back to look for you and saw what was left of the boat . . ." She trailed off again. "He told us there weren't any survivors. All we had to track you with were your earpods, and the last signal we got was twenty feet underwater at the wave plant. And you know he blamed himself," Clare said. *"Again."*

"Does he know I'm alive now?" I asked.

She shrugged. "We sent him a message. But I haven't seen him in the past hour. He took off."

"Took off? To where?"

I didn't wait for her to answer. I turned and headed for the airport hangar.

CHAPTER thirty-five

I walked inside the airport hangar, where students would be staying for the next few days, until they could go back home or find more permanent housing. Inside, neat rows of cots were lined up, and stacks of clothes were folded along one wall. It was amazing Clare had coordinated all of this in one week. Volunteers handed out plastic-wrapped sandwiches and bags of chips and fruit. Kids were already filling up the beds.

There were hundreds of people inside. But I could tell Justin wasn't one of them. An energy was missing.

I walked out of the hangar because I couldn't relax until I found him. I walked around the side of the building and found myself in what looked like an airplane cemetery. There were parts of planes heaped on the ground; rusted engines, wheels, propellers, and entire crafts sitting on the side of the abandoned runway. Tall weeds and grass grew around the edge of the cement. I stopped and listened. I could feel he was close by. There was a spark in the air. Or maybe I felt like I was being watched.

I turned and found him. He sat on the ground, in the shadow of an abandoned building. His hair was standing straight up, as if he'd been pushing his hands through it for hours. His arms were around his drawn-up knees. He looked broken, as if he'd fallen apart and been crudely put back together without anything aligned. He lifted his head and I could see silver reflected in his eyes. They were wide. He was looking at me like I was a ghost.

"Did you hear we made it back?" I asked him.

He nodded slowly. He was still in shock. "It's not every day somebody comes back from the dead," he said, his voice so flat it didn't sound like his.

He dragged himself up and leaned against the wall. We stared at each other. His eyes traveled down my face and back up again. They were half lidded and glassy and dull. So much of the fire I loved about him had burned out. It was like watching a statue crumble. I was careful to stay where I was. He reminded me of how I used to feel at the DC, slowly waking up out of a nightmare, when all your emotions are still singed from the heat. It takes time for your mind to cool off.

"I told you to go with Pat," he said. The skin under his eyes was puffy. His cheeks were wet. He pulled his hand through his hair. "Then," he continued, "when Scott told me what was happening, I suggested you head for the river. It was my idea."

"And I'm fine," I announced, my voice starting to get shaky from seeing him so upset. "It worked. We got out of there."

He wasn't listening to me. His eyes were dazed. He was still living in the nightmare. "I thought you could hide out until I came back for you. I thought the canyon was safe."

"We escaped. Stop blaming yourself for things that didn't happen."

He turned and looked out at the broken plane yard. His face was numb. He grinned but there wasn't a trace of lightness to it. "All I wanted was for you to be safe. I told you to risk anything. And it almost killed you."

He was scaring me. I needed him to wake up from the trance his mind was in. I wanted to grab his shoulders and shake him until his doubts fell out.

"I am safe, Justin. Look at me."

Thick tears welled up in his eyes and started to roll down his face, so large I could see each one falling. He didn't wipe them away. They looked unbelievable on him.

"I'm not Kristin," I said. "That won't happen again. You need to forgive yourself for that."

I took a couple steps toward him until we were close enough to touch, and I grabbed his arm. He didn't move. He didn't flinch. He didn't respond at all.

"Look, tonight was terrifying, I'll give you that. It was a close call. But we did it," I told him. "Haven't you heard? Everyone escaped. All the students are safe. This mission was a complete success. I'm alive. Why don't we focus on that?"

He looked down at his feet. I couldn't imagine what state I would be in if I thought Justin was dead, if I had been brooding for hours, imagining I had played a role in his death. But it was killing me to see him like this. It was worse torture than staring at the slicing wave generators. I squeezed his arm tighter, trying to jerk him awake. Couldn't he understand that he saved me? Until he stopped blaming himself, I knew he wouldn't be able to see me.

I took a deep breath and focused my eyes on his. "Look at me," I said. He turned and watched me, numb, his face lifeless.

"You're not responsible for me. I need you to accept this. I'm not going to quit, so don't even think about pushing me away again. It's not about you. Maybe at first it was. Maybe I wanted to follow you because it was exciting and dangerous and I wanted to break ties with my dad. But now it's just as personal for me. So you can say anything you want, but I'm not backing down. Ever. So why sit around wasting time dwelling on what could have gone wrong? Shouldn't we be celebrating all the things that went right?"

He reached his hand up and touched my cheek, delicately. His fingers were cold. He cupped my face in his palm and his eyes focused on mine but he still couldn't see me—he was still in shock. His cheeks were wet and light glistened off of them. I wanted to wipe them dry but instead I put my hand over his and we stood like that. I closed my eyes and leaned closer to him but his hand went limp and slipped out from under mine. He turned and I watched him sleepwalk away.

I wanted to yell after him, but I thought about all the times he'd stood in my shoes over the last six months, all the times he'd wanted to pull me back and rescue me. I realized how hard that must have been, how much it hurt when you know the only way to help someone is to give him distance. So I let him go.

❖

The next night, everyone celebrated. We built a bonfire on the beach and set up speakers for music. I sat on a blanket next to Scott and Molly and watched the students in the firelight. It was the mangiest group of people I'd ever seen. The girls all had ratty hair, and some of the guys still had scruffy beards growing in. They were wearing borrowed clothes that were too big on most of them, hanging off their lanky bodies, but they didn't care.

News started to leak out about the DC break-in. Molly anonymously sent a press release containing all of our research and evidence. We watched the story unfold on a wall screen Scott hung in the airport hangar. The cops pulled out the weary staff from the gates. The staffers looked battered and traumatized. They had the same expressions we wore for six months.

Journalists and police were investigating the LADC, as well as other detention centers around the country. All centers were on a lockdown and until investigations were over, no new students could be enrolled. At the same time, no students would be released. The news avoided giving information about Molly's reports. Even the honest journalists Justin said we could count on were hesitant to speak out against the DC.

I knew who could make a difference. One person. One man could set the record straight. Even though I wouldn't admit it, I knew my father still held the torch in his hands. He could sway the public either way. One memory gave me hope: the anger I saw in his eyes at the detention center. He would have to choose DS or his daughter. It finally was coming to a head and it was time for him to make a choice and show where his true loyalties lay.

I tapped my feet to the music and watched Gabe dancing with Clare. He had obviously grown up dancing—he smoothly spun her around and caught her hands, only to spin her back again. Even Scott and Molly got up and joined the crowd. I wanted to join in, but my thoughts were still weighing me down. I felt like Justin had said goodbye to me last night. I kept thinking back to what Pat pointed out to me, that Justin never told me he cared. Every time I remembered those words, it felt like a sting.

I'd hardly seen him during the day. A trail of students always followed him, eager to introduce themselves. After all, he was one of the founders of this group, he brought people together, he sacrificed more than anyone. There was always a line of people pursuing him, thanking him for inspiring them. It was like what Gabe said: he had become a household name. He was a spark that shot through the air. He was an event, a zephyr, a force. Now he was tangible for the first time. I watched girls shake his hand and hug him and giggle like they were meeting their celebrity crush. But I felt like I couldn't touch him.

When he wasn't being idolized, someone was bugging him to

take a call or answer a message. Our eyes met a few times throughout the day. But it was only for an instant and then he was distracted by someone tugging on his arm or shouting his name. And I couldn't read what was in his eyes; it was the intense look he always gave me that had thousands of meanings.

I tried to focus on the students. Gabe eventually dragged me into the mob of dancers. The music helped me forget. I let my problems escape through my pores and more light filled in the spaces. I let myself laugh and dance because I earned it. You have to take the time to celebrate your miracles.

I was flushed and sweating and headed over to a stand stacked with water jugs. Before I got there, warm fingers grabbed my arm. I looked over and Justin was there and his face was impatient. His eyes were lighter; he was finally seeing me again.

"I've been trying to get you alone all day," he said, and I let him pull me away from the crowd. We walked fast through the sand, avoiding the bonfire and noise to find some privacy. I stumbled over a mound of weeds and he pulled me up, his hand wrapped tight around mine. He didn't say anything. He didn't even look at me. He just breathed hard and focused on a spot ahead of us. We finally stopped in a shallow valley of sand.

He grabbed my face in his hands and I looked up at him but only for a second because then his lips were on mine. He lifted me up and pulled me closer until our chests pressed together. I jumped up and straddled my legs around his waist and we fell back on the ground and kicked up sand all around us. We started coughing and brushed the sand away.

"I'm sorry," he whispered in my ear, but I found his lips again because I didn't need to hear it. I already knew.

"Wait," he said, and pried my hands off his face. He rolled me over so he was leaning on top of me. He eased off enough to let me breathe but I grabbed his arms so he couldn't get far.

"You know what I realized last night?"

"That you're an idiot?" I asked.

He brushed his hand against my cheek. "I realized when I couldn't get to you, when I was too late, I realized I never told you I loved you," he said. My stomach fluttered at the word coming out of his mouth.

I shook my head slowly.

"I thought I'd never get the chance. God, Madeline, that almost killed me. That was worse than anything, to think that I never told you how I felt. And how much you deserved to hear it. I've never hated myself so much in my life. I felt so selfish and stupid for holding that back."

I opened my mouth to argue but he interrupted me.

"I love you so much. I need you to know that."

I nodded because I couldn't say anything.

"I always have," he said. "Since the second I laid eyes on you. No one's ever had that effect on me. You made my head spin. You changed my life."

I smiled at him and touched his lips, but he pulled my hand away.

"I'll always love you. Forever. Do you believe that?"

I nodded. "Forever."

"You're the only thing that matters," he went on. "Nothing can ever happen to you." I pressed my fingers over his lips because he was going to make me cry.

"I know," I said, and I pulled him down close to me so I could taste his words.

CHAPTER *thirty-six*

Two days later we left for Eden. The good news was the students who'd escaped were safe. The list of enrollment in each DC was confidential, so the police had no way of acquiring the students' names. The only person who could release that information was Richard Vaughn and the news reported he was still recovering from a serious health incident and wasn't available for questioning. For the time being, we'd won. No one was going to order students back to the DC until more investigations took place.

We arrived the night before the spring festival. It was an annual all-weekend event to honor the spring equinox. Stores closed down, shuttles stopped running, and the streets became an open promenade to welcome a parade of music, food, and art.

About two hundred students were relocated to Eden. They were scattered around the city in hotels and volunteer homes. The entire city donated food and supplies. Justin and I escorted about fifty students to a hotel downtown. His parents were covering the expenses.

"How can your parents afford all of this?" I asked Justin after we checked the students in and were heading back to his parents' house. Now that I thought about it, it occurred to me his parents didn't even have jobs. They had been full-time volunteers most of their lives.

"Are they independently wealthy?" I asked.

"More like dependently wealthy," he said. "Remember, my dad invented the Cerberix. And it can hack into anything."

He grinned at me and I caught on. "They're stealing the money?" I asked. "From bank accounts?"

He shook his head. "Not exactly," he said. "My dad owns the rights to a dozen patents. He does pretty well. But we get a little help from a private investor." He looked at me. "Your father."

"You're stealing from my dad?"

"We tap into the digital-school corporate accounts and draw money out when it's needed. Your dad's got a couple hundred mill in there. Might as well put it to use."

I couldn't help but laugh. "So, my dad's company funds everything you guys do?"

Justin grinned. "We don't feel too bad about it," he admitted.

❧

The next day, Clare and I got ready for the festival at Justin's parents' house. The late afternoon was warm and humid, so we both wore sundresses. The house was swarming with visitors and guests. A blues band was performing in the living room and music filled the house like light. It warmed and polished everything. The front door was propped open to let anyone inside.

I followed Clare downstairs and we headed to the kitchen and Elaine was sitting at the table drinking a glass of wine with two of her friends. When she saw us she smiled.

"Madeline, you're wearing makeup," she told me. "And a dress."

"Sometimes her inner girl breaks through," Clare said.

"I was just trying to cover up this bruise." I pointed to the narrow scab on the top of my forehead, just below my hairline, where my head had hit the boat's windshield.

"Well, you look gorgeous," she said. "And Clare, you grew your hair out."

Clare nodded. "I've been too busy to cut it," she said. She'd curled her hair tonight in soft waves, and her coral lipstick made her blue eyes stand out. We sat down at the kitchen table, and Clare and I helped ourselves to handfuls of sugar peas.

"You both look refreshed," Elaine noted.

"It's hard not to be when I'm here," I said.

"Maybe you should come out here more often," Elaine said.

"Why is it so good to be here?" I asked. "What is it about this place? Is it all the ocean air? Or the climate?"

She smiled and shook her head. "Nope," she assured me. "You can bring this place with you anywhere."

"How?" I asked. I needed to know her secret.

She took a sip of red wine. "Look around you, Maddie. It's the people. That's the energy you feel. That's what you're reacting to. We slow down and enjoy life." She pointed to the sugar peas in our hands. "When you rush what you eat, you hardly taste it. You get a stomachache, right? It's the same with life. Just slow it down and enjoy every bite. Eat at the table. And fill up all the chairs around it with people you love."

Noah came through the door and raised his hands. "There you two are," he said. "Can we get going? I'm starving."

We stood up and followed Noah outside, where Justin and Pat were waiting for us in the front yard. We walked downtown and followed a path through the street lit by tin-can luminarias decorated with vines and leaves. The candles inside flickered and moved with the breeze.

I asked Justin why Eden celebrated the vernal equinox.

"*Equinox* means 'equal night,'" he told me. "It's the first day of spring, when there's equal amount of day and night." He explained that cultures have been superstitious about it for centuries. It honors the idea of lightness and darkness and of death and rebirth.

I discovered quickly that the spring festival revolved around eating. When we reached downtown, the streets were filled with food stands. I tried baked apples, gooey with caramel and brown sugar drizzled on top. There was barbecued pork, grilled portobello mushrooms as big as my hand, roasted sunchokes, and squash. For dessert there were chocolate truffles and apple and marionberry pies. There were fruit smoothies and home-brewed beer and wine. There were deep-fried doughnuts and dried plums, pears, cherries, and apricots that tasted as sweet as candy.

The food alone was intoxicating. It made my taste buds scream, since I had barely used them in the last six months. I wanted to try everything, so Justin and I ended up sharing portions. We split pizza and crepes and doughnuts and cake. All my senses were on overdrive after being dulled for so long.

The DC students paraded through the streets like they were in a movie set, stunned to the point of surreal. Wherever we glided, Justin and I were stared at and pointed out like we were some celebrity couple sauntering down a red carpet. Between the two of us, it took an hour to walk one single block. People stopped to thank us or congratulate us on what we did. Secretly, I loved the attention. In my gut I had a feeling this was the way it would be when we were together and I realized I loved all the eyes on me. I was fine with being in the spotlight. It might be a lifestyle I was cut out for. And one year ago, I was just a single girl sitting in her room, staring at a screen.

Clare and Gabe caught up to us and we ran into Molly and

Scott and the six of us stayed in a group as we walked down the street. I pointed out a booth with a line of people ranging from toddlers to elderly. It was the busiest tent at the festival.

I asked Justin what they were doing and he told me it was a long tradition.

I watched people sorting through boxes of seeds and bulbs and shoveling dirt into small brown pots. People took turns watering the pots after the seeds were planted.

"It's symbolic," he said. "You're supposed to think about a goal you want to achieve in the next year, or a wish you hope will come true. That seed becomes your goal. So, you plant it and see if it grows."

I looked back over at the stand.

"Have you ever done it?" I asked. He nodded and said when he was little he did. He said every year he wished for telepathic powers but since it never came true he stopped trying.

I told him I wanted to try it and I pulled Clare's hand and got in the back of the line. When our turns came, we both looked over the seeds and tried to choose something that represented us. I didn't know flowers very well, but my mom loved lilies and she'd sometimes splurge on a bouquet of them. I liked that they were tall and confident. I chose a lily bulb and they handed me a bowl full of soil. Clare chose a tulip bulb.

I rolled the bulb between my fingers and thought about what I wanted to accomplish this year, what wish I wanted to see grow. I put my thoughts and energy into that wish and let it travel through my hand and imagined it floating through my fingers into the bulb itself. I planted it a few inches deep and poured water on top and I liked the idea my wish was safe and secret but had the potential to burst through.

Clare and I found Gabe in one of the food lines. His eyes were wide, like he was trying to soak in as much of the atmosphere as he could. I asked him if he was overwhelmed with the choices and he shook his head.

"Not with the food," he said. "It's the women. They're everywhere." He pointed out the tan girls around us in dresses and spaghetti-strap tank tops. "For the last six years all I've met are girls that get weak in the knees every time I come near them. And not for the sexy reasons." He handed me a piece of paper. "Look what someone gave me."

Clare and I ducked down to read a plastic business card. A lot of single people carried these, to list their favorite profiles and contact numbers.

"She told me she's visiting here from Sacramento for the weekend and I should *chat her up*. Does that mean I should call her?"

Clare pointed to the loopy black print. "She gave you her CMO."

"Her what?"

"It's her profile number for Contact Me Online. It's a really intimate friendship site. And she gave you her ID number on date2go.com." She raised her eyebrows like he should be impressed.

"I don't speak robot," Gabe replied to her look.

"She's interested," I explained. "She wants you to find her online so she can study your profile. Then she wants you to go to this dating site and request a questionnaire to see if you're compatible with her to meet for a virtual date."

Gabe still looked baffled.

"It's how most people meet these days," Clare said.

He frowned. "Why didn't she just talk to me?" he asked. "I was standing right here."

Clare and I looked at each other to try to explain. "Because that's backward to a lot of people," I finally said. "Most people think you're weird if you want to meet face-to-face. You don't talk in person until you know each other first."

"No, thanks," Gabe said, and threw the plastic card into a trash can. "I've been waiting six years to meet girls. I don't want to date a computer screen."

When we found the rest of the group, Justin grabbed my free hand. We passed more tents full of activities: people painting eggs and ceramic mugs and making bookmarks and decorating photos with dried flowers.

We walked down to the beach where there were bonfires burning as far as you could see. We sat on a blanket and started discussing things we wished for, one thing we wanted to accomplish in the next year.

I didn't mention what I really wished for, I didn't want to jinx it, so I said I wanted to learn how to read sheet music and play the guitar. Clare wanted to travel to Europe. Gabe wanted to mountain bike. Pat wished Angelina Jolie would be reborn.

"Angelina Jolie *Salt*, or Angelina Jolie *Tomb Raider*?" Scott asked.

"Definitely *Tomb Raider*," Pat said.

We asked Justin what he'd wished for and his eyes went straight to me. He paused for a second and smiled.

"Ninja powers," he finally said.

"Poor choice," Noah scoffed. "Ninjas are overrated. They have such limited weapon selection."

"They don't need weapons," Justin argued. "They're cunning."

"They don't even wear armor," Scott pointed out.

"They don't need it," he said. "They're too fast. And their senses are so heightened, they can smell something from three miles away."

"You made that up," Pat insisted.

"So? It's my dream," Justin said.

We made yearly goals for each other. I gave Scott the goal of fine-tuning his people skills.

"You're really not a bad guy, you just come off as such an ass at first," I told him.

"He has to work on his interpersonal communication," Molly agreed.

I told Molly she needed to water down the science jargon.

Gabe nodded. "You sound like a medical dictionary," he informed her.

"I think it's sexy," Scott argued.

Gabe told me I should learn to work on my patience. Or to give in once in a while. He dared me to try and stay out of trouble for a month.

We sat around and talked about life and dreams because they all felt in our grasp that night. Fireworks erupted over the ocean, in shapes of blooming flowers and showering branches of trees. The flowers opened and blossomed and then the petals fell over the water into a shimmering pool of light. People danced on the beach, their arms gliding like waves, like they were following some path in the jet stream. Happiness followed behind me like a loyal shadow.

CHAPTER *thirty-seven*

The celebration carried into the next day and there was more live music and festivities and art shows. Justin and I stood on a wharf packed with sailboats and watched a band performing on the stage of a pavilion at the edge of the beach. Hundreds of people gathered around the stage, but tonight we wanted some privacy. I was on my third baked apple. Justin leaned over and grabbed it out of my hand and took a bite. He handed it back to me and licked his sticky fingers.

"After this whole mess is figured out, with the DC and digital school, do you think our lives will ever be this simple?" I asked.

"God, I hope so," he said.

"Really?" I looked at him. "It's hard to imagine you slowing down. It seems like you're happier chasing."

He thought about this for a second. "You stop chasing when you find what you want," he said, and studied me. "What did you really wish for yesterday?"

"You tell me first," I said with a smile. His face turned serious. He stared at me. Really stared.

He pursed his lips together and stalled.

"What is it?" I asked. Before he could answer me, his phone beeped.

"I need to turn this off." He frowned and reached into his pocket. But when he looked at the screen, his hand paused.

"Look who's keeping tabs on you," he said, and showed me the screen. The message read: *I'd like a conference call with Madeline. Alone. Ten minutes. —Kevin Freeman*

"Great," I said. Usually a message like that made my stomach churn because it meant one thing: I was in trouble. But this time, I was more annoyed to be interrupted.

Justin slid the phone in his pocket and grabbed my hand. "You can use my parents' basement," he said, and pulled me away from the dock.

"How did he get your number?"

"I think your dad has access to anything he wants," he reminded me.

I let him lead me back to his house. We passed groups of people screaming and laughing on the beach, gathered around fire pits. We headed up the sandy hill to his parents' house and climbed up the front porch steps. Justin opened the screen door to a group gathered in the living room, lounging on the couches, drinking wine, and talking in candlelight.

We walked down the hall until we came to the basement door. He opened it for me and I looked between the cool stairwell and the warm, welcoming hallway like they were two different worlds.

"I'll be right upstairs," he promised, and I headed down to the basement. The room was cold and full of computer monitors and wall screens. I dialed my dad's number on the screen, sat down on the couch, and waited.

"Madeline," my mom cried when she saw me. She leaned forward like she wanted to reach through the wall screen and grab me in her arms.

I looked from her to my father. They sat next to each other in his office. He didn't look especially happy to see me. But he didn't look angry either. His face was bare of emotions.

"Are you okay?" my mom asked. I stared at her like I was seeing a memory, a place that you don't realize how much you missed until you come back to it. It had been nearly nine months since I'd seen my mom. She looked the same. Her light brown hair was tied in a braid, and she wore a loose red sweater and blue jeans. It didn't occur to me until now that even though we had our differences, even though we drove each other nuts on a daily basis, she had been a best friend. For so many years it was just the two of us.

"I'm fine," I assured her with a confident nod.

"You need to put on some weight," she informed me. "You look scrawny." I rolled my eyes. Leave it to my mom to lecture me on my appearance right now.

"I missed you," I told her. I thought about all the things I wanted to say to her when I was struggling in the DC and trapped on the boat, seconds from my life ending. I wished I could crawl through the screen and talk to her for hours, to catch up on life. "I'm sorry about everything I've done. I never meant to hurt either of you."

Her eyes filled up with tears and she nodded quickly. "It's all right, Maddie. We love you," she said, her hand clasping my dad's tightly. "I'm just relieved you're all right."

"How's Baley?" I asked.

My mom sighed. "She sleeps in your room every night. I keep promising her you'll be coming home soon," she said, and her eyes looked hopefully back at me. They started to fill with tears again and so did mine. What I couldn't say was no, I wasn't going to be home any time soon. I didn't belong in their world anymore.

My dad's eyes locked on mine and they softened. "You look much better than when I last saw you," he said.

"Luckily someone helped me escape," I hinted, wishing my dad would try to see the good in Justin.

"I wanted to talk to you before I head down to Los Angeles tomorrow," he said.

"You're going to discuss the detention center?" I hoped.

He nodded. "The media wants to interview me. Word got out that I was there last month. People think I know what's been going on inside. They're investigating how much I'm tied to all of this."

"Well, you do know what's going on," I said.

He slowly nodded. "I've been doing my own research."

"So, you believe us?" I asked.

He didn't answer me at first.

"We have the evidence," I said before he could argue. "We have about eight hundred witnesses," I pointed out, my voice rising. "We have blood tests, exams, proof of drugs."

My dad held his hand up to silence me.

"Are you going to help us or not?" I demanded.

He stared at me. "That depends. There are a few practical things you need to face."

"Like what?" I asked. Everything else in the room seemed to fade away. All I could see were my dad's eyes.

"Have you ever considered you might be wasting your time imagining what your life *could* be instead of accepting what your life *is?*"

"I'm not content with what my life is."

My dad thought about this for a few seconds. He took his time to answer me. "This real world, as you like to call it, is no better than the digital one. I've been out there, I've seen it. You're fighting for the choice to be miserable. I wish you could understand that."

I opened my mouth to argue but he cut me off. "No one is happy in that world either," he argued. "That world is just as fake, just as plastic. Did you know, before digital school, everyone needed to be medicated in order to survive? People just wanted to forget. Having so many choices made people sick. It drove them mad. So everyone wanted to be numb. They took drugs to cope. People couldn't handle the pressure of living. Freedom is a paradox, Maddie. It doesn't exist."

"That's not true," I said.

"What exactly do you want?" My mom interrupted the argument. I took a long breath.

"I can see there are things about DS that work. I know technology has its benefits. But some things need to change. Maybe we can meet me in the middle? Combine our ideas?"

My dad was silent for a few seconds as he considered this offer.

"You can't have everything you want in life," he said. "It simply doesn't work that way and the sooner you accept it the less trouble you'll make. Some ideas, some relationships, you need to give up."

I narrowed my eyes. I knew who he was referring to.

"Justin is dangerous," he said. "Every time he walks into your life, you nearly get killed. If he really cared about you, he'd leave you alone. I can't accept him, Maddie."

"What are you saying?" I asked.

He laced his fingers together, his signature move that a bargaining chip was in store, and I knew in my gut I wouldn't like it. His mouth formed a tight line. This wouldn't be a negotiation. It would be take it or leave it, like it always was with my father. I'd forgotten an important fact. He made a career out of getting his way.

"How would it look if I agreed to work with you, and it came back that I was tied to these radicals? To Justin Solvi in particular?" he said.

"So you're going to side with Richard Vaughn instead? You're going to let this continue?"

"Not if you agree to a few terms," he replied calmly. "If you want me to work with you, you have to compromise as well. We need to meet halfway." I knew what he was going to say and I cut in.

"No," I said. "I'm not backing down. Not for a second."

"Neither am I. Maybe you're right. Maybe we can work on changing the system. On developing a face-to-face system to exist alongside digital school. I would be willing to listen. If."

"If?" I waited. One small word hung in the air and had so much weight it pressed my shoulders down.

He opened up his arms. He was wearing a suit and tie, as if this conference call were just another business deal. "You must see the condition? The future of DS aside, you are my daughter. If you expect me to cooperate, you're going to have to join my side."

I shook my head as his words sank in.

"That means cutting off your attachments. All of them," he said. "It also means moving back home. Following my orders. Behaving for once without temptations around to get you into trouble."

"You mean, choose you over my friends?"

"I think it's a fair compromise. I can't have my daughter running with the crowd that's trying to overthrow a system I built. I especially can't have her associating with the leader of that group."

I raked my mind for any excuse. "You said yourself you see things wrong with DS," I pleaded. "You wouldn't know half of what was going on if it wasn't for people like Justin," I said. "Why can't you work with all of us?"

"No."

"But Dad—"

"I gave you your option," he interrupted, his voice rising. "If Justin's smart, he'll convince you which side to take. If you're smart you'll let all of this go. I've known you your whole life. These people have known you less than a year. So who do you think knows you best?"

I looked at my mom and her eyes were pleading with me to accept the offer.

"I don't know anymore," I admitted. "I feel like you see what you want to see and they see me for who I am."

"Do these people know you're insecure? Shy? Timid? Do they even know your weaknesses?"

"I don't have those weaknesses around them," I said. "Maybe you bring them out in me."

He shook his head. "You're not a rebel leader. It's fun right now, it's exciting, but you can't maintain this lifestyle because *it isn't you.* You will fail. I'm giving you a choice. I hope you make the wise one."

"Dad—"

The connection cut off. The room was silent and the wall screen faded into gray.

How could I choose? I had two families now. Justin, Clare, Pat, Gabe, Justin's parents, people I truly loved. My mom and dad. I couldn't live without either. But I knew I couldn't have both.

April 30, 2061

I'm not scared anymore. When I was in the DC, I was dying every day, slowly, like I was dying of thirst. I could feel myself disintegrating one cell at a time. I watched all my friends and my family die in all my dreams. Every night a piece of me died.

It's a relief to know life can't be more painful than that. If I can survive that, I think I can survive anything. I used to be scared in the DC and wonder what tragedy was lurking next. It was like they turned my pain threshold on high and watched me convulse. There's a relief in knowing you've hit the bottom. It makes you immune to fear.

I think Justin's right, that it takes pain to realize your strength. Maybe it takes tragedy to create paradise.

There is something so encouraging about the idea of starting new. You can start new every day. I just have to let it go. I need to remember my past in order to imagine my future. I'm learning that the two go hand in hand. But I'm determined to use my past as a guide, not as an anchor.

I know what my decision needs to be.

317

Justin stood on the other side of the car in the driveway. The wind gusts blew my hair across my eyes and I tucked it behind my ear.

"I'll be back in a few days," he said.

I nodded. I knew it wasn't safe for me to join him in Los Angeles for the conferences dealing with DC investigations. I had to stay out of the spotlight right now. But it was getting harder and harder to be left behind.

"I have some thinking to do," I muttered with a frown. It had been two days since my father's call. I hadn't given him an answer yet.

"What's there to think about?" he asked, like choosing families was an easy decision. "I think the answer's obvious." Justin walked around the car until he was standing next to me. "Let's review your track record. Do you ever give into your father for very long?"

"No," I mumbled.

"Then why start now?"

He picked a duffle bag off the ground and tossed it in the trunk.

"Because it's occurred to me he still controls my life."

Justin shook his head. "Only if you let him. Your dad's full of scare tactics. I think he's bluffing."

A year ago I might have believed that. But every time I thought I was stronger than my father I always got shot down and put in my place. Every time I thought I gained my freedom I was only baited into another trap.

I was his daughter. His property.

Justin shut the trunk and leaned against the side of the car and studied me. He grabbed my hand and pulled me next to him. He leaned in close, until his shoulder pressed against mine. "Do you want to join your dad's side?"

I glared at him. "Of course not. But it's the only way to change anything. Isn't that what we wanted? He's finally willing to work with me."

"In exchange for you never speaking to us again," Justin reminded me.

"That's his trick," I said. "He says he's making me a deal, but he isn't. If I stay here, I'll just get arrested again. And you and your friends are next in line."

Justin rolled his eyes as if this were just an inconvenience.

"And he knows where to find us," I pointed out. "He found your number. He knows more than we can probably comprehend."

I waited for Justin to nod and agree and tell me to give up. But Justin never backed down from anything he wanted. I just hadn't grasped, until now, that the thing he wanted most of all was me.

"I told you a few days ago this is forever. You think I'm going to let your dad call the shots?" There was a challenge in his eyes.

I wanted to believe him. But he never fought for people before. "But you told me love is about letting people go," I said.

"That's what you believe. It's what you always preach. So shouldn't you be telling me to go?"

Justin ran his hand through his hair. "Yeah, that was a load of crap," he said.

"What?"

He smiled. "I didn't know what I was talking about," he admitted. "I'd never been in love when I said that. Now I am. And I was wrong. I think love is something you have to fight for."

"You really believe that?"

He shrugged. "Letting go is easy. Anyone can do that. Love is fighting for someone to stay. That's what takes work. I know that now. I used to think I was better off alone, but alone is the worst place to be. It just took me this experience to figure it out."

My mouth fell open with shock. Justin Solvi changed. For me. I opened his eyes to possibly the most important thing in life.

"Your dad doesn't actually think he can keep us apart, does he?" he said with a smile.

He made it sound too easy. "So what are we supposed to do?" I asked. "Flee the country so we can be together? Hide away the rest of our lives? I love you, but I don't want that. I don't think you do either."

"That's not what I'm talking about," he said.

"Then what do you want?"

He looked at me like it was obvious. "I want you to fight for me, too. You fight every day. You never back down. So let's make this work. We'll figure it out."

"What about digital school?"

He frowned. "You'll always come first, Maddie. You always have. It just took me a while to realize it."

I stared at him, shocked these words were coming out of his mouth. "I still don't know what to tell my dad."

Justin waved his hand in the air like he was brushing the idea away. "He's going to be in L.A. for the next week. We'll figure something out."

I nodded and wanted to be as assured as him.

"I need to think about this," I said. I looked up at the sky and wanted to see birds. I needed an omen that something would help carry me through this. But the sky was gray and thick clouds crawled slowly by, in no hurry to move.

"What do *you* want?" he asked me.

"I want to be with you," I said because at this moment, that's the one feeling I could count on. That was my one certainty.

He took a deep breath of relief and he leaned down and rested his forehead against mine.

"Thanks," he breathed. "That all I needed to hear."

Acknowledgments

Okay, first I need to thank my husband, Adam, because none of this would have happened without your support. I would also like to thank my agent, Helen Breitwieser, for reminding me that I don't actually live on a deserted island. Thanks to my editor, Julia Richardson, for helping me to spin a manuscript that I was simply happy with into a book that I am immensely proud of writing.

Thanks to everyone at Houghton Mifflin Harcourt for their care and time on my books, especially Carol Chu, Candace Finn, Rachel Wasdyke, and Betsy Groban.

Thanks to my core four (you know who you are) for inspiring me to get out of my writing zone, and also for so many great book recommendations. Thanks to Ryan for so much writing inspiration (all of our crazy times together manage to make it into my books). Thanks to Imagine Coffee for your amazing espresso and positive energy.

Thanks to my sister for answering all of my exhausting phone calls and taking every word I say with love and patience. Thanks to my mom for hand-selling *Awaken* to practically every resident in Wisconsin. Thanks to two fans that have really reached out to support me: Natasha Fulton and Heidi McLaughlin Bennett.

And, if you're still reading this, thanks to YOU, my readers. You make this all possible.